I0599011

TURN TO PAIGE NEVER

ADAM P. KNAVE

Turn to Paige Never
Adam P. Knave

ISBN: 978-1926946-115

Trade edition.
This book is also available in ebook formats.
©2020 Adam P. Knave, all rights reserved.
Cover by Valentine Barker ©2020 and Cover Logo
design by Frank Cvetkovic

Published in Canada by Creative Guy Publishing
Victoria, BC, Canada

TURN TO PAIGE NEVER

ADAM P. KNAVE

The Amphidromic Sequence

CULTURE'S SKELETON (stand alone)

TURN TO PAIGE NEVER (stand alone)

THE RISING TIDE (stand alone)
Coming soon!

*This book is for all the wrong roads we follow
to find the right ones.*

CHAPTER ONE

THE FIRST TIME I met Anders, I killed him. I didn't do it on purpose. That was the problem, I really do try to only kill people on purpose. Some of my family thinks this is a huge character flaw, but to hell with them.

I'd been chasing some Quantum Butterfly Hybrids who'd learned to fold space a bit. They'd started opening portals and charging through them, making me give the stupidest of chases. I landed on a roof in some suburban neighborhood, obvious from the overpowering smell of freshly cut grass and emotional despair, and caught sight of them, hop-fluttering to another house.

As I landed, I saw Anders out of the corner of my eye. Ten years old, the kid reeled on the edge of the roof, set off-balance by the appearance of the QBHs. He'd managed to just start recovering when I showed up. My foot came down too close to his and he took a step back, annoyingly, right off the roof.

I watched the stupid, beautifully winged idiots start to call up another fold portal as they spotted me and knew I had to make a choice: see how the kid was, or keep up with these flapping jerks.

I leapt off the roof, like a damned professional, and landed near the kid. He'd fallen backwards and hadn't even bothered to right himself, or roll, or anything, just like a ten-year old. The broken tree branch against his neck on the ground told me everything. Kid had maybe a few minutes left.

"Hey, hey kid," I said, kneeling next to him.

"Chris Anders," he replied, having the stupid presence of mind to introduce himself as he died.

"Yeah, sure, Anders — you're gonna be all right," I lied.

"Where's my mom?" he asked.

I sighed and looked around, but didn't see, or hear, anyone coming to see what the source of the noise was. I mean, it isn't like a kid falling off a three-story roof didn't make a noise.

Humans.

"She's on her—" I stopped talking when I realized he'd already died.

Above me, I heard the fold portal snap shut. Great. I had a dead kid in front of me and had managed to lose the trail. Tuesdays sucked. But Anders. I felt bad. Who wouldn't, right? So I considered my options.

I had, in my jacket, a single charge Reversal Capsule. Now, just to be clear, a Reversal Capsule wasn't some sort of cure-all for death. They just bent hypotheticals enough to undo some localized mistake. Expensive and almost impossible to get, I had exactly one, which I'd carried with me for the last ten years. You know those little things that you think you'll need but never want to use because the minute you do, you'll find a better use for them?

Exactly.

So I hadn't used it. Shit, I hadn't even paid for it.

But I got the damn thing out and broke the shiny seal along its middle. A burst of vapor fizzed out and tickled my nose, making me sneeze even as I tried to inhale it. Save me from cutesy effects layered over helpful devices.

Forming the idea in my mind, I touched Anders' neck and undid the break, then stood and waited. He coughed, the break never having happened, and started to cry as we both realized one of his legs had also been broken. But hey, that would heal.

"Hey, Anders," I said, "nice to meet you." I smoothed down my burnt orange suit jacket and looked back toward the roof. "I gotta go, though."

I did. I couldn't manage a fold portal myself but I had the WarBoots on so at the least I could FastWalk and, if I was lucky, find the Butterfly Hybrids, Quantum realized or not.

Spoiler: I didn't find them, got lost somewhere around Spokane, I think it was, and ended up tangled in a totally different problem. I did forget about Anders, though. The kid was fine, if once dead, after all.

CHAPTER TWO

THE SECOND TIME I met Anders, he thought I was dead. I get why, but still, annoying. The whole thing started, as too many things do, I think, with a knock at the door. I ignored it. No choice, really — I couldn't have moved just then if I'd wanted to.

He knocked again, not that I knew Anders owned the fist banging against the cheap wood and flaking paint of the door to my apartment. Anders swears here that he said something, called out or whatever, and I guess I'm inclined to accept that. From my end of things, I sat in a chair and kept dying, the way I'd intended to.

The door smashed open, the shitty doorjamb not bothering to do its job. I opened one eye, just enough to see a gummy, hazy version of a human standing there, light spilling in from the hallway behind him. I thought about cursing, about telling the stranger to leave, but my lips didn't work right.

He came in, rushing to my side, and even through the miasma that clouded my vision I could see the concern in the motion. His distress, which I could almost physically sense, served to make me angrier yet. Grabbing my hand, he took my pulse, and I weakly moved my arm away from him.

Other shapes came in behind him, and he turned to call out to them, waving them over to help him. I could feel my anger fighting the chemical cocktail that drifted through my veins. My body started to fight back, just out of a primal need to tell someone off. To tell a whole room of someones off. Pettiness is a hell of an anti-drug, it turns out.

The other shapes drew closer and lifted me out of my chair. One of many hands on me left and returned quickly, jabbing a flat disc of metal against my neck. I felt a pinch as the disc extended a thin needle into me. Chilled liquid flooded into me. Well, all right, it dribbled into me, a few drops of bullshit entering my system. The taste of lemons coated my tongue and I sighed, audibly.

First of all, the genuine concern of the first guy to rush over to me was misplaced for good. He'd meant it, I knew that, but the people with him sure as fuck didn't. That little bit of liquid, the taste coating my throat now like slime, I knew that poison. I also knew it would interact with the drugs in my system in exactly the wrong way.

If I'd been annoyed before by the interruption of my slow demise, I found myself flat-out angry now. Not at the attempt on my life, that sort of thing happened. No, they'd done it stupidly, that was the source of my anger. They hadn't bothered checking what I had in me already, and they'd rushed the job, and now I would have to make them regret all of it, from breaking in straight to waking me the hell up.

Because that's what the drug combination did. The liquid, a blend of several animal-based neurotoxins and two poisons developed from the blood of plants that didn't occur naturally, destroyed most of the drugs already in my system, burning them out quickly. Knowing that wouldn't have been hard to work around if these idiots had done their homework. Because they also should have known that the combination of what drugs remained plus their own poison would in no way kill me.

If I felt like being generous, and I so very much did not, but if I did, I would give them partial credit, because that leftover chemical sludge could easily stop a human's heart in a few minutes. But anyone coming for me also knew I wasn't human, not really. Human-adjacent. Human-ish. But not, strictly speaking, human.

No, the resulting crapfest in my veins didn't kill me. It woke me up. It pissed me off. It gave me a headache the size of a yeti. But it didn't kill me. I looked at the five people in my space. One of them, the one who had rushed toward me, wore a blue button-down shirt and slacks, paired with generic sneakers, with a satchel hung across his body. The other four all wore the same outfit: green slacks, black blazer, black turtleneck. They also had the same haircut, the sort of cheap bowl cut your mother gives you to save time and money, and because she probably couldn't care less about what your head looks like.

"You stupid fucks," I slurred, my voice still wobbly from a month or so of non-use, "just messed this all up." They dropped me then, in surprise, and I hit the floor with all the grace of a wet kitten fired from an air cannon. I propped myself up on my elbows, feeling new aches, and shook my head at the five surprised people around me. "Did they decide to send the C Team out today? Is that what happened? Do you need me to write a letter to your bosses explaining what went wrong here for your report cards? It's the sort of mistake that," I continued, my voice growing in strength and speed until I was spitting words out faster than my brain could keep up with, as I too often did, "a porcupine makes when it decides, 'Hey that puppy wants to cuddle and be friends,' because, oh no, it doesn't want to be friends with you, you dumb spiny loofa on legs. Which, wait, where was…oh come on," I said as my brain caught up and I remembered the only people to use that particular poison. "Don't the Subtle Knives of the Endless Blossom have anything better to do than try to kill…no wait, hold on."

I stood up and smiled darkly at the five faces looking back at me. None of them had moved an inch, captured by the sheer Noah-esque flood of words coming from my mouth. Why did they think I let myself run at the mouth that way?

"The Subtle Knives couldn't have found me. So," I pointed a long finger at the oddly familiar face in the room. The one who came in with honest concern for my well-being. "You led them to me. You're…" my brain struggled, still not fully online, to place the face. I got it and felt a single bark of laughter escape my throat. "Anders! Holy shit. Well that makes less and less sense. Anders," I asked him, my finger still aimed directly at his face, "why did you lead a shabby, badly planned kill team of Subtle Knives soldiers to my…no, how did you find me? Then, why did you lead *them* here?"

Anders just stared at me.

"Oh, stupid dead Anders," I said, warmly, "you didn't mean to, you didn't know who they…all right so just…how did you *find* me?"

7

"I've been looking for you," he said, smally, nervously. "And then I got here and you were *dead*..."

"No," I corrected, "*you* were dead, well, what was it fifteen years ago? Fourteen? Something like that. You were dead, stupid dead Anders, but then you weren't and I never have been, and now we're here and these guys," I lowered my hand, gesturing in an arc at the other four as I did, "are about to realize they have a *big* problem on their hands and try to kill us for real — not," I shook my head, annoyed, "with a shitty poison that, I just have to point out, wouldn't have worked anyway, and you guys should have known that, you flaming amateurs. That just gets to me, you know what I mean?" I asked Anders. "It's insulting. Show some respect if you want to kill someone, bring your A game, rise to their level."

"What?" Anders asked. "What is...you were *dead*, I mean, almost at least, and I..."

"Anders, keep up. Come over here," I curled my fingers and urged him to leave the pack. He did, confusion on his face, and I nodded, "there we go. Now, in about two seconds these guys are going to realize they've let me get to my feet and they've just stood there, and this is going to get bloody, unless I do..." I reached for my inner jacket pocket and then laughed. "That move," I said over my shoulder to Anders, "works better if I'm wearing a suit, and not," I looked down at myself, realizing I had no clue what I was wearing, "a tank-top and sweatpants." I shrugged. "We'll do this the hard way, then." I clapped my hands in front of me, feeling the energy start to grow.

All eyes were on me, as no one knew what would happen next. I drew my hands apart slowly, leaving trails of light hanging in the air. Light dripped from my fingertips, allowing me to form complex sigils in the room.

The Subtle Knife nearest me took a half-step back. He waited — they all did — for some sort of explosion, maybe, or a burst of energy, some sort of big effect to come. Suckers. I had nothing on me, not even sleeves. Sure, I could fold enough spare energy to draw pretty shapes in the air that would last — I wasn't sure, maybe another thirty seconds at best. That's all they were though — light.

I glanced behind me at Anders and smiled. Then I mouthed "Door" and turned away without thinking to make sure he'd understood me. One deep breath in, hold it for two seconds, then exhale, and I ran the other way, right into the Subtle Knives.

I heard Anders's footsteps moving away from me, good. He got that, at least. The Subtle Knives startled as I charged, moving into some sort of fancy fighting stance or another, I couldn't tell you. I had zero intention of fighting them. Instead I barreled through them and to the closet.

Yanking the door open, I stood with it between me and the Subtle Knives who were, I'm sure, recovering and turning to get to me. In front of me, however, hung a dark orange suit, torn to shreds. Like someone with a knife had had a very personal, and lengthy, conversion with it that ended the way a soulful talk with a tiger ends.

Me. The suit had had a talk with me.

I didn't care about that, though — I reached

down and grabbed the WarBoots sitting below. Boots in hands, I dropped to the floor in a squat and turned as I did, causing the Subtle Knives reaching for me to grab nothing but air.

Standing again, I took off at a run, heading for the door, chasing Anders, making sure they saw the Boots in my hand. The Subtle Knives followed, after a few beats. Anders had worked his way down the four flights to the street, and I gained on him easily.

"Right at the door," I said as softly as I could while still making sure he heard me. He didn't reply but managed to turn the correct direction as he left the building. I could've grabbed his shoulder by then, but didn't want to slow either of us down. I still almost grabbed the strap of the bag crossing his back, wanting to make sure.

This, right then, the running, the being chased and having to think of four alternate plans because you always know the first few would fall flat, this was what I had been trying to put behind me. I was done with it. Having the whole mess of that life find me made me want to claw the eyes out of the world.

Instead I just said, "Duck into the next building," and followed Anders as he did as asked. I held an arm across his chest, pushing him further into the shadows in the lobby of the building we'd entered. I set the Boots down softly.

White, they came up a good eight inches, looking, mostly, like any other pair of beaten-to-crap boots in the world. Cracked and scuffed, the WarBoots were unique on Earth. Small black boxes dotted the outside near the top, each one about an inch square. They sat open, their fasteners split down the middle. I stepped into them, slowly, almost reverently. I fought, the entire time, the urge to curse really loudly.

I should've destroyed them when I turned away, when I did my suit in. I know I should've, but destroying WarBoots isn't easy and even if I could've just tossed them into a fire and walked away I don't think I would've. We'd been through too much together, these Boots and I.

My feet fit perfectly, the fasteners hanging open. Waiting. I closed my eyes and lifted my heels inside the boots, bringing each down in a quick pattern — tap, taptap, tap. The boxes on the side of each WarBoot glowed softly and the fasteners snapped shut by themselves.

I shoved Anders back harder as the Knives ran by, not even glancing toward the building we stood in. They went by, and I waited. Sure enough, they came back, looking around and talking to each other. Frustrated, they headed off. I stood there, arm against Ander's chest, breathing slow and deep, feeling the strange, constant background hum of the WarBoots in my bones.

"They didn't even look?" Anders whispered.

I turned, letting my arm drop away from him, and gave him a grin I hated even as I did it. The grin came from the old me, the one that enjoyed this sort of thing, and I'd be damned if I would let it get a toehold in me again. "I made sure they saw the WarBoots," I said, pointing down at them, "and knew they would assume I'd put them on during the run and use them. This group, they're low-level, the sort of team you send to deal with a kitten up a tree when you need to set fire to the tree. They're not bright enough to track a FastWalk."

"You mean running?"

"No, you can track running, you just sort of... well, you look and see where someone went, because people don't tend to run so fast they vanish from sight in a second or two. FastWalking — well, shit, you're about to find out." I pushed open the door and stepped out into the cool Regina afternoon at a perfectly leisurely pace. "What I need you to do is hold my arm tight. Do *not* let go," I told him, holding out my right arm for him to grab. "Now," I thought about it a second, "you've walked before. I mean that isn't a question, I'm just telling you. You've taken steps. This will be the same thing. Watch my feet, don't watch where we're going. It'll be easier. When you see my foot start to swing forward, match my step. Bring your step down as I do, and repeat. That's all you need to do, match my stride, all right?"

"Sure," he said casually, and I could see the thought race across his face as he considered that I might have some sort of problem causing me to need to explain walking.

"This will be exactly like walking, just put one foot in front of the other, ten miles away," I said.

"Wait, what?"

"Simple," I said, and started to swing my foot forward, "just match my steps." I knew if I gave him too long to consider, to ask questions, we'd be stuck there for days, and though I didn't see anyone around looking for us, frankly that meant less than nothing considering how the day'd gone so far.

The world around us jumped into fast forward. The WarBoots hummed louder, the vibrations traveling up my legs to my spine. I put my foot down, looking to make sure Anders kept up. He did fine and I lifted my back leg, watching him copy me quick enough that the step continued smoothly. We walked like that, carefully so Anders could get used to the ride as much as anyone with absolutely no idea what was going on could.

Back leg swinging forward, we took another step together. The WarBoots did their job perfectly, undamaged by sitting in a closet for a month or two. Not a surprise — they were the one thing left I could trust with my life.

Also, let me be clear here, the drugs I had flowing through my system when Anders and his "friends" broke in wouldn't have killed me. I wasn't suicidal. Not really. At worst, if I let it, the chemicals could've put me in a coma. Some people play chicken in strange ways. You have to test your limits. That's all it was.

Which is, of course, a lie. I could've died. I probably wouldn't have. Let's be realistic and pin it down at a seventy-five percent survival rate. That twenty-five percent, though — I could tell you I didn't root for it, but if I didn't, at least on some level, want the drugs to win why play the game, right?

It's complicated. That's what I told myself as I kept walking. We'd walked in a basically straight line so far, heading south. We needed to turn a bit, and turning while FastWalking can be tricky if you don't know what you're doing. It's worse when you have a passenger. I warned Anders, best

I could, and turned, feeling the skid try and pull me off course to the side. I fought it, yelling, "Lean into the turn!" to Anders, who did as he was told well enough. We only *almost* skidded out.

No one wants to find themselves moving sideways and dropping back fully into regular space like that. You don't tend to limp away. We held course, though, and kept walking. I glanced over at Anders and saw he was studiously watching my feet and not looking up.

I guessed he had looked up at least once and realized why I'd warned him. The world flashed by, a giant Technicolor blur that hurt to stare at. You needed to learn to, and wearing the WarBoots helped some, but I wore them and Anders didn't, plus I wasn't new to this ride. Which was as it should be. There wasn't anything special about it, I just owned the damned things.

We took a few more steps, around seventy in total since we'd started, and I told Anders to stop as I stopped, no sooner, and gave him a countdown on how many more steps we had. We stopped, and I looked around, pretending to ignore the sound of Anders throwing up. The sun was already on its slow descent and the air was fresh as I took a big, deep gulp of it. FastWalks always leave you breathing stale air — you get wisps that are slow enough to breathe caught up in your wake, but it's like breathing twelve-hour-old airplane air.

Anders recovered enough to stand up straight and look around. "Where are we?" he asked, and I grunted at him in mild surprise. Most people would ask *how* before where, after something like that. He was proving to be an interesting one.

"Cheyenne, Wyoming," I told him, turning around on the spot. "Do you see a cheap hotel, maybe?"

"You need to rest after," he waved his hands in search of a description for what we'd just done and came up empty, "...that?"

"No," I told him, only kind of lying. "But I do want a shower."

"Oh," he said, "well I don't know the area..."

"It's fine," I said, and took off walking, "most towns are basically the same. There's a main strip, right?" I gestured around us at the sparse shops. "We're obviously not really on it, but probably close. So we go a bit and find the center then work our way out. Someone will be trying to let people take a nap near the action, just so they can get back to it and spend more money." I turned a corner, Anders a step behind me. "And I know that sounds mercenary and you're thinking, 'Well a lot of towns aren't just trying to take tourists' money,' but really of course they are, that's the job of a small local hotel like that. Anyway, we'll find it, and you can explain some stuff, then you can leave and I can have that shower."

"Uhm, all right," he said, hesitant. I ignored the tone and kept looking for a hotel. Whatever his reasons for being around, I'd find out soon enough. What I didn't want to happen was me finding out that the reason landed me in a bad spot, something that I might have to deal with, while standing in the middle of a street. For the next few I'd play along, and use it to get us somewhere enclosed, in case.

Then, after dealing with him, I could go back

to working out if I wanted to be here, or anywhere, anymore. What good was it? I needed to figure it out, and I wouldn't do *that* while running around.

About fifteen minutes later, which was passed with mostly silence, we found a place. Anders didn't seem inclined to talk, or at least all he wanted was answers I wouldn't give him yet. Maybe he realized I needed my own answers first. Whatever the reason, I didn't really care. I led us into the small, four-story hotel and past the aggressively beige walls and chrome door accents to the front desk.

The desk clerk looked as bored as a human could get without dissolving into a puddle of goo. I shrugged at him and he nodded. "Anders," I said, not even looking at him, "pay the nice hotel for a room."

"Me?" he asked, fishing out his wallet anyway.

"Stupid dead Anders, you're why I had to leave in a hurry wearing just this. Do I look," I gestured at myself, "like I have a wallet on me?"

Desk Clerk didn't even raise an eyebrow at that. Couldn't have been the third strangest thing said around him this week, though. He traded us some keys for a swipe of Anders's credit card and we rode up to the third floor in a rickety elevator that seemed old enough to be the building's original one. I leaned against the back wall of it, while we rode up for what seemed like...elevators are supposed to be faster than stairs, is all I mean.

The room itself, when we got there, was so tiny the double bed in it took up over half the floorspace. We could get around each other, if we needed to, but would have to work at not touching when we did. The paint, that special off-white that hotels love, had just started to fade, and the single bare bulb light in the ceiling did the place no favors. I pulled the curtains shut and sat down in the single chair next to a tiny round side table. Anders sat on the edge of the bed and just looked at me as he took his bag off and set it on the bed.

I picked up the phone that sat on the end table and called downstairs. Reluctantly the desk clerk agreed to order a pizza to our room and have the guy deliver right to us. I thanked him and set the phone down, looking at Anders. "What?"

"I thought you just wanted a shower," he said, perched on the edge of the bed and nervously still.

"And then I realized I was hungry," I said, "and that you probably are, too. What's the problem, outside of you having to pay for it?"

"I just...no, nothing," Anders said, looking away from me to stare at the floor.

"Out with it," I said. "I mean think of it this way, you could tell me or I could sit here and ask you a whole lot more questions. Because there's something going on here that doesn't add up. You're obviously not with the Subtle Knives of the Endless Blossom."

"I don't even know what that is," he said.

"I believe you," I told him, "which is part of my problem here. So what the hell, Anders? What's your problem? Right this second, what is it?"

"All right!" he yelled, standing. "You're just..." he waved his hands about in as loss for words, pacing in a tight formation around the end of the bed, "...less than I thought you would be."

"And what," I asked, leaning as far back in

my crappy chair as I could, "is that supposed to mean?" I also worked to ignore the smell of the cheap carpet wafting up toward me. A small gag felt appropriate but right then I felt Anders would take it the wrong way, and I wasn't sure yet why I would even care.

"You clearly remember who I am," he said.

"Clearly."

"Thirteen years ago," he said, "I died, because you startled me off a roof. Then you brought me back. I remember it. My parents said I imagined it but I knew. So as soon as I was old enough to leave home, I started looking for you. Asking around, after an impossible woman, teleporting around rooftops. It didn't go well, at first." He shrugged.

"I imagine not," I agreed.

"But I kept at it. That was all I did. I heard rumors, other people who had run into you, forums with strange cases — a lot of people making stuff up, sure, but just enough truth to keep me moving. Across states, whenever a sighting happened close enough for me to get to."

He stopped and took a breath before sitting back down on the edge of the bed. He clearly wasn't used to speaking this much, never mind all in a rush. He stared down at his feet and started talking again, softer now. "I've been washing dishes, stocking bookshelves, waiting tables, whatever I could to keep going, just to find you. Just to find the magic person who saved my life and made it all look like such *fun*. And instead I find..." he looked up then, letting his glance take me in, all of me in my disheveled state. "I find you."

"I sort of — I'll be honest here, Anders — I

sort of wish I was offended, but," I looked down at myself, "no, I get it."

"I had a lead, quit my last job, and started up into Canada. Nothing. My visa had run out, I was going to have to deal with that on either side of the boarder, but there was utter silence. No sightings in a few years. I explored Canada, went back to older sightings in the area, everything. No luck. I was about to give up when these guys approached me, looking for you. They sounded just like the other people I knew who hunted down references to you, except they all kept dressing the same. Like a uniform. But some people have strange religions I'm not privy to, so..." He waved his hands again.

"All right, but come on. Why were you looking for me at all?" I asked. "You had a whole new life to live and not spend falling off rooftops. And you spend half of it wandering around looking for me?"

"I wanted to be *like* you," he said, hurt.

"So why weren't you?" I asked. "I mean, let's say — fine, let's say I get it. You had an idea of what I am, who I am, from a ten-second interaction, and wanted that thing for yourself. So why not just do it? Instead you chase down a fiction in search of, I'll assume, meaning — and come on, Anders, I didn't save you so you could just waste yourself like this."

"It wasn't a waste," he insisted. He kept his voice small in the room, still looking at his feet, though I suppose he could have been studying the rug and wondering why it smelled as strongly as it did.

A knock as the door made him jump, but I just raised an eyebrow. "Pizza," I told him.

ADAM P. KNAVE

"Couldn't it be those — whatever they were? They found us already?"

"Then they better have pizza with them," I told him. "Go get the door and let's see." I didn't want Anders hurt, but I figured if the Knives found me that fast they really wanted me dead and I could use that to trade for Anders's life. Or I could give in and think of something else fast. Either way, I didn't care. I couldn't work up the energy to.

The pizza guy was just a pizza guy and Anders paid him and set the pizza on the table near my chair, shifting it so it sat nearer the bed before he sat back down and took a piece. "It wasn't," he said as he chewed, "a waste of my life. I saw a lot of two countries, and met a lot of people, and—"

"And helped people when you could?" I asked.

"Of course," he said.

"Then what the hell do you need me for? Go on," I waved him away with a piece of pizza, "get back to it."

"What happened to you?" he asked.

"Nothing," I lied. "Like you would even know. Anders, you don't know me. Seriously."

"I spent years looking into you. Paige Never, the woman who shows up when you need her the most and expect it the least. The person who will save you, and leave the unexplained behind, so no one will ever even believe you if you tell them about her."

"So you know some press clippings, and obviously people do believe you if you tell them or you wouldn't be here. So there's that whole argument put to bed. Sure, sometimes I helped people, but that was then. You don't know me,

Anders. Just go on, live an actual full life, and leave me to it."

Anders sat there, finishing another slice, thinking. After a minute or so of silence, when I was almost sure I'd figured out what chemicals were being misused to make the rug smell terrible, he smiled. "Aren't you at least interested in why they were after you?"

"Trying to stoke curiosity to get me to do what you want?" I asked. "Lame, Anders. And who cares why? I've made a lot of people angry over the years. Most folks don't need much more reason than that."

"You seemed confused, though," he said, pressing the matter.

"Well, sure," I said, my mouth running away with me before I manage to stop it, "the Subtle Knives of the Endless Blossom don't normally hunt like that, much less have a reason to try for me, I'm way above their pay grade."

"So then why did they?" Anders smiled as he asked his question and I considered punching him. I didn't *care*. He was so seemingly invested in making me be the thing he thought I should be that he was ignoring the reality of the situation. Alternatively, reverse all that and blame me, I guess.

"Who knows, or cares, Anders?" We'd eaten most of the pizza by then, and the last slice hung out in the box all alone.

"I care," he said, sharper than I expected. "Don't you get it? They used me to get to you. I spent years trying to find you, wanting to be like you — do you really not get it?"

I held up a hand palm out in supplication. I did get it. He felt he had somehow betrayed me — me, the goal of his life. And even though, wow, I shouldn't have been, I still was that goal for him and finding out you'd been used to almost kill the thing you wanted more than anything — that hurt. I did understand. So why couldn't I just tell him that?

And there it was. If I didn't understand him, I could push away any sense of responsibility. Admitting it, though, knowing exactly why he cared, that made me complicit, at least in my own head. Personally, I didn't care why the Knives were coming for me. Hell, if they managed to do me in then they did. I wouldn't just roll over for them, of course not, but if they pulled it off, then they did. I could accept that.

But they'd done Anders wrong, and he just wanted to help. To help other people, of course, in some broken sense of following in what he'd decided were my footprints. More than that, though, Anders wanted to help me now. Partly to make up for what he felt was his part in me almost getting killed, as if that was a rare occurrence, and partly because that was simply who he was.

That *did* get to me. His desire to help on a few different levels, most of them utterly, consciously unselfish, spoke to me. I didn't want to snuff it out, even if I no longer wanted to partake myself. Which left only one answer. I took the last slice of pizza and dropped the empty box on the floor, near my feet.

"Let's say, for the sake of argument," I said, after I swallowed, "I do get it. And fun fact," I added, "if you consider all the times pizza has brokered understanding, I mean it stopped a war once. Not some ancient Roman war, I know you're thinking it, but no, this wasn't some old-timey people sitting around a fire going 'Let me show you what we invented' and sharing one of the first pizzas as a way to bring about peace. That would have been great, I agree, but I've never heard of it. Back in the 1960's, though," I said, gesturing with the last quarter of the slice in my hand, "there was a group who created a Slide Dimension. One of those stupid things people think is a great idea, they can create a section of their own reality and rule it and to hell with everyone else." I laughed and took another bite. "Anyway, they always — and I mean always here, I've never seen someone create a Slide Dimension who does the math correctly before they whip the stupid thing into existence — they always leave a drain hole, because you have to. Slide Dimensions don't function well by themselves, there's an entropy leak, so they keep sucking on the nipple of the actual universe like the milk is free.

"Milk," I said," is never free, Anders. Not for the cow, or goat, or I don't know whatever it is you like to milk. Rattlesnake. The damn rattlesnake milk isn't free for everyone, even if you can force it from the snake, see? So they forget this and a small war breaks out right on the border."

"What does this..." Anders started to ask, but I shrugged and gnawed on some crust.

"Short war, though, because the drainage hole was even bigger than normal, and once you create a Slide Dimension for yourself you're not going

ADAM P. KNAVE

to be the type of person inclined to just break it down because you messed up. But a bigger drain meant everyone noticed, and when I say everyone, I mean the Ascension noticed, The Collective Twitch started asking questions, hell, the Subtle Knives probably noticed, but fuck them. So yeah, war, and fast. But we..." I stopped, closed my eyes and corrected myself, "but I came by, delivered some pizza. Exactly like you don't, to the border of a growing war. It stopped everything, though, partly because who does that, but also because the energy drain, the entropic flow, really sped up near the border given how badly things were constructed, and people were seriously, deathly hungry because the various factions hadn't thought to take *that* into account even.

"Yeah, so while people gobbled pizza like starved hamsters, peace broke out and we were able to refold the Slide Dimension back harmlessly. Without it there, and with the idiots who'd tried to create it in the first place also so hungry they'd lost most of their body mass in only a few hours, they realized the problem and had to stare at it, too. So no more war, just pizza and some light incarceration.

"Which is why," I said, finishing the slice and looking at Anders, "pizza is a really good idea to help you settle some shit." I nodded and looked down at myself. "I still need that shower, and I'll need to change."

"Wait, I'm still..."

"I'm going to go look into this, all right?" I took a few quick shallow breaths and looked at the pizza box, preparing.

"I'm coming with you," he said, as I admit I knew he would.

"Then you need to change, too," I said, not fighting it yet. He'd earned this, to an extent. "But understand, we're just going to go talk to one friend, maybe raise a flag, and leave it there. This isn't a *thing*, and it won't become one."

"Sure, sure," he said, far too quickly. "But why do I need to change? I didn't see a store around here when we came in."

"We don't need one," I told him, and kicked the pizza box with intent. The kick wasn't hard, but the intent behind it helped refold the universe, so I had that going for me. Anders jumped at the kick, but I ignored him.

Opening the box, I took out a suit and a pair of shoes. Black suit, green shirt, matching green tie, and a pair of simple black dress shoes with good, biting tread on them. Setting them down on the floor, I looked at Anders. "This should fit. Unless I'm seriously rusty, which I am, but still — should fit." Closing the box, I kicked it again. I opened it and took out another set of clothes, this time for me. I didn't need shoes, since the WarBoots weren't the sort of footwear you replace.

"Wait, what?" Anders stared at the clothes in his hand, and then looked at the second set I set on the table, and then again at the box. He repeated the three-stage look a few times.

"It's nothing," I reassured him.

"That wasn't *nothing*," he insisted, "you just pulled two sets of clothes from nowhere."

"No," I said, "I pulled them from this box." I nudged the still-open pizza box with my foot.

"That's impossible."

"Obviously it isn't," I said. "It's a simple causality fold. Normally you do a thing and then something happens, you push a book off a table and it hits the floor. Simple universal rule. This just inverts it. The book is on the floor, and so now, at some point, it needs to be pushed off the table."

"That doesn't help," he said. "How does the book get back *on* the table if it was already pushed off?"

"It wasn't pushed off, that's my point," I said.

"Then how can it be on the floor, and if it is on the floor, how can it also be on the table waiting to be pushed?"

I stood up, picking up the bundle of clothes. I tapped my feet inside the WarBoots in the right pattern and the connectors opened. I didn't take them off, which wasn't a sign that I didn't trust Anders so much as that I didn't like the idea of the Boots being out of my sight anymore. "So long as you close the loop, make sure you commit the cause eventually, it's all fine. The universe sorts itself out. So long as you close the loop," I repeated with a shrug.

"So you can do magic. Show me again?"

"It isn't magic, it's applied science, and before you say it, no, any science advanced enough doesn't look like magic. That's flat out wrong. It doesn't *look like magic*. The right way to say it is that advanced stuff makes people stop thinking and so they assign the magic label so they don't have to work out the logic behind it."

"There's no logic behind..."

"Oh, fine," I said. I snapped my fingers. "Look

under the bed."

Anders got off the bed, knelt on the floor, and pulled the pizza box out. He looked at the box in his hand and then at the identical box still on the floor. "But that's the same…it has the same grease stain and—"

I kicked the box still on the floor so it slid under the bed. "There, now it's under the bed where you found it."

He set the box in his hand on the bed and looked under for the one I had kicked. There was, of course, nothing there. "Where'd it go?"

"You just pulled it out and put it on the bed," I explained.

"No, but there were two boxes and then you—"

"And then I completed the loop. You grabbed the box from under the bed. So I put it under the bed. Once I completed the loop, the one I put under the bed became the one you had already pulled out, so it can't be in two places at once."

"But it *was* in two places," he insisted.

"Until I completed the loop. That's what I mean. You need to complete the loop," I said, not sure how else to explain it. I stood up. "I need a shower, or I'll be forced to gnaw my own arm off just in protest. But go, you shower and change. I need to make a call first." I herded him into the bathroom before he could protest about causality looping making no sense again.

I grabbed the phone and dialed. Wrong number. Right, it'd been a few years since I'd called Smythe. Just meant I'd have to show up unannounced, but it wouldn't be the first time for that. I heard water running from the bathroom and stood there, thinking. I considered leaving, just ditching Anders. I didn't really care about the Subtle Knives problem, outside of a spot of curiosity, and digging into it at all could put him at risk.

Of course, if I left him, there was a good chance they would, if they were serious about finding me, find Anders again instead. And this time they wouldn't use him to find me, they'd just kill him.

Thanks to me, another person was in danger. Once again it all came down on my head. I needed to keep Anders safe now, at least safe enough to get him clear of this. Which led to the question of how safe I could make him. Let's say I found out why they wanted to kill me — I didn't intend to do anything about it, really, because to hell with them. But that didn't put Anders in the clear.

I started to get angry. This is how it happened, you tried to make sure someone was safe but you couldn't ever stop, could you? Being safe, like being happy, was a fleeting concept. I couldn't be expected to protect everyone near me for the rest of their lives, much less the rest of mine.

Anything else, though, and the blame came crashing down on me. "You said I'd be safe," as if I controlled everything. The anger looped around to point right at my own heart, because that sort of all-powerful bullshit, that persona remained the one I happily draped across my shoulders without considering the fallout. It felt good, the superiority of it, the power and joy it could bring. The way it made people feel safe could be used as a weapon as much as anything else. If people believed in you, they didn't stop to question you as much. You could do things the way you felt like getting them done.

It cut corners I liked cutting. Feeling like the hero was, even for a few fleeting moments between fighting for my life, a really seductive thing. Shit, most of the fighting for my life, at least here on Earth, tended toward being my own fault. I could've just ignored things, not burst into the breach like some sort of hero. Some sort, indeed. The sort of hero who wanted to make sure you knew she was the hero of the moment, and not anyone else.

Fuck. All of that noise, all of it, had led to me sitting in a chair, doping myself to the gills so that even if I didn't die, at least my brain turned off for a while. I wouldn't fix any of my shit here, standing in a low-end hotel waiting for a shower. I tried to shut my brain off on my own for a second, harder than it might sound, and looked around.

Anders had left his bag on the bed.

I listened for the sound of the shower running, and yup, water still rained down in the bathroom. I opened his bag carefully and drew out a small notebook, pen clipped to the cover. I flipped through and glanced at the writing on the inside. He'd been keeping logs of his search for me. Noting down what people said about me, loose thoughts about how true the stories were and where he could go next.

It's a strange experience to read about yourself as if you were a myth. Stranger, in fact, I could say easily, than acting like a myth and seeing it in people's faces. That anger from before never left, didn't have time to, really. No, it lingered, and found a new outlet in Anders's writing.

I found myself mad enough, possibly just annoyed enough, to not notice the shower stop. Engrossed in reading entries I was standing there, flipping through pages, when Anders came out of the bathroom, dressed in the suit I'd provided.

"That's private!" he yelled at me, crossing the small room in maybe three steps max, to snatch the book from my hands. Anders was short, shorter than my five foot ten probably by a good three inches..

"The suit mostly fits," I said. I didn't reach for the book back, looking Anders over critically. "I mean it fits enough, it fits good even, but I wouldn't call it perfect. That's on me, bad visualization on my part."

"Don't ignore me," he said, "you can't just go through my things."

"Everything in there seems to be about me, wouldn't you say? I think that gives me some leeway." I gathered up my own clothes and shrugged at him. "I'm not an animal to be studied, Anders. Just stop with the note taking."

"Paige," he said, using my name for the first time, and didn't that feel odd? It really did, I can't explain it fully, but he made it sound both familiar and distant at the same time. Addressing a monster from his closet that he'd known about for too long to be fully afraid of anymore, but still respected, I guess. "This is my journal. Mine."

Intriguing to watch him stand up for himself, out of nowhere. Ashamed of the journal, maybe? Or ashamed of being caught with it? Possibly neither, of course, but it didn't matter. I shrugged.

"Sure thing, Anders," I told him, and wandered into the bathroom, clothes and WarBoots in hand.

Anders got a suit and some shoes, but I got the whole package, including new underwear and a sports bra. Just looking at new clothes made me *feel* rank. The tank top draped across my body felt, suddenly, like it was actively rotting away as I wore it. I tore it off myself along with everything else and started the shower, running the hot water full blast. Let it scald me. Go for it, I dared the shower, do your worst.

I stayed under the water for long enough, scrubbing hard enough to stop feeling my skin as a particular part of me, letting it dissolve in my mind until I simply existed. My mind wouldn't shut off, of course — it never did — but I tried to let the anger go. That also never really worked, but at least half of it morphed happily into a sort of meh-like acceptance. That'd have to do for now.

Toweling myself off, I realized how badly I needed a haircut. This shoulder-length nonsense didn't work for me. I considered a ponytail and then tossed the idea away as quickly as I would've pigtails. Nothing wrong with them, for other people, but me, I wanted to not give myself a handle on the back of my head.

I started to get dressed, slowly, reconsidering my choices. I knew, when I'd grabbed the suit from the causality loop, that I shouldn't have. How could I claim to not be getting back into any of my old life and still put on a suit like this? So casually, stepping right back into things.

As I buttoned the dark gray shirt, I watched myself in the mirror. The anger swam around, toying with self-loathing, as my old self came into view. The burnt orange pants and matching jacket went on too easily, and I fought back a curse when I noticed the lump in the jacket pocket. Of course. I outsmarted myself. When you're creating a loop and pulling things forward like I had, you try to think precise, so you know what you'll have to do later to close the loop. Sometimes, though, your mind drifts a little.

Yes, I meant to bring a suit this color and cut forward. It's my default — it's who I was, if not who I still am. Like it or not, and to be clear I absolutely did not like it, dressing the part greased the wheels in my favor. But this, I sneered at the lump of fabric withdrawn from the pocket, I didn't consider. I left out, at least consciously. Not a great sign for my well-being, or my ability to work with causality loops, if I started to let my subconscious run the show.

I stood there and tied the ascot, tucking it under my collar and unbuttoning another button of my shirt so it laid correctly. The dark, blood-red color stood out from the dark orange of the suit just enough to call attention to itself, which was the entire point.

Wear one odd object, a strangely colored suit, and people might notice you. Add something else uncommon — a monocle, a funny hat, some vegetable in a breast pocket, or, say, a cravat when no one wears anything like that for serious these days — and you stand out as some strange social exception. It can, if you play it correctly, give you power in a room, just for standing there and not being self-conscious about it.

This couldn't be who I became again. On the other hand, this persona, this outward shell, would make a brief excursion simpler. So fine, I could wear a shell once more, in order to speed by how long I'd need to pretend. I put the WarBoots back on and secured them, feeling the hum in my bones, and tried to let it relax me.

I stepped out of the bathroom to see Anders trying to hide the fact he had just been writing in that notebook of his. Oh good, that wouldn't get on my nerves *at all* in a constant, background-radiation sort of way. Nope.

Anders looked over at me when I stepped back into the room, looking up from his journal, and the look on his face…it made me want to change again, into anything else. He didn't give me adoration or anything — no, his look managed to encompass a balloon of emotion I could only really settle on calling 'contentment'.

"Can we," I asked, "just go? Unless," I added, "you've come to your senses and will let me just deal with this myself."

"No way," Anders said, shoving his notebook in his bag and slinging it over his suit. "I'm part of this, too."

"You're not, but fine."

"I am *now*, I mean," he said, opening the door.

"Let's just get this over with," I said, heading for the stairs instead of the rickety elevator.

CHAPTER THREE

I TOOK ANDER'S elbow in hand once we were outside, and we did a short FastWalk to Boise, Idaho. Destination of all the greats, Boise still had strips lit up for truckers but otherwise slept as night settled across it. Smythe loved the town, swearing it gave him everything he needed.

He lived on the outskirts, in a small brown house, surrounded by far too many stone figures. Angels, gnomes, birds, a few cats, and even elephants — if you made it out of stone or a particularly good plaster, and it sat no more than about two feet tall, Smythe seemed to demand it live somewhere around his house.

Every time I'd been here the collection had grown. No reason behind it, according to him, except for his pleasure at collecting them. I assumed the 'everything he needed' part of the town was that no one had run him out yet for his decorating sense.

What grass there could be, straining between ever-encroaching statuary, grew tall and stupid, with no way to really cut it except to get in there between each statue with a pair of scissors, I guess.

Anders, still getting used to the aftereffect of a FastWalk, looked around and then stared at me. "You know a crazy statue guy?"

"Smythe," I said, "isn't a...all right, he has a thing for lawn statues, I will not deny that. But you have to admit," I waved a hand to encompass the mad collection, "it's distinctive. Most people, you have to guess, wonder if they moved or died. But not Smythe, nope. You know where he is, because anyone else would've called for an exorcist and a dumpster, in that order."

"And this is the guy you think can help?" he asked as we walked up the path to the door, which was, obviously, lined with statuary unblinkingly watching us go by.

"Just because a guy has a...slight stone fetish...that's no reason to discount his ability. His judgement in lawn decoration, sure, I wouldn't ask him to help me with landscaping. But we aren't here for landscaping, are we?" I asked. We stood at the door. "The Subtle Knives of the Endless Blossom are a thing for Smythe, one of those nagging burrs. Like when you bite the inside of your cheek and you keeping rubbing it with your tongue but each time you do, you tell yourself it won't heal if you don't stop?" I knocked on the door, turning to look at Anders. "It's like that for him, that nagging sore spot, when really, to hell with them."

"If they're so meaningless, then why are we here?" he asked.

I laughed, loudly. "Because you insisted," I told him, trying to not yell. "I was fine letting it go and ignoring it, but no, you needed to know, you tried to convince me to find out, and here we are. Don't go telling me you don't care *now*."

"No, I didn't mean..." he searched for a way to back out of the corner he'd planted himself firmly in.

"I get it," I said, letting him off the hook. "Like I said, they're a nagging burr. Don't worry about it. Smythe will know what they're up to and then we can go our separate ways with this settled."

"If he's home," Anders said, nodding at the still-closed door.

I knocked again. "I hope he is—" but as I said it, as if I conjured him, Smythe opened the door. He looked terrible. Gaunt, eyes deep set, his six-foot-two frame possibly invisible from the side. Too many days' beard growth lingered across his jaw like weeds, and his hand shook as he held it out to me.

"Hello," he said, voice devoid of any recognition.

"Smythe, it's me, Paige," I said, shaking the offered hand.

He nodded absently and offered a hand to Anders as well. Anders shook it and then shot me a quick glance. I shrugged. Smythe turned away from us and walked back inside his house, not bothering to invite us in or close the door, or even to tell me off. Not a good set of signs, honestly.

Inside his house seemed...fine. That was worrying in a whole different way. Smythe always liked a messy house, full of stacks of papers and books and whatever else he found himself working on. This, though, was clean to the bone, and sparse, everything put away. As if a different person lived here now. I pressed on, trying to act like everything was just this side of normal.

"Hey, Smythe, I figured you might know the answer to a simple riddle," I said to his back as he continued to ignore us and wander into his kitchen. I held an arm out to stop Anders and we stood there in the entranceway as I closed the door behind us.

No reply.

"Is he...I mean is this normal?" Anders asked, whispering to me.

"Wasn't the last time I saw him," I said. "Hey, Smythe!" I called out louder now, watching my old friend make tea from across the house. "A riddle, a mystery, a thing to be solved. You might even need a book or two," I said, trying to tempt him back to us. Then to Anders as Smythe continued to ignore us, "No, this isn't right at all."

I crossed the entranceway into the living room, Anders right behind me, and fairly threw myself down on the couch. I settled in as comfortable as possible, noticing Anders sitting painfully straight next to me.

A mystery, a thing to be solved. I hated it. Something had happened — not a good thing, either — to Smythe and I'd have to work it out. This, I told myself, was how it started, how it built. You get back in the game for a second, and suddenly you realize the world is upside down and you're the one who can see the switch to flip. So you flip it, except that never sets things right, just right enough for today, because there are always other switches, always other problems.

I still insisted, to myself, that I would get an answer from Smythe, help a friend, and then stop again. Because this shit was exhausting. But fine. Fine. We'd do this.

"Some...thing," I told Anders, "got into Smythe, or replaced him. Right now it's a bad sock puppet over an old friend, just lumbering around, going through motions that don't even add up to close to who he normally is."

"So what do we do?" he asked.

Oh, sweet Anders. You do nothing. I do things. You sit there. But I didn't say that. "I need to feel for soft spots," I told him. "Think of reality as a goat. A really loud, shitting-everywhere, eating-your-socks goat. It goes about its day all normal, and sometimes, there's a—"

"A soft spot? In a goat?"

"All right, no, but reality really is like a shitting, bleating goat, all right? That much is true. It's also like a plank of wood. Not a wooden goat — although the case could be made, you would be hard pressed to make a wooden goat as smelly or annoying as a live goat so that whole idea just falls apart — let's stick with the plank of wood for now. Wood gets a soft spot, some rot, and if you're not careful it will grow and then you'll have to start over, whole new plank of wood."

"Wait, this thing wrong with Smythe, it could... destroy all of reality?" Anders asked.

"No, I mean — I don't think so, at least. It's a metaphor," I said. "Relax. I just mean I have to find the soft spot, the source of the rot, and then I might know what we're dealing with."

"Might?"

"Might. I'm sorry, Anders," I said, shaking my head with amusement, "did you think there was a handbook to this madness? You just sort of hang on, and hope for the best, and learn when to duck and when you have to fight a duck, and..."

"You've fought ducks?" he broke in. Smythe

stirred tea in the kitchen and started to turn back toward us.

"You *haven't*?" I asked. I shrugged. "We've met very different ducks, you and I. Regardless. Let me work."

Anders shrugged a fairly petulant shrug, or at least I read it that way quickly, and I thought about Smythe. Most people, you look for a soft spot, you feel out the world around them and something sticks out. Smythe, like me, happened to be one of the people who did a lot of that exact sort of digging in their free time. It lends a certain…chaos…to the environment around you. So I couldn't just feel for anything off in the environment, because Smythe collected that exact sort of thing.

What I needed to find, then, would be the gun in the room full of guns that not only still had a bullet in it, but also had a bunch of powder residue around it. I cast my mind wide, eyes closed, feeling the room out. Nothing. Great.

I stood up, letting my eyes open slowly, and started to wander the house. I waved Anders to sit down and stay, hoping whatever remained of Smythe would be easily fooled. From the noises behind me, he had been.

The door to Smythe's workshop tempted me but I rejected it for now. Needle in a haystack could be a fun game, but I really wanted to rule out everything else first. So I kept wandering, slowly, letting myself remember how to feel out a wobble in the spin of the world. I really hoped the rust I'd let myself grow hadn't managed to make this all harder. I knew that it had, though, and I also knew that was the entire point. I didn't do this anymore.

I told that to myself a few times, as I kept on doing it all through Smythe's house.

I found the culprit in the bathroom. As soon as I came close to the room I could feel it, a cold, almost damp feeling that ran through the air with a charge. Tendrils of it, seeping through the door. I opened it and went right for the source, wedged between the wall and the toilet tank — a small, highly dangerous bag.

I couldn't just grab it. Being this close to it already threatened me. I could feel wiggling spikes of energy, freezing cold, stab along my brainstem. If I focused right, I could see the light bending a bit. Not good. Powerful, dangerous stuff.

I backed out of the room, not wanting to take my eyes off of the toilet — not a thing I normally think — and tried to stroll casually back to the living room where Anders still sat on the couch. Smythe sat nearby in an armchair, ignoring him, a cup of tea on the table in front of him. It steamed along, and Smythe just looked into the brew, absently.

"So what is it?" Anders asked me.

I sat down on the couch and winced a little, letting my face show it nice and slow. Anders didn't take that well, but I leaned forward, elbows on knees, and smiled at Smythe.

"Hey, Smythe," I said, "how's the tea?"

He picked it up as I named it, and took a sip. Setting the cup back down on saucer, he looked into the middle distance. "Still hot," he said at last.

"Good, good to know. Did you have other company recently?" I asked.

"Oh, who could say," he told me, still not really

looking at either of us.

"Of course," I said softly. "I found the source of this, I'm pretty sure — too damned sure," I said to Anders, keeping my voice low, "but the problem now is dealing with it."

"You can't just...fix it, or destroy it?" he asked, continuously glancing at Smythe.

"Not this, no. I can't even get close enough to touch it, and before you ask, no, you couldn't either." My fingers drummed on my knees as I thought. "Smythe, we'll be back," I said suddenly and stood up, pulling Anders with me.

I led him to the hallway to the bathroom, stopping short of getting close enough to let that thing get a grip on me. "Smythe is acting strange," I said, holding up a finger, "save all questions for the end," I put in quickly as Anders started to say something. "He's drifting, he's not himself, just a shell — mentally at least. Still drinks tea, so I doubt he's been replaced by a hive of beetles."

"That happens?" Anders asked.

"Questions at the end, but yes," I conceded, "on occasion. But no, he seems human." I held up a second finger. "Still, everything just seems to glance off him. What would do that? Normally the list would be stupidly long, Smythe plays with a lot of dangerous items. But from the feel of that thing when I get close to it, and the fact it had to have been placed there by someone else, we can narrow it down. Keep in mind they didn't want to kill him." I held up a third finger and shrugged.

"They just wanted him useless," Anders said, after I stayed silent just long enough for him to decide I'd finished.

"Right, and not in a way that would necessarily bring attention to that fact. The neighbors, I can't imagine they come over often, but they could get proof of life, delivery people wouldn't notice a problem. No, they just—" I groaned as it finally surfaced. "They wanted to make sure he wouldn't notice a problem, and that, even if someone noticed and investigated, they would ignore it."

"But you didn't," Anders said.

"No, but the people who did this expected to deal with me separately, see?" I said.

"The Subtle Knives," he said, and I nodded.

"It hangs right. Smythe would have noticed them moving, and doing something big. And he would have been just annoying enough to find me and drag me back into it. They didn't know that last part, they just assumed he'd reach out. Conversely, if I noticed first I would've gone to him. But if they took him out, for real killed him quickly, then they would have to know I would've burned the ground they slept on. So no, they wanted to incapacitate him, and ensure he died, slowly, after I was taken care of. Which they tried, remember?"

"How could I forget?"

I grinned. "Exactly. And that's what they did to Smythe. A memory leech. Took me a while to recognize the feeling, but that's what it is in there. Every time he goes to the bathroom it gets worse. First he'd have started to forget appointments, or what he wanted to dinner. Then he would start to lose closer memories. Shuffle like a zombie, always slightly lost in his own time frame. Eventually, if we leave him alone, he'll forget how to eat, and breathe. I give it another two weeks, say."

"So we stop it, destroy it, whatever — right?" Anders asked.

"Sure," I told him, "except we can't get close to it and I don't have anything on me to help."

"Wouldn't Smythe, though?" Anders asked. "And, wait, why didn't he notice this thing before it could really affect him?"

I looked down the hall, happy to see nothing, no Smythe or anyone else coming for us. Smythe probably sat in the living room, sipping tea, having forgotten we were there, of course. But eventually he'd need to pee. I snapped my fingers and pointed at Anders. "Right, they would have had to surprise him when they got here, which — that would not have been easy. Or they've just gotten way more powerful recently. I mean, the idea that the Subtle Knives are going after Smythe, not to mention me? That's punching way out of their league. I didn't feel anything else, though, so let's assume, for now, we have to just deal with this. Sure, Smythe would have what I need."

"So..."

"Yeah, yeah," I said, already walking away from the bathroom, "come on."

We passed Smythe on the way to his workroom, and I waved. I felt anger growing again. Working the case, elbow deep in problem solving, I could lock all the compartments, even for minutes at a time, and feel nothing. That's what you do. And I didn't want to be doing this, regardless, but what they did to Smythe got my blood riled. I walked, all right I stalked, on down to Smythe's workroom in the back of the house and considered the very locked door. I'd fix it later, I decided, and hauled off and kicked the door in.

Well, I tried to. The door shook a bit, and held, and my leg hurt. I saw sparks come off the wood and shook my head at them. Smythe, that clever bastard, had locked the door in a few different ways. Still, I had WarBoots on. I tapped my heel on the ground and twisted, keeping the pressure on as I did. I felt the boots gain and hold a charge and I stood there, facing the door down. If it knew what was good for it, it would just open.

The door remained closed, though, so I kicked it again, the small boxes along the side of the WarBoot glowing brightly. The doorknob and lock assembly, under the sole of the boot, simply ceased to be solid matter, reduced to a hot cloud of particulates that only dreamt of someday being coalesced into metal and wood again.

Pulling the door open, I stopped at the threshold of the room and waited. Smythe wouldn't secure just the door, he would set up defenses in the room. We couldn't count on him remembering them, either, so there remained no point in dragging him over to try. The hell with it. I walked into the room with purpose, bracing myself for anything nasty. Standing in the center of the small, cluttered room, I took a deep breath and waited for...nothing? I could feel the pull of energy from multiple directions in here, but nothing that reached out to me specifically. Smythe must've worked in exceptions once you got into the room itself.

Why he'd do that but leave the door warded against me I couldn't begin to explain, outside of a sense of humor on his part. I searched for other protections anyway, not looking for anything aimed at me, but aimed around the room in general, waving Anders back before he could walk in behind me. After turning off a few nasty, ugly little surprises, I waved Anders in and started to catalog the space.

"I'll need something to protect me when I get close to the bag," I told him, looking around, "and something to pick it up with. I can destroy it easily, but making sure it reverses, that's the key, otherwise Smythe won't remember what he's lost."

"They reverse?" Anders asked. He grabbed me a sheet I pointed to and handed it over.

"Some of them," I admitted. "But only some. I have to work under the assumption it will, though. It's like when you go and get ice cream, you know the creamery gets creative and will only have good flavors about half the time, but damn it you want some butterscotch chocolate crunch, so you have to just brave the odds and hope they didn't make a batch of seaweed-and-jalapeno–flavored crap again. Anyway," I continued, "hand me that stone elephant and let's go deal with this."

"The elephant will restore his memory?" Anders asked, following me out of the room.

"Hmm? No."

"Oh, I thought, because it was an elephant—"

"Pachyderms, in general, have really good memories, sure — mostly because of brain size, if nothing else, but that whole old adage about elephants never forgetting is frankly species profiling, Anders. No, you know what has surprising memory capacity? Pangolin. You wouldn't think of it to look at their silly lizard-looking mammalian butts, but they can...I once knew a pangolin who had memorized pi to the millionth digit. Of course, what good is that, to a pangolin? None, really — they're not strong in math, I find. And I know, more species profiling."

"I'm starting to just assume at least half of what you say is made up on the spot," Anders said.

"I'm hurt. Sure, if you want to think of that way, it's all made up. I don't have a script, Anders. I'm making up this very sentence as I say it. So sure, fine, you got me."

"That's not what I—"

"Oh, I *know* what you *meant*, Dead Anders. And I'm hurt by it, like I said. I can't help it if my life has been full of things you consider strange, but you wanted to come along, and you even said you wanted to do what I do, so maybe I was trying to pass along some kind of earned wisdom or something."

"By talking about terrible ice cream flavors?"

I smiled at him as we headed down the hall to the bathroom. "All right, fine, I just like to talk while I think. I work better when my brain and mouth are doing two separate things. Don't worry about it."

"So what *is* the elephant for, then?" he asked as I stopped us outside the bathroom. The cold stabbing feelings came back, radiating out of the room worse now that I expected them.

I unwound the sheet I'd taken and held it up between us and the door. "Take this, grab a corner from underneath so your hands aren't exposed, and hold it up in front of us both as best you can," I said. "But put the elephant down first." He did, and I carefully passed the sheet over, corner by corner. The stabbing in my head diminished and I reached down to grab the elephant.

"We're going to go in there, you first, holding up the sheet. It'll protect us for a few minutes. But if we tried to pick the bag up directly — wrapping it in the sheet, say — things would just catch fire. By 'things' I mean the sheet, and then us."

He nodded, and I noticed he didn't wince when I explained, just accepted the sheet and stood ready. I gestured for him to move, slowly, and we walked into the bathroom. I told him to take a step right, or left, to navigate the small room as best I remembered. Tripping and walking face first into a sink wouldn't do us favors, and I couldn't risk Anders dropping the blanket.

We made it close to the bag before the sheet started to smolder. Urging Anders to move a bit faster, I pressed the elephant against the bag wedged behind the toilet tank and squeezed it. The bag stuck to the side, thankfully, and I was able to lift it clear.

"We need to get outside," I said, holding my arm out so it was on the other side of the sheet. The bag still radiated, and my hand slowly started to go numb, but we backed out and headed down the hall. Which is when the sheet caught fire.

Anders dropped the sheet and took a few steps back quickly.

He dropped to his knees, face a snarling rictus.

I felt it, too — the bag had protection against movement and was fighting back, growing more powerful. Good and bad, I figured. I dropped the elephant, and by extension the bag, on the flaming sheet. Tearing off my cravat, I bundled everything up and secured it as best I could while fire snapped and licked at everything.

I blinked. Why was I—?

Damn it, no.

I grabbed the bundle. And ran. I kept forgetting why I ran. Luckily holding fire works as its own reminder. I hit the front door with my shoulder. Threw the bundle, cursing at it as it flew in a high arc across the lawn full of small statuary.

There was a reason I was out here. I'd been doing something. Oh shit, a bundle on fire sat on the lawn.

Right!

Right.

I grabbed a stone swan by the neck and beat the bag, sheet, cravat, and elephant package until the fire went out and the bag laid there, dead to the world.

Anders came out a few seconds later at a full run. "Are you all right?" he asked, stopping next to me. "Is it...dead? Destroyed?"

"Shit!" I said by way of reply and ran over to kneel by the bag. What energy it still had wisped around, and I tried to gather it and redirect it, sending it to Smythe. I sat down hard when done and took a deep breath. "All right, now it's good and dead, and hopefully I was able to return some of it to Smythe. Bag didn't have a storage, really, but the energy it did have, I could at least send it toward him, and maybe, hopefully, it'll help." I stood up, slowly, and brushed off my pants.

Frowning, I noticed my jacket cuffs were

singed. I tried to brush them off and some soot, along with some fabric, drifted away. My hands were red and sore, but not much more than singed. I flexed my fingers slowly, drawing a look from Anders.

"How aren't you burned?" he asked, shaking his head.

"I don't burn as easily as you do," I said, "and the fire wasn't all that hot, really. Most of the flames you saw, they weren't really fire, just a bleed-through light show while the energies interacted between the bag and the sheet."

"No, I felt the heat," he insisted.

I shrugged. "Still not as bad as you might think."

"And you don't burn easily," he said.

"I do not. But," I said, turning back toward the house, "we should see if Smythe is all right." I kept my voice light, at least lighter than I felt. I'm sure the tone hit Anders, who, like me, had forgotten about Smythe for the briefest of moments. For me, though, the entire thing was over. Smythe would remember or not, and there wasn't anything else I could do. I kept telling myself that as we walked back to the front door.

Smythe sat in the living room, still looking into his tea. I called his name, twice, each time louder than the last. He didn't respond at first, but managed to eventually look up. "Paige?" he asked. He took a deep breath. Let it go. Took another. Stood up, unsteady on his feet.

"Smythe," I said, dropping into his couch, forcing myself to look as relaxed as he'd expect me to be. "Feeling better?"

Anders just stood there, watching. I patted the couch and gave him a look. He sat, keeping his back straight, arms stiff at his sides, fists resting lightly on the couch to either side of him.

"Paige," Smythe said again, staring at me as if I'd just teleported in, which I suppose to him I had, "what—"

So I explained. At length. As best I could, at least. Smythe shook his head through most of it, obviously absorbing what I told him, but finding it hard to locate his own memories of it. I tried to go further back, recalling a few times from our shared past, and those he smiled at, nodding.

"So, you're telling me," he said when I gave in and wound down, "the Subtle Knives pulled this off?"

"Seems so," I said, "last I heard of them—"

"Before," Smythe said to Anders, "she left the world to rot, she means."

"Don't start," I said.

"By the way, hi," Smythe said, leaning forward to hold a hand out to Anders. "You're the new one, huh?"

"New what?" Anders asked, relaxing a fraction, enough to shake Smythe's hand before he returned to his uncomfortable posture.

"He's not a new anything," I broke in, "and don't worry about him, Smythe, worry about you. There are still gaps. You sure you can't remember anything about someone coming in and planting the bag, anything of use?"

"Well, her bedside manner is still fucking *spectacular*," Smythe said to Anders.

"Hey I also owe you a door," I said, "if we're

counting reasons I'm terrible." I went on to explain how we got rid of the memory leech, and Smythe, standing and starting to pace as I told the tale, laughed.

"Well when I redo all the *other* security around here, I'll add that to the list. I mean I only secured the door against you because you snoop," he said, taking the dregs of his tea to the kitchen and setting the cup in the sink. "I figured if you got in, you'd mean it, so why stop you after that? Still, doors aren't cheap."

"If I had money, I'd pay you for it. Anders, do you have door money on you?"
"I...how much does a—"

"Don't listen to her," Smythe said coming back to join us, "and, really, you'd be better off not traveling with her, regardless."

"I've told him. But it doesn't matter, this is the end of the line." I stood up and held a hand out to Smythe. "Don't be caught off-guard again."

"I could say the same to you," he said.

I nodded. "You could, but you won't."

"No," he said, "I won't."

And there it was, for me. Smythe had gotten into shit because of me, even when I'd tried to stop being involved. He'd tell me — anyone I knew would make it clear — my deciding to leave the game didn't mean the game stopped, and I got that. I understood it deep in my bones. But I hated it.

The ripples would keep washing ashore regardless of what I did. That meant I had no real free will in the game. I mean, sure I could walk away but then...then what?

On the other hand, the truth-telling hand, I could still walk away, and had, and intended to keep doing so once I left Smythe's. It hurt, having him caught up in this at all, but he was an adult. He'd made his choices, as had I, and we both lived with them.

"Come on, Anders," I said, nodding at Smythe. I tried to pack my apology into that single nod, along with my friendship, and I knew he'd catch all of it and accept it. Anders looked confused, but that seemed to be par for the course. Not surprising — the kid found himself way over his head and I refused to toss him a rope. I wanted him to learn these waters had sharks and that he should get out of them as fast as possible. I didn't think it was working, though.

"So now what?" Anders asked as Smythe closed the door behind us. I looked at the scorched remains of what we'd just been through as we passed them.

"Now? Nothing. I suppose maybe lunch, then I go find another small room to hole up in, and you go home." I turned a random direction on the street and kept walking. Anders, of course, kept up by my side.

"But we haven't found out what the Subtle Knives wanted," he said. He didn't whine, or sound plaintive, he just started it as an obvious fact. Precious.

"And we won't," I told him. "So I'm going to get some lunch—"

"We just ate, remember the pizza?" he said.

"And then we—look, Anders, oh Dead Anders, this stuff isn't free. It costs. If nothing else, it's exhausting and burns calories. I'm *hungry*. I'm sorry that bothers you." I shook my head and looked around for a promising direction to find a diner in.

"That doesn't bother me," he insisted, "what bothers me is you just ignoring what happened."

"I'm not ignoring it, Anders. I'm openly choosing to walk away. A place I was happy in before you led them to my door. So let me get back to it. I'm done. I'm retired. That's it. You wanted to come along to find out what happened. I let you. What happened is that we'll never know what happened. That's it. Sometimes that's the answer you get."

"That's not good enough," he said. That time there was a bit of a whine added in.

"That's life," I told him, "it's messy and stupid and doesn't make sense, and no one really likes it. You must have been so much fun at birthdays when you were a kid. Expecting only the best cakes and sad when friends didn't show up to share some cake with you, all full of tiny, impotent rage at the world."

"Weren't you sad if people didn't come to your party?" he asked.

"No, because that meant I didn't have to look out for them killing me." I answered. "Oh, look," I said, gesturing, "a diner. Lunch? On you?"

Anders sighed and shrugged.

CHAPTER FOUR

THE CRACKED VINYL seat squeaked under me as I slid into the diner's rearmost booth. I leaned back, draping an arm over the back of the seat, dipping into the booth behind me. Diners remained one of humanity's greatest inventions, right up there with a good bar. I grabbed one of the upside-down coffee cups on the table and set it back down right-side up.

Anders sat down across from me and I nodded toward the other cup. He shrugged, so I flipped it over as well. The incantation complete, a waiter came over with menus and a pot of coffee. I didn't even look at the menu, just looked at the kid with his pad in hand and ordered some breakfast: eggs, bacon, sausage, the works. Enough for two.

Anders ordered a salad and fries, and the waiter went off to deal with someone else. Or maybe not, didn't seem to be many people in the place. Not surprising, given the size of the town, but it felt somehow sparser than it should be. An emptiness hung about the place — a miasma of sorts.

"Hey, sorry about this," the waiter said as he came back with Anders' salad, "but I'm going off shift. Don't worry though, Suzette will help you guys out just fine." I thanked him and he wandered away again.

"So this is it?" Anders asked after a few bites of salad.

"This," I said, "is it." I gestured broadly around the diner.

"Not the diner, I mean with you," he said.

"Oh," I said, sipping my coffee, "yeah. I think it is. Some things are better left behind. Not every road — it's like when you go out to buy new shoes, you know?"

"I—"

"You have a shoe in your head, maybe it's one you've seen in a catalog, or on a friend's feet, whatever the case, and maybe it's just a platonic idea of the type of shoe you really want. But you go out and you search and search and you find every other type of shoe there is. I mean you still need shoes, right? So you can either stay with the ones on your feet, or you can spin the wheel and settle. Nothing *wrong* with either choice, not really, but it's a choice. And you need to make it, because otherwise you'll spend the rest of your life looking for shoes."

Anders shook his head. "You could just order the ones you saw online, and even if you buy some shoes, you'll need more later. It's not a final choice."

"You're saying my heart isn't in this metaphor?"

"It's not your finest, no, and I've only heard a few."

I drained my cup and set it down, looking around for Suzette. No one looking like they could've been a Suzette hung around anywhere I could see so I turned back to Anders. "Harsh but fair. Look, I'm tired. I've been tired. I'm *still* tired. I turned away from this for a reason. Can't you accept that?"

"Can I know the reason?" he asked.

I thought about it. Did I want to go into the past right here and now with some...let me be honest... stranger? Not really, no. I didn't want to go into it with friends, either. "No," I said, and turned to look around for Suzette again. This time I spotted her, coming right for us with food. Good timing.

She set the plates down and smiled at Anders, who gave her a perfectly polite smile back, and went to grab the coffee pot. As she left I noticed a feeling leave with her. I closed my eyes and waited for her to return.

"Fine, I get it," Anders said. "But I think people still need help and you—"

"Hold on," I muttered.

Anders, for his part, got quiet instantly. I couldn't even hear him move. Good on him for that. I reached out mentally, trying to sense the whole of the diner at once. I felt stiff, sore — the normal ways I used to do this were vastly underworked and atrophied. Still, old habits and all that. I knew, in a general sense, what I was looking for, and that helped immensely.

Suzette came back, refilled my coffee cup, and left without a word, I assume seeing me in intense closed-eye concentration and Anders doing who knows what. None of that mattered. What mattered were the swirls of force left in her wake. Suzette didn't travel alone. I opened my eyes and saw Anders staring at me.

Draining my second cup of coffee in a single go, I set the cup down on the table and turned, catching Suzette's eye and waving her back over.

She came back, refilling my cup again.

"Sorry about that," I said, smiling at her, "don't know the strength of my own caffeine habit, I guess."

"Oh, no problem," she said, "I'm the same way." I looked her up and down — waist-length red hair, the color from a bottle, average height, two arms, two legs, a head, nose and eyes in the right places— she looked perfectly normal. To my eyes. To that twitch in my brain, the part of me trained to feel the off-center bits of the world, there was so much more. I knew she had no clue.

Damn it. Damn it to fuck and back.

Anders looked at me. I looked back at him. I could see the muscles in his jaw flex repeatedly as he fought the urge to ask. I shook my head at him, and he took it to mean I didn't want to talk about it. His head started to drop, looking down at the table, but I laughed, holding up a hand and making him reconsider.

"No, sorry," I said, "I didn't mean anything bad."

"I *get it*, all right?" he said, letting his own annoyance creep into his voice. Frankly, about time. Hey, it wasn't lost on me that my behavior was terrible. I won't claim innocence, or that I didn't know I kept shoving Anders aside in an attempt to make him just go away. I'd even told him as much. But outside of staying around, he'd managed to keep the sheer frustration out of his body language and voice, at least to a large degree. I found satisfaction in seeing it then. Not in any sort of "ha-ha I made you mad" sort of way, mind, but more in a "thank goodness you're actually human" way.

"No, Anders, no," I said, resting both hands on the table in a none-too-subtle way, "the waitress. Suzette."

"What about her?" he asked.

"Something's not right." I leaned back, sliding my hands off the table and watching him, waiting for the reaction.

"Sure," he said, shrugging and picking at his salad.

"Maybe you're not understanding me, Anders. There's something wrong here, with Suzette. Not like she has mismatched socks, or anything, I mean wrong in my sense of the word. Wrong in a fancy font, maybe some old special curly ends off the letters that go way up and out and make you wonder what drugs the calligrapher took, mostly because you're pretty sure you want to find his dealer and strike a deal. That sort of wrong."

"So you're going to let Smythe know, and I should go bug him if I'm interested, I told you, I *get it.*"

When I said I understood the annoyance and felt sort of glad for it, that time passed. "Anders, you need to stop right now or I won't buy you a toy."

"What?" he asked as he set his fork back down.

"Smythe needs to recover his own shit, so I can't punt on this," I told him.

"But you're done, remember? You literally just told me, I mean literally *just told me* how done you were. And now, what, a minute later you're saying—"

"Yeah I'm a fickle fuck, I guess. I don't know

what's coming for her, but *something* is, and," I waved a hand around, aimlessly, "I'm right here, and—"

"And you want to help her," he said.

"Ugh, fuck, fine, yes, I want to help her," I said. I speared a sausage link with my fork and bit at it angrily. "So I guess I'm here for a bit."

Anders took a mouthful of salad and muttered "I knew it" to himself.

"I heard that," I said, and had some eggs.

He swallowed. "I'll help," he said.

"Is there anything sort of...I don't even know what it would take to dissuade you at this point."

"Exactly," he agreed. "So now what?"

"Now we finish eating," I said, and went back to exactly that.

"Shouldn't we be helping her?" he asked.

"We will," I told him, "but we need to eat, too. So finish up — we have to find a hotel to base out of, after." I went back to eating, glancing up at Anders periodically. He looked slightly confused, trying to parse out what he thought I meant. After a few minutes I smiled at him. "No, really, we finish eating and leave — no trick here, Anders, I mean it."

"All right," he said, and went back to eating. "Though," he said after a few more bites, "can I ask—"

"Really, Anders? Really?" I laughed and set my coffee down and leaned forward, elbows on table, chin in hands, staring at him. "Let's have it then."

"You — I don't know how to even ask this," he said. He glanced all around as if the diner itself could help him.

"Just spit it out, no spin," I said.

"You use my name a *lot*. Like, I mean, most people, they don't repeat your name over and over when they talk to you. But you, you just keep doing it. It's odd, I just have to — it's odd," he said, all in a rush, the words spilling out of him as if they would tangle up going any slower.

"Is there a question in there, somewhere?" I asked.

"Why?" he asked. "I mean, why do you do that?"

I blinked several times at him. "Wait, really?"

"Really. It's not normal. I don't mean it's sinister or anything, just that it's...noticeable."

"I never thought about it, but hey if that's your thing, I just — Anders, I'm old. I like using names, so I remember them. That's all. I'm sure it'll wear off. It isn't like I'm used to talking to people, either, much less having them around a lot."

"You're old. That's your answer." He shook his head. "You're not much older than I—"

"Anders," I said, laughing as I did, "Dead Anders. I'm just over two hundred. Two hundred and fourteen, if you want to be precise. I'm old."

"You," he sputtered, dropping his fork, "are *not* two hundred and—"

"Shows what you know, and if you really want to know, it's habit. When you're helping people—" Anders reached into his bag quickly and grabbed his notebook, starting to write down what I was saying, "—stop that," I told him, uselessly, "but when you're helping people, it reassures them if you repeat their name. That way they know you're not dead. Like you were, Dead Anders. So yeah, old habit. Plus, it helps to remind me that you *aren't* dead, in this case. Because, let's face it, last I knew, you were totally dead."

"You need to stop bringing that up. You claim I was dead, but I don't remember it that way at all." He put his notebook away, not taking his eyes off me.

"We'll agree to disagree there, but if it bothers you so much, I'll try to stop saying your name." I shrugged and started in on the bacon. Suzette came by and refilled my coffee again, Anders still on his first cup, making me feel like I had some kinda problem. Not making me feel it in any way that would stop me from drinking my fourth cup, but even so.

"I just had to ask," he said, salad finished and reaching for some fries. I considered explaining his priorities were out of order, you eat the hot thing first, but hey, maybe Anders liked lukewarm fries. I would try to not judge. Much. "And," he continued after another minute, "are we really just going to find a—"

"Yes, Anders," I said.

After that we finished our meal in silence, which, at the very least, sped the process up considerably. Anders paid, thankfully, and we walked out, my sense of the world getting calmer the further we got from the diner. I'm not sure how I didn't notice when we walked in. No, that's not true, I knew exactly how I hadn't noticed. So rusty I couldn't even tell when the weirdness encroached on lunch, never mind exhaustion from dealing with Smythe's problem. There'd been days when this would have all been second nature.

Now, I would have to regroup and go back to the start if I wanted to help anyone. Treat it like I used to when I knew nothing.

We stood on the street and looked around for a few before I let Anders pick a direction to start walking. I hoped the town was small enough that any hotel would be close, at least. It was, though calling it a hotel was being generous. Not that it mattered. Two beds, a bathroom, a door, and electricity were all I needed. We needed.

I sat down on the vomit-colored bedspread and leaned back on my hands. "You know why this all happened. With Suzette, I mean."

Anders looked at me, reaching for the flap of his bag. "No, but you already know? That's great."

"You," I said, letting myself fall backward on the bed, legs dangling off the end at the knee, "take all the fun out of me. I was *going* to say the lack of cravat did it. Threw the world off its game. But now, if I stick with that, I sound cold and uncaring."

"Well, only kind of," he said. He took a chair, one of the two in the room near the tiny presswood table, and looked through his notebook. "So do you really have an idea, or...?"

"None at all. I'm not even sure what could have caused the feeling."

"All right, fine," he said, "so what do we do?"

I lay there, staring at the ceiling. What do we do, indeed. I knew he wouldn't like the honest answer, but hey, he wanted to come along on this ride. "We go for dinner in a few hours, catch the end of her shift."

"Wait, really? And until then, we do what? We prep for—"

"Nothing to prep for, Anders. Not yet. We need to go, and I need to feel it out. Get ready, this could take a while."

"Well, what are we looking for?" He took off his shoes, getting comfortable. I sat up and took off my jacket, laying it next to me so it wouldn't continue to crease.

"It's hard to explain. Like I said, I need to feel it out. There's no big sign — well, normally no big sign. There was this thing, once, I say 'thing' but really if you want to know it looked like a giraffe and a tractor got tossed in a blender. Anyway, the thing made signs. Actual, handwritten signs. Not handwritten, really, it had no hands, but you know, written. I guess, if I think back now, it must've written the signs out holding the pen in its mouth? You know, I'm not actually sure. But the point is, most things don't leave signs."

"Fine," he said, and started to write in his notebook.

"Can I see that? What are you actually writing in there, huh?" I asked, hoping to turn the discussion away to something that wouldn't just dead-end in my fumbling to explain a system I didn't fully understand myself.

"You looked through before," he said. The memory of it twitched across his face.

"Not for long," I said, "and I'm curious. Come on, Anders, what is it?"

"Paige," he said, saying my name almost as a sigh in and of itself, "it's my journal. Mine. Just leave it alone."

I didn't reply, just laid there, staring at the ceiling listening to his pen scritch across the pages. Hours passed in silence like that, until I sat back up and looked over at Anders, who was reading through old bits of his journal.

I pulled my legs up onto the bed and crossed them, turning to sit facing him. "Remember how I said there is no magic involved in this, only science?" I asked.

"Sure," he said, closing the journal and looking at me.

"That's kind of the problem right now," I said. "In terms of me explaining things, I mean. Look, if you only had pre-relativity physics in your head, no idea that anything else could exist, and I needed to do some math based on quantum string theory, you'd not only be lost, you wouldn't even have the building blocks – you'd be whole giant mental shifts behind, and that's multiple shifts-with-an-S. That's the translation problem."

"So give me the building blocks, in order. How did *you* learn it, if not like that?" he asked. He wasn't wrong, but I wasn't a teacher.

"Just because you know how an internal combustion engine works doesn't mean you can show someone else how to build one," I told him. I rolled off the bed with something approaching ease, but never quite getting to grace, and grabbed my jacket.

"So explain it — and I can ask questions, Paige, come on," he said. He shoved his journal back into his satchel and secured the flap as I shrugged on my jacket and smoothed it down before buttoning it.

"You wanted to tag along, I didn't invite you, remember," I said. "I never offered to teach you things. I keep telling you to leave — you won't, but no where in there does that require me to buy textbooks I couldn't even buy, rent a chalkboard, etcetera."

"That's not," he said, following me out of the room, "what I'm asking and you know it. You're deflecting. Why?"

"Because I don't want a sidekick," I told him, flatly. "I like working alone."

"Working alone? Like you killing yourself slowly in a hotel room? Was that working alone?"

"That," I said as we walked back to the diner, "was my retirement. Which you forced me out of, and now, fine, this is my choosing, but you still aren't."

We sat down, after I made sure Suzette was still working. The place still stood mostly empty and she seemed to be the only staff on the floor, so I didn't worry about sitting in her section or not. There were no sections.

"So do you feel anything?" he asked as we waited for Suzette to bring us coffee. "Do you know what it is?"

"I swear, Anders, if you ask me that again I will get up and leave you here. This takes the time it takes."

"If you won't explain why, though..." he started, letting the end trail off as Suzette came by and poured coffee for us.

She smiled with recognition. "You guys back so soon?" she asked. "Car trouble? Or y'all staying in town for a while?"

"We just couldn't get enough of the coffee," I told her, returning her smile. "No, our uncle lives nearby, and we decided to set up camp here while we visit. Don't want to be so close we can't escape, you know how family is."

She nodded, scooping up our menus off the table quickly. "For sure, but it's nice of y'all to visit your uncle. So you all family then? Cousins?" She looked at Anders as she asked this, and I wasn't sure which of us she'd pegged as the one to actually flirt with for a bigger tip. Nothing wrong with that, mind you, all part of her job.

While she stayed close, though, I focused on the air around her, feeling for a wobble of sorts, something in the fields, for a clue. Nothing. Just the same wrongness I'd felt earlier.

I looked at Anders and shrugged. He nodded, taking the meaning. We sat, drinking coffee, in silence for a while. I used the time to feel out the diner and think. I decided, for Anders' sake, to think out loud. I didn't want him here, I didn't want him going down this path, but he'd refused to even flinch to date, so fine, let him go off the deep end a while and maybe that could convince him of the actual depth.

"You think in three, maybe four dimensions," I said, after Suzette refilled our cups, "the normal ones: length, width, depth, and hopefully time. Your normal space/time coordinate system." He nodded at me, trying to hide his pleasure at getting anything from me.

I didn't acknowledge it and kept going. "There are, of course, more than that. M-Theory gives you eleven dimensions, which is a good idea but also wrong. There are seventeen I know of, and don't worry about naming them, you don't need names for them. You just need to know they're there and they interact with the four you know of in all sorts of ways."

I stopped to sip coffee and order my thoughts for myself. Start at the start, I reminded myself. Don't go off what I used to be able to do, but act like this is the first time. Right. "Something like this is generally easier to think of like an incursion. Some being, or force, that moves, generally, along an axis you couldn't — humans can't, natively — spot. Right up until an intersection hits and then it's like an ant seeing the shadow of a boot just before getting stepped on.

"Something that moves like that, off the beaten path, can be fine and harmless — things do it all the time. If you took a brick, hell, take a whole city, and have it move—"

"How do you move a city?" he asked.

"World. Stranger. Trust me on this," I said, "but if you take one and have it move along time as well as space, you couldn't see it except for where and when it intersected things you could see. Now, if you take a being who doesn't normally exist in the three spatial dimensions — or even in time as you think of it, at least — what happens?"

"They, uhhh, they don't look like anything. Until they do."

I lifted my cup in soft salute. "Exactly. And there's a lot of that. There are larger forces out there, things that most humans simply aren't equipped to understand. No fault there, no implication. Dogs see far fewer colors than you do, that doesn't make dogs worse than humans."

"But you can?" he asked.

"I can," I said. I set down my coffee cup and looked at him. I got it. I did. I understood it so well I wanted to ignore it. Looking directly at it just sort of hurt, in ways I couldn't be honest about, not yet.

"So it doesn't matter," he said. "It doesn't matter that I want to help people when I can't. I can't see the right dimensions; I can't understand the world correctly. This isn't Air Bud."

"Excuse me?" Suzette came back over before I could ask anything else, much less get an answer. Like clockwork, this one.

"You two want something to eat, maybe?" she asked, and smiled at us.

"Oh, sure," I said, "don't want to just take up a table for coffee all night, huh?"

"Oh that isn't it," she insisted, "I just figure we all gotta eat, right?"

"I'll have a burger," Anders said, not even looking at the menu she offered.

"I'll do the same," I said, smiling at Suzette until she wandered off again.

I shook my head at him. "I know you're upset, but you could at least be polite to her. None of this is on her, and really, being rude to waitstaff is one of those *things*. It shows what you—"

"Paige," he said, sighing the end of my name and drawing it out. "I'm not rude to waiters. I just — all right, I may have been a bit rude there, but all I've wanted to do is help people like you and you just showed me how it can never happen."

"Well..." I trailed off, considering how to explain. But Anders wasn't about to let me dawdle on that precipice for long.

"Yeah, life isn't Air Bud," he said.

"All right, that's twice. What is an air bud?" I asked, as Suzette came back with bottles of steak sauce and ketchup and the like.

"You've never seen Air Bud?" she asked me.

"Am I being pranked right now?" I asked the ceiling.

"It's about a dog who plays basketball," Anders said.

Suzette nodded, chiming in, "And they don't want to let him, but there's no rule that dogs *can't* play basketball so they have to let him."

"That's..." I shook my head. "That is a thing. All right. Thanks, Suzette, for clearing that mystery up.

"Oh, it's nothing — you should watch it, I mean, we spoiled it for you but it's cute, you know? And that dog was really good at basketball." She laughed as she walked away and I found myself joining in without meaning to.

"You aren't Air Bud, this isn't that movie," I said, laying my hands palm down on the table. "Can we table this for now and I'll explain when we get back to the hotel? I promise."

Anders took that to heart, his face softening. He nodded and started to fidget with the ketchup bottle. "And how long are we here for? Tonight, I mean."

"A while," I said, with a tiny hint of a shrug added on for emphasis. Truth was I didn't know. Long enough to get some kind of read, but even then I knew it wouldn't be enough to end this.

"So, fine," he said, "larger forces, you were saying, from other dimensions."

"Oh, right. They often don't mean harm.

Maybe they follow someone around, on purpose or not, for a while, but it's generally harmless. If every single press against the window was a threat, you know — endless, and unstoppable. But every now and then, probably more often than I want to admit, but not by too much, one of them tries to actually come through. They want to be *here* as well as *there* and it's never a good fit. But some kids burn ants, right?"

"Tommy Friesel," Anders said before he could stop himself.

"The worrisome neighborhood kid?" I asked.

"He liked his magnifying glass a bit too much once he learned he could focus the sun and burn small things with it. If they were alive, all the better."

"Yeah. Exactly. Yeah."

Suzette brought our burgers not long after that, and we ate in silence. Anders thinking Anders Thoughts I guessed, while I reached out and kept feeling for that soft spot, hoping it wasn't a Tommy Friesel situation, even as I felt pretty strongly it had to be.

Out of practice, idiot, I chided myself. I couldn't make that call, not yet. Biasing myself wouldn't be helpful to anyone, not even Suzette. Starting a fight with a creature just sightseeing would still be a fight, and put her in the middle, not to mention harassing a perfectly innocent being.

We've all done that, or so at least I like to think, so I don't feel so alone, but doing it on purpose smacked of a type of meanness I didn't feel comfortable with. I needed to be right, for all parties involved. I also needed, for myself, to not get in so deep I forgot why I didn't do this anymore.

There remained a lot of pressure, doing this sort of work. Saving people: a reductive way to look at it, really, that I wished Anders would get past. Maybe he would with time and, frankly, explanations that only I could give. Except I wasn't explaining, was I? No, I kept acting like a petulant child toward him. I resented him, truly, at least a little bit, for putting me in a situation that'd led right to here.

That resentment didn't need to be fair, and it certainly *wasn't*. I tried to pack the feeling away, to box things small enough for shipping, but brains will be brains and until I faced it head on, I knew that color would always abstract into my conversations and interactions with him. So I would make a point of working around the resentment and minimizing it that way.

None of which helped me work out why the invisible pressure following Suzette around set off my last damned nerve. There was a familiarity to the thing, one I couldn't place. Couldn't name or catalog.

"The hell with this," I said after I finished eating. "Let's go back to the hotel."

"You're giving up? Again?" Anders's face did that complicated dance of emotion where he tried to look perfectly fine with a thing and hide his disappointment. That specific set of twitches were a thing I'd grown too used to seeing throughout my younger days. I didn't want it now, when there wasn't even a call for it.

"No, I just know when to retreat to think, and not push my luck for the night. Also I promised you an explanation." I flagged down Suzette and got the check. Anders paid and I made a mental note to work out getting some money of my own again. He didn't mention it, but who wants to feel like a leech? No one, that's who.

I still planned on this being a short-term gig and then going back to my old life, the avoiding-reality-and-just-letting-the-years-pass-me-by sort of life, but even then money would be needed to set me up.

Outside of getting a job, something I knew I didn't have the time or patience for, money didn't rank high on the "easy to come by" list for most people. Me included, but only sort of. I knew a few tricks, but they generally took time. Add it to the list of things, I guess.

We left the diner and headed back to the hotel.

CHAPTER FIVE

THE ROOM HADN'T mysteriously changed into nicer accommodations while we were out. I sat at the table and Anders joined me, setting his bag down and taking out his notebook. Laughing, I shook my head, and he slid the thing back into the bag, closing it and setting it on the floor.

We both knew he'd write stuff down later, anyway, but the presence of the notebook, the idea of him taking notes and learning, it still made me want to set small fires. He understood, or had started to, I guessed. It'd do. For now.

"So this is where you—"

I cut him off, biting back my annoyance. He was right, kind of, to be snappish at this point, and I had to remember that. "Don't assume, Anders," I said. "You have questions, and fears, and all of that. You want to know...well, right now you want to know if your dreams are total unreachable garbage."

"Hey, they—"

"No, let me finish, please," I said. He nodded and leaned back in his chair, managing to not cross his arms, though I think we could both feel the phantom echoes of the gesture regardless. "I just wanted to explain a bit more. What I am, what you are, all of that."

"To let me down easier?" he asked.

I did the math in my head. If I told him the truth, I knew, I just *knew*, he would follow me doggedly even after this finished. And I planned to go back and hide. So which would be fairer to him: tell him the truth unvarnished or phrase it in a way that cut him off and left him angry and sad but safer?

I knew which I wanted to do. No question that making Anders go away worked better for me. Something in him, though — it reminded me of me a bit, not much, all right? I am in no way admitting to having ever been this sort of hopeful puppy wanting to save everything.

He'd also risked his life helping me, and from his point of view was still doing that even now. And that made a difference. Given all that, he deserved the actual, full truth. As much as I didn't want to give it to him and encourage his behavior.

I sighed, slowly, letting my lungs empty as fully as possible and holding myself there, without oxygen, for a good minute. Then I sucked air into my body greedily and ran a hand along the surface of the table, just feeling the old, slightly sticky varnished surface. Fuck, why was it sticky? No, not the point now.

"I refer to myself as not human," I told him. "The people I come from, the folks that birthed and raised me, they call themselves The Ascended. Before you say it," I said, tapping a finger on the table lightly, "I already know it is one of the most absurd and pretentious things you could call yourself."

Anders nodded, apology written on his face. I laughed.

"No, really, I know. Imagine growing up and being told you were 'one of The Ascended' and having people take it seriously. Hell of a trip. But here's the thing. We're human. Or were, at least. We just, they just — it's hard for me to think of myself as one of them, really, but at the same time—"

"At the same time it's hard to erase history, even when it comes to identity that doesn't fit?" Anders offered.

I nodded. "So anyway, yes, The Ascended. Human, at least at one point, but they learned things. Science, mostly, but it boils down to cheat codes, tricks to do things like extend lives, and see further than most people, to bend the laws of what you think of as reality, to pull off all sorts of tricks. One of the first things they did with that information was to create a pocket dimension — a really stable one, big enough to house them all — and move there. We're talking the size of a small state here. It took incredible power and coordination. They even named it The Ascension. The sort of thing that could have been used to make the entire human race better, but...did I mention they're generally pretentious and self-serving? "

"I am getting that impression," he said. "So how come you aren't...I mean..."

"I got over their line of bullshit. Leave it at that. They're a pocket dimension full of assholes. I'm an asshole-of-one."

"That sounded really good in your head, didn't it?" Anders asked, stifling a laugh.

I didn't bother stifling mine. "Not really. But that's all it is. I promise. Sure, I'm two hundred and fourteen. But only due to things I learned as a child. I can sense those extra dimensions because I was taught how."

"So you're saying I can learn it, too?" The spark of excitement blossomed in him, then. It radiated out and filled the room with hope.

"Theoretically? They don't have many kids, honestly, but there were new faces at times, so it has to be a thing. But the learning curve, it's not something I know about."

He nodded, trying to keep the joy from his face badly. "But it's possible."

"If someone were to teach you everything, if you could learn it, if...there are more variables than there are — look, think of it like otters. They love to hold hands and can stack cups and do all sorts of pattern recognition, but could you teach one math? I think it's been done, I'm sure they have the capacity, but fuck, I don't know how you'd go about it."

"So I'm an otter to your human?"

"No," I sighed, "except in the ways you are. Can you stack cups? See, you also have hands, totally otter behavior. Seriously, though, I just don't know." I stood up and moved to one of the beds, laying back on it. "But at the least, I promise, while we're doing this, this *one job*, I'll at least explain as best I can what's going on and why."

"That's fair," he said, standing and stretching slowly. "So what's next with this one, then? What is it? Do you know?"

"As much as I did last time. We sleep. We go back during Suzette's shift. Maybe follow her a bit, see if the incursion is tied to the diner or to her. I don't know. It's been awhile for me, remember, I'm rusty. We're in this for the long haul. This, like it or not, is what the job used to be. So get some sleep."

"Sure," he agreed quickly, as if I wouldn't notice him taking his bag with him and dropping it near his bed. We traded off getting ready for bed, and I remembered we should have bought more clothes, but whatever, we're adults. We slept in what we had and I muttered something about needing to at least find more underwear and socks tomorrow, as well as everything else needed to live in a crap motel for a while.

The next day happened much like the previous: Light shopping at some roadside outlet, diner for breakfast, room to sit and think, then diner for another meal. Suzette didn't seem to be working that day, which let me feel the diner out. Nothing that would count as abnormal. Didn't bother me, and it certainly didn't make me leap to the conclusion that whatever this happened to be, it was targeting Suzette. One spot on a graph couldn't be enough data for that sort of conclusion. Took a bit of convincing to make sure Anders understood that, though.

He remained bored, even if he tried to hide it. All fidget and twitch, he managed to bite back on any childish whining, but that energy, that insistence on doing things, it radiated out of his every pore. Ignoring it still took a small toll on me. I tried to be understanding, but, damn it, the anxious puppy needed to settle before he peed the rug.

Two more days passed and we got no further. I felt fine about that. Anders didn't, starting to pester me with questions, slowly at first. I ignored the useless stuff, the when's and all, but tried to keep him in the loop on everything else. The truth of it remained simple: We were gathering information, slowly, but consistently. It took a lot of data to get a good result set, though.

Sometimes, as I told Anders at the end of the fifth night, you get lucky, for a very special use of the word lucky. The thing you're investigating will attack, make itself known and move itself into the Problem To Be Dealt With category, instead of being a giant question mark. And yes, that could be good — for you, personally. But generally not for the person you watched. They were, after all, the one being attacked. Hell, even then you were throwing yourself bodily in the way of a problem, so nothing exactly screamed safety. No, the calm remained the safest of moments. Even as you looked actively for the storm so you could evacuate people as needed.

A picture started to emerge though. With the almost-endless possibilities of what this event could be, it felt good seeing them dwindle with time. We learned that whatever it was, the possible incursion did seem to follow Suzette around. That took some doing, not wanting to just stalk her and creep around in the night.

I ended up talking to her outside the diner one evening and explaining my job as an undercover IRS investigator who needed to talk to her about her bosses. Given the general way people treat waitstaff — mostly their bosses, even when well meaning — she agreed pretty fast. Anders came along as my assistant, and the whole way back to her shabby apartment we were followed by something pressing against the curtain between worlds.

Every day the pressure against the barriers seemed to increase a fraction. The thing on the other side definitely wanted in. But more than that, whatever being was hunting over there took its time, not wanting to create a noticeable tear. Which meant they'd done this before.

Always possible this was a friend-of-a-friend situation, of course. One creature comes over, escapes back, and explains to the thing next to it who also eventually becomes curious. Or hungry. It happens. Not as often, but it does happen. Either way, the fact remained, everything so far pointed to experienced hunting. Learned or told, that experience didn't mean shiny good flowery things at all.

As to what could be pressing in, that mystery still eluded me. I explained all of this to Anders, who wanted to know all sorts of details. I gave him what I could, explaining how I could feel the difference in pressure along the spaces between worlds and all of that. I tried to teach him the simplest ways of feeling for disturbances, but he didn't seem to feel anything.

I knew from experience that you could always feel something: the firmness and safety of those spaces was basically faked. I realized that my own sensitivity remained screwy due to disuse — focusing so hard on this one specific instance would blind me to others, so I knew why I felt I could only feel the one disturbance, but Anders should have felt something if he'd been receptive. And maybe it just took more time. Also always possible, and I made sure he knew, even if I couldn't be sure I was telling him the truth. I told him the truth he needed.

Like any other sense, learning to feel the actual state of the world around you in a new way proved hard to explain. There were receptors in the human brain that could notice the pressures, though — the cracks and swells in the walls of the world. The idea relied on knowing, deep in your being, that these things could be felt, and then learning to ignore false signs from your own brain. Learning to see new parts of the spectrum, basically. Putting it into words proved hard, as always, but I tried to remember what I'd been shown as a child.

The world, I told Anders, felt smooth as a marble to us. But in reality it stood shot through with cracks and warped bits of paint, giving it a texture unlike anything else. Not a texture you could feel with your hands, but one you could only feel with your mind. Relax. Close your eyes, stop trying to see the world with them, and instead work on seeing the world as it really is. Feel the air around you, the pressure of it and how it moves. The heat of light on your skin, and the cooling areas of darkness.

Now focus on how the wider world feels in your memory, that smooth marble. Everything in its place. Hold that in your head as you feel for texture outside of yourself. Just as a wood table can look smooth until you run your fingers over the surface to reveal the bumps and cracks and whorls, so can the universe. It takes focus and concentration — the sort that, initially, only comes from relaxing yourself enough to be receptive.

I also explained the problem with what we were looking for.

The biggest issue with not knowing what intended to come through, assuming it truly meant to, remained how to push it back. You can't fight a penguin the same way you would fight a full-grown seal, even if they live in the same area. Penguins you just push over and roll around until they give in, but a seal will bat you to your ass without warning and crush you. On the other hand, a penguin, given half a chance, will peck you to death, hence the need to roll it around. Helps sand down the old stabby-face bit.

If they both made the same shape of shadow — and I realize penguins tend to be far smaller but work with me here — you wouldn't know what to prepare for, and leaping into the fight to push and roll a seal will get you killed. But waiting to see cedes ground in the fight before it begins. You give up your chance to prepare.

In the old days, when I did this and enjoyed it, I stayed prepared enough I could mitigate the problem. But now, that same lack of preparation might easily kill me, Anders, or Suzette.

As much as I didn't want to admit it to myself, and would refuse to admit it to Anders, there remained something comforting about taking this on. The old ways, even with a week of slow, plodding boredom as the facts slowly unraveled in front of my eyes, had a way about them. There was memory-based emotional response to it all, and yes, that is one hell of a clinical dodge, but I need to do that at times, as anyone does.

No plans to continue, though. My heart couldn't take it. You have to *care* about people to do this sort of work. That kind of compassion — constant, throbbing along your skin like an open wound — cost. A price I couldn't afford anymore, and even if I could, frankly, not one I felt interest in offering up now.

None of which actually mattered, because right then what mattered was saving Suzette. I crawled up my own ass and got lost a minute, but the focus of the week remained fixing this one incursion. Then I could find a new place to sit and stare at the walls and live a quiet life uninterrupted by background radiation pinging in my ears all day.

All I could do until then was keep grinding away and showing Anders what I did, as meaningless as that felt.

The eighth day was when it happened. When I failed.

CHAPTER SIX

ANDERS AND I left the diner after dinner, like we had every night. Suzette was still working inside, now taken to giving us what she felt were sly nods and winks as she served us, thinking her boss would get raked over the tax coals someday soon.

The soft breeze agreed with me, hushing a whisper across the road that could be easily mistaken for trucks going by on the highway — ghosts drifting past, leaving only dust eddies in their wake. Anders started to ask me how much longer we'd be going back, and if I'd learned anything new. Wanting to sigh, I looked over my shoulder at him as he let go of the diner's door and watched it swing shut, the metal frame slicing through the night, catching light from the exterior flood lamps designed to give the parking lot a feeling of safety.

A spark sizzled as something in one of the lights shorted. Then another, a louder pop-and-bang as bulbs blew. I went still, Anders comically almost colliding with me before he, too, stopped, wondering what was happening. No storm nearby — the soft, almost too-gentle breeze contained no portents.

Inside, the diner lights flickered. Maybe, the thought flashed through my consciousness with the desperation of the unready, the power grid simply had issues. A new employee had spilled coffee. A rabid racoon had gotten hungry and decided insulation would make a fine snack.

But I knew. Hell, Anders knew. The problem stood, though: No one in the diner knew. We both turned, looking in through the large glass front of the place, and sure, the lights flickered, but power outages happened. No one screamed, or ran, or even really worried. As a status quo, that wouldn't last.

"This is us," I said to Anders as I started to walk back to the door.

"Just tell me how to help," he said. I could hear his footsteps align with mine. Which was great, except I had no idea what we were about to walk into or how to cope with it.

"We go with plan B," I said, opening the door and walking through.

"There are plans?" he asked. Smartass.

"To the emerging life form," I said loudly to a mostly empty diner, "this is your one warning to turn around and stay home." The few people eating turned to look at me, confusion growing quickly even as the lights inside started to spark and pop. "And don't play dumb as if you can't hear me. I know how the membranes work. So," I continued as Suzette hurried over to us with concern in her face, "if you would, simply turn around — you would be saving us both a lot of trouble, and I could stop drinking so much coffee that my bladder hates me." I shrugged at Suzette, who stopped in front of me.

"Hey y'all, scaring the customers isn't cool, all right? I mean I like you and all, but—"

"Suzette," Anders said, holding a hand out toward her, "why don't we go sit over there and

I'll explain."

I admit I hoped her concern had been for us, not for the diner, but you get what you get. "Tell her the truth," I told Anders, "but get ready to help."

He nodded and walked Suzette, who willingly followed him, her puzzlement taking control, to a table where they both sat. Smart kid, he sat them so they could both still see what went on.

All of my waffling, my apprehension over even edging against this life again, dropped away like a weight. I could feel my focus narrow down until only this diner existed. Breach energy flooded the space, tasting like carrots, oddly enough, and lighting the place up like a shitty cop movie for a second. I squared my shoulders and waited. Maybe the idiot on the other side of this felt like ignoring me. Maybe they deserved one more chance to listen to reason.

"...and I know it sounds totally out there, but trust me when I say the monster is real..." I heard Anders say off to my side, explaining stuff to Suzette. It wouldn't go well, that part never did. But he had to learn, and see how most people were closed off to what they decided remained impossible.

"Listen up," I said to the swirling air and light show growing in the diner, "I'm Paige Never. I'm the woman your friends warned you about when you wanted to come here. Maybe you thought I'd died, or retired — fair play. But I'm *right here*, jerk, so it's time to rethink your plans and go get brunch on your side of the curtain. We both know what I can do, and what my standing in your way ends up costing you. Trust me when I say neither of us wants that. I just want to leave here, and I want *you* to leave here as well. Simple. But if you don't, I will bring down the force of the Ascended down upon you. Worse," I grinned a fake grin, "I'll enjoy it." I clapped my hands together, and then slowly unbuttoned the one button on my jacket, letting it start to whip in the growing wind. "So what do you say? Just back off and this is over."

Anders appeared at my side. "Will they listen?" he asked.

"First of all," I said without looking at him, "shouldn't you be with Suzette?"

"She's fine — well, as fine as you can be when you're half convinced of what's actually going on here but still fighting it with what's left of your old, thought-to-be-rational mind."

"Anders, you wanted to help and I—"

"Gave me a job that I did. What next?" he asked.

"Well, since this piece of shit," I waved as the breach started to fully form, knowing I had nothing on hand to stop it easily, "isn't listening, I guess I have to play traffic cop for real and turn their ass around."

"Right, and?"

"And nothing," I said, patting down my empty pockets and growing annoyed. "I don't have anything to use," I said softly so only Anders could hear me, "and I'm having to improvise here — not the best-case scenario by about a mile or two."

"So what can you use, what can I prep for you?" he asked. I stuffed the anger I could feel at his pestering down deep and thought, instead, about ways he could help.

"Go find something iron in the kitchen, just in case," I said.

"Iron, really? Like for fairies?"

"Just go." I waved him off and watched as he made a wide curve around the swirling mass growing in the diner. I figured he had a less-than-stellar chance of finding anything useful in the kitchen, but if he did, it could help, and either way the kitchen was behind the problem and not between me and whatever might force through the breach.

A fuchsia tentacle emerged slowly, slithering along the fake tile floor. Another followed, and then a third and forth. They went up and met at a fuchsia torso, and from there up the creature looked like anyone else, if anyone else happened to have fuchsia skin with porcupine-like spines sticking out of their elbows and shoulders, and an elongated jawline that seemed as if it could swallow a pig whole.

"Really?" I asked the intruder, "You're a...no, I'll get it. It's been too long, but I know you folk, you're a...Kindeleet, right? The tentacle lower body gives you guys away every time."

The Kindeleet snarled at me and slithered forward, letting the breach slide closed behind them. Great, now I knew what the beastie was — I just had to remember how to deal with one. I'd faced a few, ages back, off the coast of...nope, couldn't remember, just that the place had lovely beaches and a problem with invading Kindeleet tentacle fuckwits.

"The smug child of the Ascended," the

Kindeleet said, hissing their way through the sentence, "all alone you stand, and you think you can stop me from slaking my hunger here in this..." they looked around, taking in the surroundings.

"It's a diner. And no one here is on the menu," I said.

Suzette stood up — I caught the motion out of the corner of my eye — and grabbed a chair, standing there, waiting. "Kill it!" she shouted. The few other patrons started to stand, realizing this was, in fact, a thing happening to them and not a terrible prank or whatever strange type of dream they'd decided on.

"No!" I responded, holding a hand out toward her to make her stay. "I'm here to stop *anyone* from getting killed. That means them as much as you. If we start killing things out of fear, what does that get us, outside of having to hide a whole lot of bodies over time?"

"It wants to eat me!" she insisted.

"They, first of all," I said, and looked at the Kindeleet. "You have a name?"

"Parthainju, first of my fam—"

"Don't need a title, thanks." I looked back at Suzette. "Stop calling Parthainju here an 'it.' No need to be rude. And sure, they..." I looked at Parthainju. "Hmmm I don't even know if you use gender. Up to you, Parthainju. What do you say?"

"I am male, obviously."

"Got it. So, Parthainju here, he wants to eat you, sure, and I intend to stop that from happening. But that doesn't mean I'm gonna let a mob kill him, either. That's not how this works. Now, look, let me handle this and we can all get out of it intact."

"Why must you dole out lies to these meals of mine, Ascended child?"

"The name, again, is Paige Never. Anyway," I turned my full attention back to him, "I dealt with a host of you guys once, and turned you back. There's just one of you. So maybe rethink this and just skulk back to your own place. I'll even help you reopen the barrier, gentler this time."

I sniffed the air, and the smell wafting around keyed a memory. A good one, as far as this situation went, at least.

"Never mind the iron," I said loudly so Anders could hear me, "I just need some vinegar. No oil, or salad though. Well maybe a salad, this place does decent salads, really. Yeah, bring me a salad, oil and vinegar, but also a bottle of good pure vinegar, all right?"

Anders didn't answer but I heard rustling from the kitchen. Either he was making me a salad or the chef had freaked out on him, or both. I pressed on, regardless. "But if," I said to Parthainju, "you keep pressing me, you'll regret it. No, I won't kill you, not unless you make me, but that leaves a whole wide world of hurt open to me. Really though, you could just leave now and everything would go so much simpler. I mean, can I be honest with you?" I asked, stalling for time.

"Proceed, while you can," he said, the hissing subtle but present.

"I retired, all right? I don't want to be here. This is on you. You had to go and decide to try and snack on some humans, I'm assuming because a friend told you they were tasty or whatever it is you get out of it, and so you found the weakest point you could and pushed. For a week now I've waited — watching and trying to work out who wanted into this stupid dimension and for what dumb reason — and it's all just a case of you having the munchies and demanding some takeout. So, yeah, I'm mad. And yeah, this is all extra annoying. But if you think that somehow makes me less of a threat? Check the math."

"You are rusty," he said, slowly licking his obnoxiously long jaw. Ick. "You are alone. You are also," he wiggled forward on his four tentacles, "stalling for time, trying to think of a way out of this."

"No, you fuck," I said, seeing Anders coming out of the kitchen with a bottle of vinegar, "I was stalling for time waiting for this."

Anders ran over and handed me the bottle, shrugging when I raised an eyebrow at him. "Like I had time to make a salad?"

"I gave you time," I insisted, and then instantly felt a dagger of anger aimed at myself for enjoying this. "But thanks." I undid the cap on the bottle and smiled at the Kindeleet. "As for you, know what I remembered? The smell of you. Kindeleet have a serious alkali problem. Your blood and your sweat both, you're just a giant walking hydroxide problem. Which is also why," I looked around the diner, "no one should step in your sweat or touch you in *any* way. Chemical burns suck." I smiled at Parthainju. "Speaking of chemical burns — you know, I'm *sure,* what this bottle of vinegar would do to you."

"And yet you said you would not kill me," he said.

"Oh, don't get worked up into a lather, this wouldn't kill you," I told him, shaking the bottle a bit. "Scar you? Sure. Hurt for weeks? Easily. Kill you? I mean I could manage to, but by default, no, not at all. So, again, go. Shoo. Scram. Or else." I poured about a drop and a half of the vinegar onto the floor. Parthainju recoiled out of fear. Perfect.

What wasn't perfect was his next move. Spooking him into leaving, that plan felt solid. Spooking him so much he lashed out, that edged into mistake. I caught the movement of one of his rear tentacles just a second or two too late. He'd grabbed and ripped up a stool from the counter, flinging it right at me, whipping it around in a frenzy and letting it go to fly out the glass front of the diner.

I dropped to the floor as the stool passed me by and worked on capping the vinegar. Yeah, I could have stopped this right then — and scarred the Kindeleet for good, and probably should have — but I still wanted to solve this neatly. That mattered to me, if I was going to step back into this, even for a minute. I wouldn't do it like I had Smythe, leaving the job only partly done. Failing other people.

Stupider yet, overthinking this shit would get me killed trying. I needed to focus. "Anders, *don't* touch him!" I yelled, seeing Anders start to rush in. He skidded to a halt and looked for a chair to grab, anything that might help, and I got to my feet.

Parthainju whipped a tentacle at my head, but I didn't move, knowing he couldn't reach me. I stood and faced him, one hand held palm out to him. "Yeah, scared and angry, I get it. But—"

"No more of your meaningless words! You show only your fear! You can not stop me, and so you try to make me back away, knowing nothing else will work!"

"The vinegar..." I reminded him, giving the bottle a little shake. My dive to the floor had spilled some, but not much. We both watched the liquid slosh in the bottle for a second.

"If you had the stomach to use it, you would have, No, Paige Never, you are a shell of what you once were, and now I shall—"

The rest of whatever speech he wanted to give cut short in favor of a scream as a splash of vinegar landed on the tip of one of his leading tentacles. "Do I have your fucking attention?" I said. "I am in no way kidding. Leave before this gets uglier." I caught Anders just in the edges of my vision, working to keep Suzette and the others back. Good. Except I'd need both hands free for my next trick.

"Anders," I said, holding the vinegar out to him, "hold this, but don't throw it unless I specifically tell you to. Got it?"

He nodded and took the bottle, standing ready to splash the Kindeleet, who turned his gaze right to Anders and kept it there, tentacles twitching and hands clenching and unclenching.

"Eyes over here, dude," I told him. I scratched my neck thoughtfully and considered my next move for a second and third time. I could pull this off, I decided, ignoring any evidence to the contrary. Rusty, so far out of practice I hadn't even thought of this until a few seconds ago, lost in my own head — I was a mess. But being a mess would get people killed. So I couldn't afford to be. Honestly, at times, it can be that simple.

I clapped my hands and refocused, feeling the space of the diner as a living thing, letting my mind tap into the wider universe. Tapping my heels inside the WarBoots, I activated them and felt their energy spread out quickly, mingling with everything else. Some breach energy lingered, as it will, and I drew it to me slowly.

"I warned you," I said, "I'm one of the Ascended, like it or not, and that means I can do…this." I pooled the energy from the beach and took it in, briefly. Not long enough to fry my own nervous system: Free tip, don't fill your cells with energy from between dimensions, it'll cook every nerve ending you have for good. Instead I focused it down, letting my WarBoots collect it.

I kicked out toward Parthainju, the sole of the WarBoot stopping well short of him. As my leg extended, I released the energy collected and watched it wash over Parthainju, shoving him back painfully and interacting with the remnants of the breach around him. "I can shove you out of here by force, if need be," I said, drinking in more energy and preparing, "and then what — you try to come back and we do this again? Boring, right? Because that kind of cycle just doesn't end until one of us either misses an appointment or dies, or I guess kills the other. And really if we're gonna go down that road, we might as well try and kill each other now. And I know what you're thinking," I told him, shaking my head, "you already want to kill me. And you know I don't want to kill you. So, sure, some of this feels kind of rote *already* and we've been standing here for too long, and did I mention I'm retired and not into this? So you're leaving one way or another. But if I have to force you, it'll be way worse, because I can make sure you don't come back here and we both know it."

While I let my mouth run, I watched the energy behind Parthainju gather. Smiling, I shrugged at him. "Time's up," I said as I brought my right foot down hard, setting off the WarBoot to release the rest of the stored energy inside. The breach blossomed to life and started to suck the Kindeleet back into it. "Anders, now! Throw it!"

He didn't hesitate, snapping the bottle toward Parthainju like a pro, unleashing a large splash of vinegar. Parthainju screamed, recoiling in fear and gliding right into the breach, which got soaked in the vinegar.

"Someone grab me a raw potato!" I yelled, snatching a fork from the closest table. No one moved Great time to go still, people. "Seriously! Now!" That got a few people moving, hopefully one toward the kitchen.

Meanwhile, the Kindeleet fought back against the pull of the breach, but each time he did the vinegar caught in the energy burned him again. He'd give up soon enough — too soon, if I didn't get that potato, damn it.

It arrived, like a missile, thrown at my head by someone I didn't see. Managing to catch it with a hand just before I caught it with my face, I stabbed the fork into it and leaned forward. Holding the quickly heating metal of the fork tightly, I swirled the potato inside the open breach like I was roasting a marshmallow.

The breach snapped shut, Parthainju closing it from his side like a good, terrified person, and I yanked the potato back just in time. It smoked blue wisps into the air and smelt like ozone mixed with clay. Perfect. I shoved it, still hot, into a jacket pocket and worked the fork free, dropping it the ground.

"All right," I said, looking around the diner. "Good job, everyone. We did it."

"We didn't do nothing," Suzette said, her shoulders bunching up, "and you shoulda just killed that thing."

"We went over that," I reminded her, "and I stand by the idea that no one being killed is far better. As it is, he can't come back. The breach energy mingled with the vinegar and his own chemistry — if he tries to breach he'll die, and he knows it. So you're safe." I looked around the diner. "All of you. From him, at least."

Looking around, I wandered over to the order counter and grabbed the pot of coffee sitting in its warming cradle. I poured myself a cup and drank it in one long, far-too-hot swallow. Victory sips need to be timed, damn it all. I couldn't even get that right anymore. "Anyway, Anders, we should go."

"You're gonna just leave?" a guy asked, standing next to his table, a plate of quickly cooling meatloaf and congealing gravy perched on it, seeming lonely.

"I mean, well...yes." I turned and walked out the door, not looking back to see if Anders followed.

The door opened and closed again behind me

so I assumed he had, confirmed when he asked, "We're really just leaving?"

"You can stay and sweep up broken glass if you really want, but I'm tired," I told him, heading in the general direction of the hotel.

"What about the potato?" he asked, catching up and walking alongside me, notebook out. He was trying to jot notes and walk, as well as pester me, and I admit to being slightly impressed. Decent amount of mental juggling there. Not Olympic level or anything, but even so.

"Breach energy, corrupted and stored in a living thing, is a good tool to have. And potatoes make great receptacles for power. Like the ancient potato grenades, they come in handy."

"Ancient potato grenades?"

"Store some energy in a potato, prime it, and throw. You know how grenades work, come on."

"But not with potatoes," he insisted.

"Same concept, trust me. They used then in ancient Rome, actually. Got rid of the Fae that way. Then they lied and claimed iron was the thing that hurt them the worst, when really the whole idea of the cover-up existed just to produce a run on iron-ore–based goods to prop up a flagging market."

"Fairies are real?" Anders asked, switching gears away from spuds.

"That's our name for them, not theirs, but yeah. Hey, Anders?" I said, stopping and waiting for a light to cross the street. "Let ask you something. I'm heading back to the hotel to rest, and answer some questions about this for you, but then I'm done, you know that. Are you going to let me be done, or will this be a fight?"

"If it's what you really want, after all this, then yes, fine. I can take a hint," he said, crossing the street while no traffic barreled toward us. I followed, easily catching him.

"No, you really can't," I pointed out. "But I'm happy to hear you'll start to."

CHAPTER SEVEN

I LAY MOSTLY on my bed in the room, WarBoots dragging my feet toward the floor. To tell the truth, I wasn't tired, not in a physical sense. Emotionally might be a different story. Anders wrote in his journal, of course, and I lay there staring at the ceiling.

He hadn't asked me anything yet, which I appreciated, even though I realized he was simply biding his time. I used that same time to work out what I wanted. Did I really want to step back and stop, right when I'd put a toe back into the water?

Yes.

Right then. Yes.

But doing so would also leave Anders out in the cold. He didn't seem to be able to learn to even feel any sort of incipient event happening — but he'd only been at it a few days, so fuck, maybe it was him, maybe it was my teaching, maybe the cause lay in a...

I sat up quickly and looked around the room. "Anders, do you feel *anything* strange?"

"Like the energy stuff you tried to teach me? I mean, I—"

"Shush, just try and feel out, see if you notice anything odd."

He nodded and closed his eyes, letting his head hang limp. I watched him try to enter the state needed, something I could do by reflex — any of the Ascended could, of course, since childhood —

he looked like he was getting there decently well. Yet when he opened his eyes again, he shrugged at me. "Nothing," he said, trying to hide the sadness coloring the word.

I got up and started to pace around the room. "No, that's it, though," I said, gesturing wildly toward nothing. "You can't sense anything." He started to reply but I cut him off quick. "Neither can I," I said. "Now I can chalk that up to being out of practice, but *that* out of practice? No. I don't believe it."

"Come on, Paige, you felt the thing at the diner," he said.

"Sure," I agreed, "but normally, like I was telling you, there are things brushing against the walls all the time, looking in, just poking at stuff and so on. There's a hum. You learn to tune it out — the more you look for problems, you want to focus on the bigger issues, like with the Kindeleet, but even so. Like the shitty electricity in this place. You can hear the sixty-hertz hum if you look for it — it's there, of course it is, the wiring in this place might be old enough to need an AARP membership. But normally, just sitting here, you won't hear it for long stretches. That doesn't mean it stopped."

Anders stood slowly, closing his journal with care. "Are you sure?"

"About the shitty wiring in this place? Fuck yes. But also about the background hum of the universe. I don't think it's a problem of you not being able to sense problems so much as there's something just...off...everywhere."

"How do you figure it's everywhere?" he asked, tapping his pen on the table rhythmically.

"Because we're in Boise. What would possibly affect only Boise? That would be like deciding that rabbits get to talk but not cats or dogs. Makes no sense, Anders. None."

"Assuming you're right, what could be causing it?"

I kept pacing back and forth in the tiny room, maybe five steps before I needed to turn back around again. My patience wore as thin as the carpet. Not with Anders, but with myself. "Who knows? And really does it matter to me?"

"Paige," Anders said, moving in front of me. I stopped, staring at him. "Stop it. Yeah, I know, you retired. You wanted the quiet life. I've heard it all, you've heard it all come out of your own mouth. But you keep going after things anyway. Can you just admit — to yourself, if not to me — that you want to do this?"

"No," I said, shrugging, "honestly I can't. I wish I could. But I can't. Either way, though, I do want to know, at least — maybe just to poke at it as a science experiment — what could be causing this."

"Sure," he said, slumping back over to sit down. "How?"

"Beyond the normal base-level hum, you can feel stiches, fixes in the world. Not always, of course, and even then not too well, but maybe — I mean look at the options," I held up a finger. "Either the world has grown slowly simpler, and things that were normal for thousands of years, breaches and the like, have mostly stopped to a really strange degree—" I held up a second finger, "or someone else is fixing things, or—" I held up a third finger, "nope, I don't have a third option."

"Well, if you can fix things — and used to, but stopped — why wouldn't someone else fix them?" Anders asked. It was a good question. A really good one. But I knew things Anders didn't.

"There are, and have been, but not to this degree. In my day, when we—" I caught myself, "...when I used to do this, there wasn't a chance in hell this much could be dealt with. You'd need a team, an operation, and even then — I don't know. Let me see if I can feel anything."

"Can I help?"

"You know what," I said, nodding, "maybe you can. I'll start, and I want you to focus on feeling what I'm feeling. Piggyback it. I don't know if it'll work, but it's the same tricks I showed you to feel energy states, so if I'm right and it isn't you but the world, you should be able to."

"How will that help?" he asked.

"Hey, if you can feel energy states, at all, it reinforces what's going on. Which is good. I'm sorry I didn't think of this first, but the idea that someone, or some group, is keeping the world quiet never occurred to me. Why would it?"

I reached out, mentally, and felt for leftover energy spent. Nothing nearby, of course, nothing in the room or even shouting distance. I kept pushing, trying to feel further. At the very edges I could sense...something...but not enough to tell what that thing could really be. Sighing, I opened my eyes and told Anders to do the same.

"We need to go somewhere else. I'm thinking a big town, coastal maybe," I said. "Somewhere there would naturally be a lot of activity. Enough to overwhelm you if you're not careful."

"So you're in, for this?"

"Stop asking and I'll stop answering. For right now, until I'm not, all right?"

"Fine," he agreed, "but also I think I felt something that time. Near the end, just a hint, like a whisper of a smell?"

"Yeah," I smiled at him, "you felt the very scant edges of the same thing I did. Useless, really, but proves we're on the right track. Somehow. Let's sleep and we'll leave at first light."

Anders nodded and carried his bag and journal over to his bed. "You know we can't go to the diner for coffee tomorrow, right?" he asked as I started to close the bathroom door behind me to get ready for sleep.

"I don't know that, Anders."

"No, seriously, by tomorrow, they'll be looking for us. Police, I mean. Faking being IRS agents has to be a crime, and the damage—"

"That we didn't do," I pointed out.

"Even so. We can't."

"Fine," I agreed, "we'll go and get coffee after we get there."

CHAPTER EIGHT

CLOSING THE MOTEL door behind me, I straightened my jacket and adjusted my grip on the paper bag of various and sundry items we'd picked up over our week stay. I stepped down on the inside heels of my WarBoots in the sequence to power them up and we walked to a corner, watching small amounts of traffic go by lazily.

I held out my right arm and Anders took a good, solid hold of it. He watched my feet without being reminded and we started the first step of the FastWalk in sync perfectly fine. The world slid by and I navigated, even though I could feel Anders drifting a bit. The last times we did this he managed it fine, so I simply carried on.

I felt his hand on my arm start to slip.

I reached over with my left hand. Reached out for him. Felt his fingers slide free of my upper arm.

No more Anders. Just gone from where he'd been next to me.

As soon as I realized he'd let go completely I skidded to a halt. I slid right into a wall, but not fast enough to break anything. I'd bruise plenty, though. Solid objects suck when you're moving at speed. Didn't matter, I turned and took a quick breath, stepping forward to FastWalk back the way I came.

I'd only completed a step after he'd let go, so I took a short step with the WarBoots and stopped smoothly, looking around. I couldn't think of a way to really find Anders, though. Sure I could look, but he could, realistically, be anywhere along the line of where we'd walked. Shit, he could be half inside a building, I supposed. Super low chance of that, I admit, but the chance existed. Right then, though, the idea loomed large.

Considering that without me to help stop him, he would've come out at speed — that worried me, too. I kept looking. No idea if taking another partial step would help or not. Assuming Anders had survived this I would have to look into getting a phone. Just never occurred to me. No one called me, after all. This is the sort of thing that flashes though my brain when faced with just enough unsolvable worry to matter: I just slide out and focus on the useless and ridiculous.

But no, I needed to find Anders, in whatever shape he'd be in, and go from there. So I stomped around, trying to work out where I stood. The road I was on seemed like a small local interstate at best. No one on the road, traffic lights in the distance, and behind me a stack of trees, reaching up into the sky as if to ask why they were left to surround this craphole of a deserted area.

I walked into the trees, expecting the worst, and pushed past unkempt branches, fallen and not, until I came to a wide clearing. Better, but still not great. At the edge of the clearing was a small lake. At the far edge of the lake sat Anders, elbows on knees, head in hands.

"Anders!" I called out, rushing over to him and sitting.

"Ow," he managed, turning to look at me. His eyes were bloodshot, and scanning the rest of him quickly, I could see some tears and scrapes but everything else seemed all right — except his left foot. It sat bare, shoe and sock gone missing. I also only counted four toes, the littlest one vanished, off to market or whatever, the stump looking fresh but cauterized.

"What happened?" I asked, shifting where I sat to examine his foot better.

"I'm not really sure," he said, wincing and pulling his foot away from me when I went to touch it. "I tried to focus and feel the cracks in the world while we were FastWalking, and—"

"Fuck," I said, sitting back and leaning on my hands, "that'd do it. I never even thought to warn you about that one, I'm sorry. But when you're moving in an impossible way, trying to resolve the layers of reality around you is like trying to juggle water. No wonder you stumbled. So, uhm," I asked, squinting a bit, "your foot?"

"I hit the ground, moving, of course," he said. "I think I was still in the trees when I came back to normal space and velocity. Luckily the clearing was here and then the water."

"So you sheared a toe off on a tree?"

"The water. I must've still been going incredibly fast — I skipped once, I'm pretty sure that's when the toe came off, but I was moving fast enough the surface of the water boiled."

"Well...fuck," I said, articulately. "Can you walk?"

"Right up until the shock wears off, I think," he said, standing slowly. "I'm going to be a giant bruise tomorrow."

"Me too, I mean I stopped with some control,

way more than you, but managed to plant myself right into a wall."

"Damn."

"Hey, I didn't lose any extraneous bits of myself, so no big deal."

Anders looked around, "Where are we, anyway?"

"I have," I said, shrugging as we both limped back to the road I'd come from, "no real idea. We need to work that out first, then we can see if we're good to travel."

He nodded and we continued to follow the road for a bit, noticing the majority of license plates read Iowa. Good enough for me. I sighted by the sun and found east. We agreed to try a single-step FastWalk first to see how it went. Anders gripped my upper arm tighter than before — I couldn't blame him for that — and we stepped forward.

I felt him wobble but we managed to stop easily and safely. We'd still need a bunch more steps to get where I pointed us, and I told him so. I didn't have anything on me to dull pain, and I knew that if my impact had started to hurt as it had — my whole side throbbed like a marching band trying meth for the first time — he must be in agony.

Still, we pushed on. The going remained touchy and we made shit time, considering, but we didn't die, either. There's an old adage about pushing too hard when you're hurt — the more you push the worse results you get. Healing up, taking care of yourself, would enable you to, in the long run, get things done in less time overall.

I can't deny the truth there, but I also know that when you meet reality, you end up, often, having to push through and just get the job done and shut up about it. Not the most efficient method, but there couldn't be a choice at times. I hated that this seemed to be one of those times — outside of my own pain, Anders could barely stand, much less walk — but I knew the more time we wasted, the longer I would be forced to sit and idle. And the longer I idled, the less I could use the momentum of simply doing to plaster over how I really felt.

There's a kind of grace to be found in simply going to autopilot, even if the reflexes are years old.

But the more I tried to show Anders, the more I found myself rethinking the exact things I taught him. We stopped for another breather and I found myself frowning. When you learn a skill, you keep the emotional state you learned it in — those feelings become the best way to access the skills your brain retains. I realized, as I showed Anders a few tricks, something I suppose I always knew: I learned a lot of this, as a child, in the worst ways possible.

Being brusque with Anders while I tried to show him how the world actually worked, and ways to survive in the darker, shit ends of it, would leave him in the same place it'd left me, eventually. Well, it might. But the idea that it even could frustrated me and made me want to turn around and leave him.

Of course, I admitted just as quickly, the other option would be to try and teach him things in a better way. I didn't know how long I could keep this charade up, how long I could keep fighting — but while I did, I knew in my gut Anders wouldn't leave unless he had to. Which made him my responsibility. And if I couldn't be better than the bastards who taught me—

I sucked it all back down and started to FastWalk us again, knowing the destination would only be another step or two. As we went, I allowed myself a brief fling with the idea of letting Anders in on any of these thoughts before dismissing it entirely.

Committing to try and teach him things in a healthier way would be difficult enough, honestly. Adding in a full mental exposé didn't feel like something I could take. Instead, I kept moving, sliding us to a halt after one last step.

"New York," Anders said, looking around. "You know, I looked for you here, heard a lot of rumors you lived here."

"I did, for a bit," I told him.

"What made you leave?" he asked. He smiled as he glanced around the city. We were in Manhattan, 90th and Amsterdam — nothing special about the place, just an intersection we stopped hurtling through space at.

"Sometimes you just know to leave a place before it takes you over. New York is great, I love it here, but also it's work just being here. That can be great, but there's also a time to cut out, you know?"

"I guess," he said, obvious in his love for the town. He smiled, looking around, and since he said he'd been here looking for me, I guess I was why he left. Or, rather, a lack of me.

"Sorry you left, huh? You could always move here, stay here."

"Trying to rid of me again?" he asked, shaking his head. I could see he was joking and didn't read anything into it.

"It's just that your love of the town, it's... physical, you know what I mean? Not in a 'Florida Man arrested for fucking a badger' sort of way, but emotionally physical."

"'Emotionally physical' isn't a thing," he said.

"Well it should be, and you know what I mean regardless, and anyway that isn't why we're here."

Anders nodded at me and looked around again. "So you wanted to come to the Upper West Side?"

"Not particularly, if you must know — no, we need to get to midtown. I should still have a stash there. Some money, some painkillers, all that good stuff. But really, I came here for exactly why you think. It's *noisy*. Not just in terms of city noise, either. The spaces between worlds — when you get this many people together, they draw attention. All the big cities have it. This just felt close."

"What about California?" Anders asked as he hailed us a cab. I looked at him and he shrugged. "I have enough space on my cards for a cab ride and I don't want to do the subway stairs on this foot, all right?"

"Fine by me," I agreed.

We cabbed down to midtown, a small building along 29th off of 6th, and I realized I didn't have the keys anymore. Laughing, I explained to Anders and he joined in. Of course I didn't have the keys anymore. Of course. I pressed my palm flat to the building's exterior door lock and concentrated.

The lock popped open and I smiled at Anders as I swung it open. "How'd you..." he asked as he entered the building. I let the door swing closed behind me, the lock auto-engaging as it always did with a still-familiar click.

"Just remembering more and more of what I used to be able to do without thinking about it. It all comes back, just at its own speed," I said as we climbed to the third floor and came to stand in front of another door.

"I meant more in the actual literal sense," Anders said.

I laughed and unlocked the door to my stash apartment the same as I had the building's front door. "Oh, sorry," I said as I walked in, flipping switches for lights that didn't work. Right, no one had paid the electric bill for the last bunch of years. "Remember what I said about small pocket dimensions, and how they can self-replicate into alternate realities if you aren't careful when you build them — which is, like, say, reason number seven to never build a pocket dimension for yourself?"

"...Not at all," he said, following me down the darkened hallway. It opened up into a single large space, the walls having been reduced to structural load-bearing columns ages ago in ways that would totally have destroyed my security deposit if I didn't have complete control of the space. "And how do you still have this space? Is this even legal?" he asked, looking at the obvious modifications.

"To hit up the latter first, it's legal enough.

I own this space. Basically. Just leave it at that. As for the door locks, look, you can create small pocket dimensions and they're often really just tightly controlled alternate realities, though most people hate to admit that so they get uppity when you point it out. That aside, they're easy to do once you know how to mess with things enough. And on a very, *very* small scale, you can create an alternate reality where the tumblers are already set to be open on the inside of a lock. The effect doesn't last longer than about a minute, but how long do you need to open a door, right?"

"You created an entire alternate reality, just to open a door?" he asked. I shrugged in reply and pointed at one of the couches that was slumping its way toward decay in the far corner of the room. The place still managed to feel like that strangest mix of cozy and utterly impersonal. Mostly the apartment stood as a big, empty, dusty space, all greys and blacks, but then it mixed in a bunch of couches and rugs, all muted colors, but colors ranging across the spectrum, huddled in one corner and threatening to spill over into the rest of the space.

"Locksmiths take forever and charge a lot," I said by way of defense.

Anders sat on a couch and worked his shoe off carefully as could be. I caught him wincing a few times, heard a bit of sucking air through a clenched jaw, but otherwise everything seemed normal.

Well, normal for my memories of this place. Possibly not a great endorsement. I wandered toward the opposite side of the place, where a small hall led into a smaller bathroom. I rummaged around for supplies and wandered back — all right, limped back — to where Anders sat, staring at his foot. He was just focusing on where that toe used to be. I couldn't read him, and had no clue if he felt sadness, or shame, or loss, or anything at all. The shock would be wearing off around now and soon everything would hurt, not just the twinges along the foot.

I sat down on the other side of the couch and let the supplies in my arms spill into the space between us. Rummaging through them, I offered Anders a small packet of pills and tore another one open with my teeth, dumping the contents into my mouth and dry swallowing. "They'll take the edge off but leave you focused, trust me," I told him.

"What are they?" he asked, opening the packet slowly and peering inside.

"Medicine," I told him, and started to open a sealed bandage package to wrap his foot with.

"No, but, I mean," he asked, pressing further, "what *kind* of pills are they? I don't take drugs, really, I mean maybe some aspirin, but even then only when I really need to."

Gesturing for him to lift his foot in my direction so I could wrap it, I shrugged. "Think of it as really *good* aspirin then — I mean, basically, same idea. Reduces pain and swelling, all of that. But it isn't toxic, or addicting, I promise."

"No, I need to wash this first," he said, looking at his foot. "But really, if you can't tell me what this stuff is, only what it isn't? I might pass."

"Towels in a box under the sink," I said, and he stood and hobbled to the bathroom. "But Anders,"

I raised my voice so he could hear me as he started to run water, "I'm sorry I don't have an ingredient list for this stuff, but it's decent Ascended medicine. You're gonna have to trust me on this."

The water shut off and Anders came back, his face white with pain. He walked slowly and carefully, barely putting pressure on his left foot, and then only on the heel. He sat heavily, automatically lifting his foot off the ground as he did, and looked at the open pill packet still sitting on the couch where he'd left it.

"I really don't—"

"Take the damned pain killers, Anders, or I have to leave you here. Right now you couldn't even put a show on if you had one. We should get you another shoe. But first, take the stupid pills and let me wrap the foot."

He nodded at me and dry swallowed them, making the face of a person who'd never had to dry swallow pills before. A tiny fit of light coughing and he sighed, slumping back on the couch and lifting his left leg toward me. I took it carefully and wrapped the whole thing, making sure the stump of the little toe got extra protection. Cauterized or not, the wound still counted as fresh.

I felt my own pills start to kick in, and my shoulder moved far more freely than it had when I'd started wrapping Ander's foot. Good, because I could hope his own would kick in soon — I knew the touching of the bandage, the act of wrapping it tightly, must've been making him want to scream. He didn't, but he stayed sheet white, with a haunted, pained look on his face.

"I'm gonna run out and get you some shoes,"

I told him as I finished, tying the bandage off and leaning back on the couch.

"Can't you just make some appear, like before?"

"I could," I admitted, "but I really shouldn't. I already have to account for one pair for you. Doubling up on that would get confusing. Besides, somewhere around here I should have some money. I'll run out, grab something for you, maybe some food too, and then we'll do what we came here for."

He just nodded, sinking back into the cushions. I stood up, feeling much better — but, still knowing my bruises and strains existed, I didn't give in to the urge to stretch. I could pop something and possibly not notice for a few hours. "Don't hurt further yourself while I'm gone, either."

Rummaging until I found some spare keys so I could get back in without needing to break the laws of physics, I looked around the place. A lot of memories in this place, people coming and going and testing the limits of help that could be provided. Along with a bunch of memories of being alone and feeling as empty as the majority of the space did. The urge to scream, to whip up a storm in the open spaces and make myself known, bubbled up out of nowhere.

Instead I just asked Anders' shoe size again and set off into the city to find some socks and shoes and food, in that order. My stomach protested that order, wondering if he really needed shoes. I laughed at myself and wandered the streets looking for a shoe store. I swear, they used to be easier to find, but taking my time meant Anders would sleep some, which I knew he needed.

I did, too, and I knew that, but I also knew I could go longer than him without giving in. No, let me take the time and give him a chance to rest. I eventually found a crappy shoe store and grabbed something basic with a slightly wider-than-normal toe box so the bandage would fit. They wouldn't hold up for too long — a month of good use, or a few weeks of serious walking — but this wasn't a perfectionist moment.

That feeling, the push to make a mark, stayed buried, and I fought a little bit to ensure it would. I'd work out this strangeness and just keep moving, not thinking about where too hard, until I could really work things out.

Right then working things out meant food. I found a cheap Chinese place on my way back and ordered enough for food for five people. The guy behind the counter started to reach for plastic forks and looked at me as he did. "Just two," I said, knowing that he didn't even begin to care.

Anders was, as expected, fast asleep when I got back. I tried to close the door quietly, pocketing the keys in my torn and disheveled slacks. The door to this place, let me be clear, never did close quietly. Ever. I mean it didn't slam by itself, but the weight of the door — I'd reinforced it, of course — and the hinges being what they were, and, well... Anders startled awake as I tried to ease the door fully shut and lock it.

We ate, and sat back feeling sleepier than ever as the food sat heavily in our guts. But no rest, wicked, all that. I wiped off my hands and again fought the urge to stretch. "Feeling better?"

I asked.

"Much," he said. "I guess those drugs worked. My foot hardly hurts at all."

"Good. But for now, stay off it. The idea here, the whole reason we came here, was to see if the silence is a real thing. So let's check."

He nodded and I took a deep breath — not necessary, but hey, breathing is good — and I stretched out my mind, feeling for incipient problems. Not much bounced back at me. The silence echoed across my brain strangely. It itched. I looked at Anders, who had his eyes shut as he concentrated, finding the headspace needed.

"Anything?" I asked him.

"Same amount of nothing as before," he said. Right then. Fine.

"This time, feel for the fixes. It's the same sort of energy but it'll be older — stale, almost. See if you can't feel what I'm doing and lean on that feeling. I know that sounds silly, but we did it before, so..."

"I got it," he told me, looking as serious as I felt but for utterly different reasons.

I cracked my neck lightly and felt outward for stiches in the fabric — repaired seams, as well as lingering proof as to who might have done the work.

There.

A hint, a burst of activity, days old already.

Fuckers couldn't hide it, but I could feel how they'd tried. Oh, clever apes. I reached deeper, and feeling Anders reaching alongside me, taking him with me. Diving deep, I knew this would all stop making sense to him, but I needed to check.

"Oh for fuck's—" I cut myself off and slapped a hand down on the couch instead. Anders opened his eyes, watching me.

"You gonna explain or just curse more?"

"Both, probably. Fuck. This makes less and less sense, Anders. I don't *like* it when things make no sense. That means they're probably true," I said, shrugging. "Wait, you felt the fixing?" I asked.

"I don't know," he admitted. "I felt something — I could sense the wall more this time, and nothing seeming to push back against it close by—"

"In itself strange in this town."

"If you say so," he said. "But then, trying to replicate what you were doing, everything felt muted, and the...what you're saying were fixes, they felt like old paper — once wet, you know that strange roughness that always feels just *wrong* along your fingers, like it'll never be just paper again? When you soak a book but dry the pages?"

"Yeah," I told him, "fixes. No fix is perfect. So, first of all, see you can learn this stuff. But secondly, there was more — could you feel anything about the fixes besides that? Anything else, maybe some of them felt different than others?"

"I'm not sure. Some of them felt blander than others? Like," he waved his hands a bit, and I could see, along his right wrist, bruising coloring up nicely already, "like they were just decaying stuff, but most of them felt more feathery than that. Redder, if that makes sense. I didn't see a color, or smell anything, I just...somehow red made an imprint."

"Oh that's fine, it's different for everyone, the

way senses crosswire about this stuff. It's a form synesthesia that some ninety-nine percent of the population doesn't even know exists. For me, that red you felt just left the taste of pineapple."

"And you hate pineapple that much," Anders said, apparently deciding that made sense.

"I do, actually," I agreed, "but even if I didn't, I would in this case. That residue is almost certainly only one group, still. They use specific methods, always have. Everyone's take on how to do this sort of job leaves a personalized remainder, a signature. This was the Subtle Knives."

CHAPTER NINE

BAADER-MEINHOF PHENOMENON. That's the name for that very special universal trick where after you learn of something, or think about it a bunch, you start to see it everywhere. Really, it's a function of selective attention working alongside confirmation bias, but "Baader-Meinhof phenomenon" sums it up faster.

Ever since I'd almost been killed by them, the Subtle Knives of the Endless Blossom had been at my heels, in spirit if not in fact. But now, this — this felt like too much. I started to curse again, and Anders just watched, waiting for me to wind down.

"I don't want to you start you up again," he said slowly, "but if they're solving problems, isn't that a good thing?"

I took a minute to sit and think about how to answer that. "I can see," I started, "where you might think so. Solving problems is good. Sure. But the Subtle Knives...they're not good guys. They're not even — look," I pressed my heels down and undid my WarBoots, slipping my feet out of them, "I'm not saying I'm a good guy, either, but there's not good and there's *not good*, right? A badger might not be a weasel, but they're both in the Mustelidae family. And let's be honest here, if given a choice, you don't choose a badger — in that situation we have an entirely different conversation to have."

"Weasels bad, badgers good," Anders said.

"Got it. You're a badger to the Subtle Knives' weasels. Sure."

I propped my feet up on the table and leaned back against the couch. "Don't dismiss this. Let me tell you about these fuckers." I started to lay out the history of the Subtle Knives of the Endless Blossom for him...

———

The name itself, of course, sounds vaguely Japanese. There's a reason for that. In 1629, Charles I dissolved Parliament. That set off eleven years of tyrannical nut-jobbery, and one Walter Humphrey Miller decided he wanted no piece of that.

So — with a few friends, a small boat, and a handful of shoddy maps — he set off to find a land to set up camp on that wouldn't be as bad as what he thought England was headed toward. He found Japan. It took them the better part of two months to do, and let's be honest, they didn't necessarily mean to land where they did, but they needed to land somewhere and restock and just get off the damned boat, so there they were.

They arrived in and stayed for the annual cherry blossom season. The sight awed Miller. No one involved spoke the language, and though they had seen the occasional cherry blossom other places, none of them had seen so many.

Not long after, they left — because of course they did, since no one *wanted* them there — and returned home. Along the way, Walter Humphrey

Miller came to a conclusion: He would help save the World. Please note: he defined the World as "civilized society" and defined *that* as "the lands he came from," initially. Why he made that leap suddenly can be attributed to another long sea journey or madness. It could also easily come down to Walter being the sort of asshole who thinks he's so special that eventually this sort of idea dawns on him. You'd be surprised, but shouldn't be, at how often it happens. Normally it dies away quickly. With Walter Humphrey Miller it stuck. He had a mission.

Once back, he gathered friends and people he decided would be of like mind and spoke, in really racist terms that aren't worth getting into, about his trip and the state of Japan and the people — but really he kept coming back to the cherry blossoms. In lieu of an actual plant, he'd commissioned many drawings of them and showed them to everyone, explaining how his new concept would center around them. Our boy Walter got a lot wrong. This surprises no one.

But his secret, unnamed society kept going, through force of will — and a good supply of beer, Miller being good friends with a brewer who happened to buy into his special brand of nonsense. And though their "official" history claims otherwise, one night after a few too many of his friend's beers, Miller decided his society needed a name. They would gain a stronger purpose to go with it, and so, drunkenly, he set their course:

Having watched people prune the trees, oh-so carefully, he felt that was what they needed to do to humanity. Treat it like a cherry blossom, his cherished image. And they would prune as carefully as possible. Their blade would be subtle, so the people would never see them in action.

But that's just where things started.

It took a little less than a century for the Subtle Knives to go off the rails. Miller long since dead, he had no say in this, of course. But his followers had kept the faith, trying to work in secret and blame others for their actions so no one would even be able to whisper their name. That didn't quite work, of course, but they did a passable job.

In 1704, Isaac Newton first put forth the idea of multiple universes. And though it would take until 1954 for Schrödinger to really give voice to a modern multiverse concept, Miller's followers worked out the basics of the idea themselves a century earlier. They didn't publish it, or talk to anyone about it, because they used the idea to expand their mission.

They considered that somewhere out in an infinite number of universes there would be one in which they ruled, and the Earth there would work exactly the way they wished it to: namely, everyone in their place and those places all considered carefully and boringly.

To get that one "true" universe to be the only one out there, the Subtle Knives, who now considered the Endless Blossom to refer to the multiverse itself, would work to take over and destroy every universe they didn't rule in — assuming they didn't suspect that they were creating the one true universe where they stood.

They could, and did, attribute anything that

went wrong to "being in the wrong universe," but everything that went right could be "proof they were in the right universe," things just having not unfolded completely yet.

That double standard let them not be very effective and fine with it. In terms of secret societies running around the globe that killed people, toppled governments, and/or tried to reduce the population to sparkly goo — and don't think the Selfless Triangle of Glitter was a laughing matter just because of their name or goal, seriously, they were a total pain in the ass for years — the Subtle Knives of the Endless Blossom were minor-leagues.

You could count on them to rant at you about the Endless Blossom of the multiverse and how they wanted to prune the whole thing down over time. How their knives were their bodies and their actions...incessantly, so on and so forth. But they weren't spectacularly effective. Mostly they concerned themselves with ridiculous, petty, arguments, and a spot of attempted assassination every now and then.

They didn't care about incursions — they enjoyed them, seeing them as proof of their own theories. Which isn't to say they caused any. Again, they simply weren't that good. They were street level. A bunch of people with big, lofty speeches and some occasional fighting skills, but that was where it ended. These were not world dominators, as much as they told everyone who would listen that they were.

They were poison users, stabbers in the night, hand-to-hand fighters who counted a few members that could pulls a couple of tricks in their ranks. They weren't a *threat*. Not really.

————

"So you see," I finished up, "why it really worries me if this is them. If the Subtle Knives have, after all this time, upped their game, there must be a reason. And for them to do it in such a short span of time to boot, that's...that's a sign they may have found some new cause, or a backer, or something that really shook them up and spurred them on."

I crossed my ankles on the table and drummed my fingers on my thighs. Anders watched me, and I could see how my own anxious twitching started to amp him up, too. I forced my fingers to lay still.

"So if the Subtle Knives," Anders said, "are now a...a what...a credible threat, I suppose — you knew Smythe, right? Do you know anyone else who could help?"

"Smythe was the local expert on them because they weren't worth multiple experts, all right? Like putting out a grease fire — if you have a bucket of sand you don't also need a guy with a dump truck of concrete. So there isn't really a back up just waiting off somewhere in the dark, looking at the sky for a light to go off."

"Oh," he said, deflating a bit.

"They went after Smythe, they went after *me*, they might be targeting anyone who's stood in their way in the past. Clearing the board. But if we assume that..."

"Then who do you know who would be on

their list?" Anders asked.

I nodded. I'd been off the board a while — by now there could be new people, but who to even ask about that? Also, if they were this good now, for whatever reason, I had to worry about something else.

When we first left, I'd half-wondered about them following a FastWalk, but figured even if they could, it would take a while. They hadn't seemed to, so I'd tossed it out. But if they were good enough to pull this sort of thing — and let's just say I got lucky, for whatever fucked-up meaning of "lucky" fit, dealing with that Kindeleet instead of them — then why hadn't they shown up yet? Easy to assume they could be that widespread right now if they wanted to be.

Which put me in the mind that their plan was still moving in a direction I couldn't see. Never a good thing. In the old days, when I was young? No — when I gave an actual shit for real and didn't just fake it to keep moving — I wouldn't have stood for it. Plans within plans that folded back on themselves and confused everyone, occasionally including my own damned self — that used to be *my* calling card.

Now I didn't care if I couldn't be shown to be the cleverest person in the room, I simply intended to find them out and stop them. Or something. Stopping them might not be my game, after all. But even if that ended up Not My Job, I could find someone who would. There used to be a decent amount of us.

"Used to be," I said out loud, "there were a bunch of people in this line of work. Not," I amended, "all gathered up, or good friends, but there were a few good eggs in there."

"A society of—"

I cut Anders off quickly. "Nope. Nothing that organized or collaborative. You just slowly met other people who lived in the strange spaces, and, occasionally, you got a beer and didn't try to kill each other. That was it."

"Well, do any of those not-wanting-to-murder-you friends still exist? Outside of Smythe," he put in at the end.

"I'm sure. Well," I said, "I'm pretty sure. Just not sure how to find them, anymore."

"Let's just go to one. There has to be one close, right?" He stood up, slowly, and gathered up the remains of our food.

"Maybe," I agreed, sliding my feet off the table and back into the WarBoots, tapping down to make them secure themselves around me. "And just put the trash back in the bag, we'll toss it at a corner."

"That's illegal," Anders said.

"So's a lot of stuff, Dead Anders. Now come on, get some shoes on and let's see how we travel."

Turned out we didn't travel great, but with the money I had stashed we could at least make headway without having to max out all of Anders's life. We limped our way to a train and headed out to Queens. I would've called ahead, but I didn't think Shealano had a phone.

At least, she hadn't the last time I'd seen her years ago, so even if that'd changed did us no good. Regardless, we went, painfully. The painkillers were wearing off, but the extras in the pills helped

heal us a bit faster. Not much — far from fully —
but we would at least stay upright. I hoped.

CHAPTER TEN

AQUILA SHEALANO LIVED in a basement apartment in Sunnyside, Queens, near the cemetery. Because of *course* she did. She specialized in...I don't want to be overly mean, here, but Shealano tended to focus on the look of a thing more than the effect. Yeah — some people were, in fact, haunted. And you learn to deal with it. She would rather you paid up front and then moved, rather than taking care of the problem.

Which would, I suppose, raise the question of why go see if she still worked in the area, given she tended to be at least half fraud. The other half, the part she reserved for dealing with non-client, actual-threat–level events — that was where she proved how serious she could be. Her abilities there, her willingness to get the job done, they made you forget she spent most of her time conning people out of their cash.

And really, when it came down to it — you took the help you could get, especially when it kept you alive. We just tried to not talk about anything outside of the problem at hand. Plus, if I'm being honest, she thought as little of me as I did of her, just for other reasons.

She thought I was a tourist, a debutante — an outsider come down from the mountain to give light to the wretches. I never said I disagreed with her assessment. And that might be why I bristled so much around her. She disliked me for the fears

I had about myself.

Regardless, out of all the names I could pull from a hat, she remained the one least likely to have moved. She had a client base. She also owned a stake in the cemetery, which sounds darker than it is. She wasn't paid to help fill it or anything.

I knocked on her door, refusing to let Anders see that I breathed a bit hard, hurting more than I'd like still. I knew he hurt even worse and didn't want him thinking about anyone else's pain.

"Office hours are—" Shealano yelled from behind the door.

"Shea, it's Paige Never. Open the fucking door, you hustler." All right, sure we were there for help, but if I acted too nice up front, she'd be suspicious.

We were treated to the standard New York sounds of four or so locks being opened one after the other before the door opened a crack and Shealano looked out through the slight opening.

"You're dead," she said.

"I'm not." I looked at Anders, "He *was*, but only for a minute. Doesn't even remember it."

"Oh, well that's...that's a thing," she said, pulling the door open fully and ushering us in. She shut the door, locking all the locks before turning to face us. We stood there, in the purple gloom of her apartment. She's done it all up theatrically to look like a Tim Burton wet dream of what someone in her line of work would live like.

"I wasn't dead," Anders said, by way of greeting.

"You were," I reminded him, shaking my head. "Shea, I need some help. Can we talk?"

"The Mighty Paige Never vanishes for years,

leaving us poor humans to fend for ourselves, and now she's back and—"

"Stop the third-person shit. You want to insult me, just do it like a normal grifter," I said, walking away and down the hall, through the black-, silver-, and purple-glass–beaded curtain and into her actual living space. Much nicer. Soft browns and whites made the space feel like somewhere you didn't want to buy candy and a plastic mask at.

Settling into a chair, I nodded at Anders, who seemed unsure at my total disregard for etiquette. I shrugged and leaned back a bit, sticking my legs out and crossing my ankles. Comfort mattered.

Anders sank into a chair painfully and took a deep breath. He closed his eyes as he exhaled and I could read the pain on his face easily. We'd need to find something to do about that foot if he intended to keep coming along with me. I just didn't know what, without a full kit, and I didn't have one of those anymore.

"Sure, just sit wherever," Shea said, following us. She sounded angry but looked amused. Good.

"Shea, look, I just need—"

"No way, Paige, no," she said, cutting me off with a sweep of her hand. "Where the hell have you *been*?"

"That doesn't matter," I said.

"Oh but it really does — you see," she replied, "the rest of the world didn't just stop simply because you went on a little vacation, Never. We kept bleeding while you hit the sauna."

"Shealano," I said, as serious as I could, "I know *all about* bleeding." I glanced at Anders, then stared at Shealano until she noticed and put two and two together.

"Wait, where's—"

"Exactly. Now leave it," I told her, wiggling the fingers on my right hand to trace a small light pattern. There was, of course, nothing behind it, but Shea caught the motion and lost her focus for a second. "Aquila Shealano, I come to you for aid, in the old and sacred ways."

We both held the silence and serious of the moment for at least a good five seconds before bursting out laughing together.

"Oh fuck, the 'old and sacred ways'? What PBS Masterpiece Theatre bullshit was that?"

"Oh who cares?" I asked. "But we do need help."

She sighed. "Fine, of course. Come back here after all this time begging for my help, *like always*, and here we go."

"The Subtle Knives are—"

"Those clowns? Hold on, let me make some coffee," she turned and vanished, unconcerned.

"See," I said to Anders with a shrug, "clowns." I raised my voice, "Shea, they came after me, and wiped a decent part of Smythe's brain already."

That got her back in the room fast, a filter already heaping with grounds in hand. "They what now?" Anders and I told her the story, though I left out how he found me and instead started from us ditching the Subtle Knives.

Shealano sat and listened, not interrupting to ask questions or get clarification on anything. Nice of her, really, since I don't think any of us wanted to drag it out longer than needed. When we finished she turned, without a word, and left the room. She came back a few seconds later, and I could hear the coffee maker hissing away.

"The quiet — I assumed seasonal issues, maybe — or hell, I don't know," she said, sitting across from us, "probably I just welcomed it and didn't give it thought. But looking at it now, no, I see the start of the quiet, about a year ago? Yeah, a year ago, roughly." She nodded to herself and then sat quietly, thinking. We let her. Anders and I had had some lead-in and a bit more time to process. Then again, if I wanted to be callous, maybe she just *really* needed the coffee.

"So are they still following you, do you think?" she asked.

I waved my hands about uselessly for a few seconds. "I don't know. I want to say yes, just because I can't fathom why they would stop, but then again I don't know why they started, either. Also, if they are, they're doing a piss-poor job of it."

"At least you haven't used anything that could be sniffed out as you since you got here," she said. "Assuming they tried to follow and were behind, or decided to play a longer game. Announcing yourself in town, in *this* town, when you have to know there are more of them here — just the size of the city, right — so low profile was the right way to go."

Well.

Fuck.

"Uhm, about that—" I began.

"You fucking tourist dilettante, Paige!" she raged suddenly, and stalked back out of the room.

Anders looked at me and I gave him a half-smile. "That lock opening," I said, loud enough to be heard in the other room. "If they were looking. If they wanted to know. They'd know."

"You made sure they could find you, and probably track you here," came her loud reply, "to me, by showing off that stupid pocket-universe lock-picking bullshit?"

The coffee maker beeped, and Shea came back with a single cup. Guess we were done being cozy. "So what's your great idea, now, then?" she asked, sipping at her coffee, one raised eyebrow away from a cliché.

"We came here for your help. That still remains my plan. See what you know about the Subtle Knives, get your help assessing the damage, and then — I don't know."

"So you're up for the fight?" she asked.

Damn it. I wasn't. I knew that. I think, deep down, Anders knew it. The sting came when I saw Shea knew it, too, and judged me for it. I could admit that — that I wanted an excuse to hand this off, to go back and retreat. But to have her know it, to see it in her eyes — I felt shame. And then anger: at her, then myself, then her again, then back at me. All within a handful of seconds, because how long does it *really* take to admit to yourself that you're just a piece of shit? Not long. Not long at all.

"We don't even know if there is a fight, yet," I equivocated.

"Your...whatever he is," Shea said, nodding toward Anders, "is awfully quiet, here. He worth anything?"

"Anders?" I prompted. He wanted to be in on this, he could learn to speak up.

"Probably not," he said, causing me to cough-

ADAM P. KNAVE

laugh quickly. "I'd love to say yes," he continued,
"but I have no idea what I'm doing. Paige is
showing me some stuff, but I don't know how to
do anything." He fell silent then shrugged. "Except
hold my own in a fight," he added.

"A real fight?" Shealano asked him, finishing
her coffee. "I'm not talking fists and bottles."

"I am," Anders admitted, "but your type of
fight? Energy and secrets and other dimensions?
No."

"At least you're honest," she told him. "Unlike
your..."

"Boss," I said, not finding another good term.

"Boss, then," Shealano went on. "She lies.
Obviously, and all the time, sure — but I mean
right now. She wants to run. If there was a fight
I couldn't trust her at all. But she wants to come
here and ask for *my* help? I guess I'm supposed to
do her fighting for her."

"That's not it, Shea," I said, feeling every ounce
a shit-heel. "I want help. I want to find out what's
going on. I don't want to charge in like you always
try to, spreading fire before facts."

She laughed in my face at that. "Yeah, the
calm and collected Paige Never, who never used to
declare war on anything that moved if it disagreed
with her."

"Will you help or not?" I asked, standing up as
I did. There seemed to be less and less reason to
stay here.

Anders stood with me, but watched Shea.
"Just so you know, she hasn't been like that, from
what I've seen, and when I was a kid she saved
me. I don't know what your problem is, the both

of you, but you keep talking like there's something much bigger wrong, so maybe you should focus on that?"

"That supposed to rally us to each other's side so we can go out into the fight together?" Shea asked him.

"Well...yeah," he admitted.

"No such luck. Get out of my place, tourists."

I started to leave the room when Anders moved and blocked me. "You know I thought for sure you two would get the point," he said, looking amused. "But no, the fact you used to be in a relationship just gets in the way. I swear, sometimes you allos make no sense to me."

Shealano and I both gave him looks set to wither. "You're just flailing, trying to rile either or both of us," she said.

"But he's right," I put in. He was. We didn't see each other long back in the day and we didn't part *terribly* — hell, we could generally work together. But I guess the years gone, and the guilt of the present and all of it, really, had combined to just make us both prickly.

"So how'd you know?" I asked him, dialing back on the annoyed and trying to shift into curious. I felt secure in both, but curious got results.

"Aromantic asexual," he said, tapping the center of his chest. "You can sense the world, well, I learned to spot these things since it isn't my natural language really — I wanted to make sure I could understand anything that might be your motivations. In things like movies, shit, if nothing else."

ADAM P. KNAVE

"Oh, I think I like this one," Shea said. "Fine, Anders. You think our past bullshit in that area is what's causing this?"

"I do."

"He's kinda right, I think," I put in.

"He isn't," she countered.

"You're both boring me," he said. This was a side of Anders I hadn't seen. The done-with-your-shit version. I agreed with Shea: I liked it.

"Hey, Anders," I said, "what's with the attitude all of a sudden? This whole time you've pushed, but never like this." I just had to know. Curious, remember.

"You keep phrasing all of this as if the world is on fire, but you just get so swept up in your own bullshit. Fuck, Paige, I think I get it now."

"Oh," Shea leapt in before I could reply, "please tell me what you've worked out. Please?"

"All your friends start out cursing you, and wishing you'd leave, because you won't commit to them," he said, letting his voice grow softer as he spoke, as if the words dragged him down as he said them.

"Exactly!" Shea said, crossing her arms and looking at me.

"You've known me for ten minutes, Anders, and all of it at my worst," I said. I took a few slow breaths as subtly as I could manage, trying to not show how hard I worked to swallow any anger and just stay normal.

"So show me the best of you," he said.

"As rallying cries go, 'be less shitty' isn't the best," I said with a shrug, "but you're right."

"You don't have to tell us," Shealano said.

"Shea, don't," I told her. "We have our own shit to work out, sure, but Anders here is right. I haven't been fair to him. You know, at least, that I'm a fuck-up at times, and this isn't…"

"More often than sometimes, and yeah, Paige, you seem worse off than normal, but even so, this is bullshit."

"And it's my bullshit to deal with," I said.

"Not when shit is going down. I think the kid—"

"I'm not a kid," Anders jumped in with.

"I think…*Anders*…is right. He wins. We have to work together on this. As he said, the world is on fire, or we think it is. Let's find out — and put it out, if it is."

I shrugged. "Fine. But, Anders," I smiled at him, "I might not be back full time, even now."

"You keep saying that and keep being here. I'll take it," he shrugged.

"Fine, let's table all the whiny shit and personal crap," I said, "and work out a plan. Shea, can you still track?"

"The Subtle Knives? Without trying hard. Or at least, the old…yeah, let me get some gear. Speaking of…"

I patted my pockets and shrugged. "I have a charged potato, breach stuff, but otherwise I'm out."

"And traveling light, got it. Let me see what I can do, for both of you." With that she walked off toward the kitchen. I assumed she went through it to her storage room and left her to it, turning to Anders.

"You're just fucking up my *whole* life, aren't

you?" I said, letting the half smile twitch the corner of my mouth.

"Guess so," he said, sitting back down. "Think Shealano will have something for this constant, throbbing pain?"

"I hope so, we both need it," I said, sitting back down on the couch next to him.

He took out his journal and made notes and I tried to not glance at what he wrote, even though I really wanted to. Fuck, that journal annoyed me. This wasn't a classroom, and this sort of thing didn't lend itself to keeping notes on — you never knew who would find it.

But I also knew he wouldn't stop. Anders would probably write stuff down on scraps of paper to make himself feel better if he didn't have the book. So I resolved then and there to make sure nothing happened to it, or at least that it got destroyed before someone else read through it. And yeah, I know it was an empty promise to myself, but it made me feel better.

Shealano came back with an old hinged doctor's case, leather cracked and split in a few places. I hadn't seen that bag in an age, it felt like. She set it down on the floor and joined it, crossing her legs and pulling it close, then started to rummage through it. "You know," she muttered to no one, "I just now put this stuff in here, you'd think it would be easy to find."

I managed to not laugh and waited as she pulled out a few small cubes and tossed them at me. "I saw you still do that useless finger light thing?" she asked.

Nodding, I added only, "It's a good distraction."

"Push it through those cubes — they won't hold up long, but they should refocus that light into something useful."

"Did you just give me laser cubes?"

"You haven't used them in a while, I'm sure," she said, "but riding a bike and all that. As for you," she said to Anders, as she held up a small, blue handball, "squeeze this hard. It's a one-shot but it'll disrupt the synapses of anyone it hits after the squeeze. Only lasts a few seconds, but hey."

Anders took the ball and gently put it in a pocket.

She closed the bag and stood up, looking at us. "I'll get some painkillers," she muttered and dashed back into the kitchen, returning quickly with some pills, handing us each a bunch. "Not as good as your strange shit, Paige, but it'll do."

I swallowed them quickly, but Anders got up, and, without a word, went to the kitchen. I heard water run, and he came back empty handed. Some people just hate dry-swallowing pills, I guess.

"We need to track the Subtle Knives, grab a few, and find out what the hell is going on. I really think it's that simple," I said. They both nodded and we followed Shealano to the front door.

She opened her bag, letting it dangle a bit in one hand, and took out a plastic bag of sunflower seeds. Taking a few seeds out, she tossed them into the air where they hung, floating impossibly. "These should start moving in the general direction of the Subtle Knives," she said. She opened the door and the seeds just spun in place. "They're supposed to..." she frowned, and I moved past her to poke at one. It just hung there.

I caught movement out of the corner of my eye and saw the knife just before it entered the space my head occupied. Pulling back, I hit the door with my shoulder. The guy went past me and right at Anders, who punched him in the face.

"Get back inside," I yelled at Shealano.

"No way," she replied, pulling something else out of her bag. "We open the door, they'll swarm in." She threw a handful of dust in front of her and it spun, picking up speed and glittering. Following it, I realized how many Subtle Knives were coming for us. Endless Blossom felt right, about then. A small horde was descending upon us.

Anders kicked the guy he'd punched to make sure he stayed down.

The air got cold. Too cold, too fast.

"This you?" Shea and I asked each other at the same time.

Shit. That meant it was them, and that meant they'd found a much stronger...leader...boss... whatever. Someone to teach them tricks. The Subtle Knives I knew wouldn't have been able to start a temperature drop this fast. This was the advanced class.

I dug deep and felt out for any energy I could use. The Endless Knives were coiling a bunch of forces up, swirling them to freeze us out. I tried to tap into them, take the energy from them and spin back out at them.

I spun the forces around my hands, tracing shapes with my fingers, while Anders and Shea kept the throng away as best they could. I knew Shealano wanted to fight dirtier still, but she let me take point without a word. She was always good at small attacks, but large, stupid things like this were where I shone.

I wove the potential across my knuckles and pulled at it, forcing whomever on their end was playing with this stuff to feed it more and more energy to keep going. We fought for control and I yanked away a large chunk, cutting it off, but losing the larger battle. Out of practice — or were they that good?

No time to think about it just then. I knit the energy into patterns quickly. "Shea, Anders," I yelled, "hold out a hand!" They both managed to, while fighting, somehow, and I threw lumps of structured energy at each of them.

Their respective hands started to shine. "Oh, Paige, you shouldn't have," Shealano said, grinning. Anders just look confused. "Kid," she said to him, "hit things with the shiny fist. Trust me."

He did, and the resulting effect — a shock of power that tore through the Subtle Knife being punched — made Anders jump back. Took a second to realize the effect was intentional, and didn't hurt him at all, before he jumped right at the next guy in the pile of bodies surging toward us. There had to be at least thirty, and in close quarters — we were pinned to the doorway. "You sure we can't retreat inside?" I asked Shea.

"We won't close the door clean and you know it, Never."

"I can buy us the time, just both of you get behind me."

Anders and Shea wedged themselves behind me, pretty much pressing against the door. That'd help. But we still needed to get them all to back off for a few seconds.

My turn.

I pushed all the energy I still had stored up from my steal into the palms of my hands and clapped. Hard. The noise startled everyone, including pigeons, and set off car alarms. I smiled at the twenty-five or so Endless Knives staring at me, and took a truncated bow. Any further and I would've headbutted one of them. They were too close as it was, in arm's reach.

"So here we are," I said loudly, at the assembled. "And I'm thinking you lot have been given marching orders but not fully prepped. So let me introduce the players on the field!" They didn't move toward me, just looked at each other, then back at me — in shifts, it seemed. Heads turning back and forth like curious penguins.

"Behind me is Anders — you don't know him. He's good at the punching, though, which is kind of news to me, too, but here we are. Next to him is Aquila Shealano, the Bane of Light. I'm sure some of you have heard of her. She's the one who once exploded a dragon out in Jersey. With. A. Nickle. So maybe don't mess with her?" I turned and smiled at Shea. She rolled her eyes and tapped on the door twice so I could hear it. Yeah, yeah, Shea, I'm getting there. Pushy. "And me? I'm Paige Never. Whoever is in charge of you goons these days, they know me, they have a serious mad-on toward me, and my friends. Right now, though? I'm still being nice and not wiping you all off the face of this planet." I heard Shea snort a tiny laugh that only me and Anders could hear.

"So I tell you what," I continued, "you saw what

I could do by clapping my hands. What you don't want to do is find out what I can do if—" I got cut off by a series of small explosions that started in the air above the Subtle Knives and worked toward me. The explosions rained down golden light onto the goons in front of me, and they started to glow in turn. This was big shit, whatever it was.

"Shea, just...now! Go!" I yelled and turned away from them as Shea opened the door. We got through and the door swung closed, only centimeters from secure when forces started being applied from the other side. Lots of forces. In large, repeating thumps. We pushed back but started to lose ground.

"Shea, get clear. Anders, push," I said, and gathered up the last of stolen energy, feeding in into my legs. I braced myself against the door with Anders and we shoved, hard enough to make the surface of the door start to creak. But it latched.

"How long will it hold?" Anders asked before I could.

"Maybe ten minutes, tops," Shea said, busying herself gathering things up. "Paige, did you give up something while you were gone?"

"What do you mean?" I asked, knowing exactly what she meant and hating it.

"You know. The mantle. You gave it up, didn't you. As part of your 'retirement,' I'd guess. You really are selfish. The only way to stop this is to go get it."

"I'm not going back there, Shea. We can—"

"We can't. I can hold them off for a few, and then get to safety myself. Even if they're after both of us, they'll assume I went with you when they sense the door you're about to open."

"What door?" Anders asked. Great, of course.

"Shea wants me to go back to the Ascension," I told him. "She's forgetting two things. The doors are all closed, and I'm not exactly welcome there."

"Where *are* you welcome, Never? Just go back there and get the sort of firepower we can use. Shit, better than that, get some information."

"The doors are *closed*, Shea," I reminded her.

"Because closed doors have stopped Paige Never before. Right."

Anders kept glancing at the door. "Whatever we do, we need to do it soon. Paige, is Shea right?" I appreciated him asking me — of course, my problem remained that she *was* right, when it came down to the bare facts. If I forced my way back, it would give her time to take Anders and get to safety, and convince the Knives that we'd all gone. Unmistakable.

"She is," I told him. "All right. Shea, you take Anders and get somewhere safe. Maybe find some other friends, stay low, make sure the Knives don't find you until you hear from me."

"I'm going with *you*, Paige," Anders said.

"Yeah, I can't travel with a stray, Never," Shea said, on the verge of a whine.

"I'm not a *stray*, and I'm going with you, Paige," Anders insisted.

I sighed, loudly, for effect. They both looked at me and I shrugged. "You know what, Anders was right, we don't have time for this. Fine, come with me, but know two things before you do, all right?"

"Sure," he said, straightening the strap of his bag across his chest.

"One, this is gonna hurt — I don't know what's keeping the door closed, but once we start we can't turn back. And two is just that the people we're about to go see will think you're a pet of mine and treat you accordingly, assuming they don't just kill me on the spot for showing my face."

He took a deep breath and nodded. Of all the things you could probably say about Anders, you couldn't call him cowardly. Foolhardy, sure. Obsessive journaler, absolutely. But he had steel in him — possibly because he didn't really understand the stakes, but that felt like selling him short. He wanted this — no matter how much he saw of it, he still *wanted* it like most people want to breathe.

I readied myself, trying to feel as sure as Anders did, as mean as Shea needed me to be, and as confident and ready for anything as I used to be. Didn't know if it'd work, but I'd find out. I focused on the Ascension, the idea of the place, the feeling of it.

You never really forgot the place, or left it, I suppose. Opening a door should've been fairly easy, but since they'd been closed and travel between the Ascension and Earth forbidden, well, yeah. Harder. By a magnitude.

My only real hope lay in remembering that the people who closed the doors did it with me in mind, at least partly. So I could guess what they'd do, and how to work around it. That was the hope. In reality, I pushed, mentally, as hard as I could.

Time, as always, worked against me. Give me an hour and I could've eased the door open and maybe even managed to sneak back in. No chance of that now. But I still had to get the passage open. The work resembled what Anders and I had faced in the diner, a breach point — but whereas the Kindeleet just needed to tear a hole in world, I needed to tear a specific hole in the world, in a spot that had been reinforced.

So fine, tackle it like any problem. *What, run away from it? Ha-ha it's funny because I'm an asshole loser.*

No, that's part of the protection — they wove a bunch of self-doubt into their barriers. Smart, actually. If I hadn't wallowed in it for longer than I cared to admit, that sort of blow could've stopped me.

I pushed aside that first defense and kept digging. They wanted anyone who tried to retake the path to the Ascension to wear themselves out. Every level I pushed at felt designed to suck more out of me. Good plan. I came at this with a mostly empty tank anyway. I couldn't talk my way out of it, I couldn't con my way through — the only road left remained skillfully applied force.

Too much brute force and the attack would bounce back at me — I knew that much. Old play. Too much trying to sneak around the defenses in place and I would waste all my short time and we'd be mobbed by the Subtle Knives.

The barrier stood as a door. I stood as Paige fucking Never. Doors lost to me. That's what they did. I kept that in the front of my brain, holding tightly to it and feeling the edges of reality around where I wanted to dig my fingers in and rip.

I could sense the shape of the thing clearly, and I knew I could do this. I'd been trained, literally, since birth, for this sort of stupidity. So think, Paige, think. I needed a road back to the Ascension, and that took opening a door. One of the first things I'd been taught was that there are always multiple doors, but only one right one in any given situation. The door I was trying to force open didn't need to be the right one — I'd just grabbed it as being sensed and a first point of contact. Stupid.

I stopped trying to pry open this door and instead sent my senses out for a door — a place in the universe I could bring to me that would be aligned better with my needs. Tears happen in a specific place, on both sides, but you can...sort of...shift them a bit if you know how. Think of it like making a choice. You choose how the spot corresponds to local and remote reality, if you know what both ends look like.

You need to know, though, what *both* ends look like. It's been one hell of a long time since I'd been back, so how could I know what anything there looked like these days? Except — the North Tower intake room. They couldn't change it. Now I had two points, one where I stood and one I knew deeply and could see in my mind easily. So now I could shift the universe around a bit, focus on connecting the dots, literally.

I still needed an influx of energy. I couldn't take it from my surroundings, so I decided to do something spectacularly dumb. I'd shown Anders that I could pull off a causality fold. Borrow from the future to get a new suit, sure. And if I didn't pay it back before I died, I could collapse the whole universe. I'd done it for a bunch of dumb stuff over the years. But I'd never tried borrowing a large amount of raw force from my own future.

I did now.

Sometime in my own future there would be a ton of energy around me. I borrowed it from myself, knowing that paying it back could quite possibly kill me. But that would be my future, and I needed to think about my present in order to get there.

I clapped my hands together, this time almost in slow motion, letting them come together as if I was praying, elbows bent, and pressed them hard against one another. Slowly drawing them apart, I felt the static charge of a massive amount of force growing between them.

Perfect.

I funneled it into the universe, shaping it and prying away at the spot I now knew I needed. I wrapped the breach in my own admittedly-stolen-from-somewhere energies to contain it and feed it back into itself. The effect grew. The barriers started to give. The locations — Shea's apartment and the North Tower — met, impossibly.

I knew that between the two, we'd have to walk a road. Most portals, breaches, and tears like this were simple doors you pried open and stepped through. The Ascended were smarter than that. There would be actual, physically passable space between them. An interesting trick, and one I admitted I didn't know how they'd done. There was, though — and this was important to me just then — no way to know what that path would look like or hold.

I knew it used to be just a long, boring walk.

That was before they shut down passage. Now, who could say. That would be a problem for a few seconds from now, though. I still had to get the door open on both ends and stable enough for us to go through.

I felt the universe shred itself a bit.

There we go.

A sliver of light appeared in Shea's hallway and grew steadily from there. It widened more and more, shimmering much like fire would, hanging in the air. "Shea, bug out while you can," I told her. "Anders," I said, looking at him, "this is us. Let's go."

We stepped into the shimmer.

CHAPTER ELEVEN

Shealano's apartment vanished as we found ourselves in a giant lump of nothing. "Just hang on," I said, as nothing went by at a speed you couldn't measure since there were no points of reference. All perfectly normal — the shunt to allow for a tunnel space between dimensions took a second to kick in. Added bonus: the shunt itself worked to disorient people. The Ascended may be total weasel farts, but they could also be kind of clever.

Nothingness started to resolve into somethingness. I figured there remained a good chance the hallway had been replaced. No one would ever guard the shunted space — the idea that anyone could ever be that punished just baffled me. Imagine it, standing around for...who knows...in a long, mostly featureless hallway, waiting to see if maybe, this decade, someone would come by. Especially once they closed the doors.

No, whatever they had planned, it wouldn't be a person. Or an animal — really, any living thing. I give them shit for, well, being themselves, but that level of cruelty they save for people. Then again, they blocked the way close to a century ago, and things might have changed. Fuck, if they'd changed that much we really were in trouble.

But no, they hadn't. The nothingness resolved into the hallway, looking the same as it ever had.

The place I occasionally saw in dreams, and nightmares. Exactly. The. Same. Which made no sense. They couldn't have just blocked the doors shut and called it a day, could they?

"Is this it?" Anders asked.

I shrugged. "I can't imagine so, but it used to be."

I took a step forward.

The world became fire.

Pulling myself back, standing next to Anders, the fire didn't go away. A single step down the hall and the entire place had erupted into flames. Flames that engulfed the structure, top to bottom.

Where we stood remained eerily calm, as well as unexplainably, yet politely, cool. Perfect. So all we had to do was walk...I tried to remember how far the hallway stretched and make a guess, I'd say a good half-mile...through fire.

And not normal fire, no, this stuff already didn't act right. No air rushing past us, so nothing to feed it, yet it showed no sign of dimming down. Inches away from our faces, our backs to the now-solid surface we'd come through, yet no heat coming off it.

The backs to a solid surface bothered me, too. We couldn't go back without some way to reopen the door we'd come through. The crack in the universe we'd walked through should've been accessible. It fascinated me. I could see how they did it, and I get why, really, but why not trap people in the nothingness of the shunted space? Why let us reach this far and trap us then?

The only way I could make sense of the idea was to picture it as a way to make the whole thing hurt more. Trap something in the space between, shunt them into nothing, say, and maybe the find their way back, maybe they don't. Probably they don't, though people who can open a rift can usually be counted on to have at least heard of the nothingness between points, and half expect to be dumped into it.

But let someone get this far, only to then set a half-mile long fire in front of them, and lock the door behind them? I couldn't open a rift from here — the hallway itself was between spaces, but not of the nothingness, either, made of stuff akin to a private sub-sub-dimension. Never quite understood how they folded space enough to make it, but I knew you couldn't breach into or out of it.

This remained an exercise in meanness. I could do mean. I could do fucking furious, which is what I found myself becoming as I stared into this fire. Fine, they wanted me to walk through fire, literally, to get back to the place I used to be able to call home? Fine.

"You trust me?" I asked Anders.

"Yeah," he said, but I could hear the fear in his voice. He suspected what was about to happen.

I held a hand out, and he took it, all clammy and nerves. Both of us, mind you, not as comment on him. I nodded, took a deep breath, and then turned to him and smiled. "This won't kill us, and it won't be as bad as you think it will be right this second. Like a needle. You worry so much about the pain, when you get jabbed it doesn't even register."

"So this won't hurt?" he asked.

"Oh, it will," I told him, "just not as bad as being fully, totally on fire for a half-mile walk."

"What are we going to do, then?" he asked.

"Walk half a mile, or so, through fire. I mean, come on, Anders, that was obvious, I thought."

I tried to draw some energy from the fire itself before we took a step. No-go. I still had a bit of reserve, a smidge leftover from cracking the breach. It would have to do. Literally, it would *have* to.

We took a step. Into fire.

We didn't burn.

The fire itself made no sense since it wasn't oxidizing anything in order to give off heat and light. Which meant that, on some level, the fire didn't exist. Unfortunately, what didn't exist could still kill you. I focused on turning the physics of the fire counter to observed reality. It could heat us some, it could blind us with light. Both these things happened.

It hurt, is what I'm saying.

But since the fire *also* did *not* exist, I curled the physics of the moment around, counting on the intersection of reality and unreality to clash enough to give me a blank space between them. The fire could hurt, but it could not heat us to a level that we, or our clothes, oxidized and caught fire as well.

Realistically, this all hurt like hell on wheels, but we wouldn't do more than lightly smolder. All I had to do was remain completely focused on that, and all of the reasons why and how. So long as my will centered there, we would continue to be fine. We could even breathe — since the fire wasn't burning oxygen anyway, there was breathable, if hot, air all around us.

Anders knew none of this. He simply trusted me and took step after painful step by my side. I did reach over and change his grip from holding my hand to holding onto my upper arm, though. My fingers flexed, both hands making complex, mostly meaningless sigils over and over again to keep my brain focused.

The first quarter of the walk proved uneventful. We didn't catch fire. The next half of the walk was mostly the same, except I noticed that my jacket started to smolder. I glanced at Anders, and his did the same. The longer we spent, the worse it would get. I tried to do the math on how long we had, but couldn't hold that and focus on making sure it didn't happen at the same time.

We pushed on. Step after bloody step, through the fire. Breathing got harder, the heat pressed in, and the smoldering along our clothes got slowly worse. I considered running, then tossed it out just as quick.

The faster we moved, the more energy we'd burn. I also wasn't really sure either of us *could* run — Anders with his foot almost certainly couldn't. I could, but it would hurt and wobble my concentration even further.

I pointedly ignored the smell of smoke in my nose as we continued to slowly start to burn. Our clothing smoldered but my hair hadn't caught, that I could tell. My skin felt hot, the sort of painful scald that turned into the ice cold of a burn, except the nerves were being fried in slow motion. I started feeling my confidence slip, just a fraction, that we would make it. That sliver of doubt took root and signaled only bad things. That sort of concern would bleed into the focus I needed and cause the very thing I fretted about.

Time for a desperation play. I reached into my jacket pocket and pulled out the potato. No clue if this would work, or make things worse, but since the alternative seemed to be death, lobbing the spud felt like a plan.

I tapped into its stored power, feeling it with my mind. Doing so leeched a bit from my protection of us and we started to get hotter. Nothing for it. I shrugged at Anders, the air too hot to want to verbalize.

The potato charged itself up nicely, even as it started to bake in my hand. I threw it, as hard as I could, out in front of us. I had to hope the fire wouldn't eat, or incorporate, the energy stored in the grenade before it could go off. I waited.

The walls shook.

The fire snuffed out.

The light blinded me.

All in the space of a second. Anders and I both hit the floor hard, knocked over by the perfectly quiet force. "Holy..." Anders muttered. My sight started to return, spots still lingering in my vision.

"Get up, we need to keep going fast before the fire recovers," I said, pushing myself to my feet. I offered him a hand. He took it. We started to walk again. My sight recovered more, and as it did I saw the light in the hallway start to shift toward reds and oranges.

"Fire can recover?"

"Fake, bullshit, can-still-burn-us fire, the shit

we've been walking through? Yes," I said, snippily, I admit. Without the fire blocking our line of sight, I could see the door at the end of the hall. We were closer than I'd thought.

Another ten minutes and we were there, just as the flames started to really come back to life. The door, of course, stood locked. Enough of this shit. I charged the WarBoots and kicked out. The thing that represented itself as a door ceased to exist.

Messy but effective.

Stepping through shunted us to the other end of the breach that I'd initially opened. The North Town intake room, just as I remembered it: Big, empty, and cold. The room stood at the top of the North Tower itself and had been used as a breach entry point for longer than I'd been alive. As such, no one ever cluttered it with furniture.

I sat down on the floor and Anders joined me, both of us enjoying the cool air. "So, this is The Ascension," I said. Exhaustion wracked me. I knew that within minutes, at the most, people would come find us — you couldn't breach here without people noticing. I didn't want to be on the floor when they showed up — but then, I also didn't want to be in a crispy, ruined suit. Can't always get what you want, so you own what you have.

I leaned back and rested on my hands as the door opened and four guards rushed in, weapons at the ready. They wore gleaming white suits, not quite metal, not quite leather — a strange mix of the two, it looked like. They carried two-foot-long batons and wore face masks hiding any expressions they might have had.

"Don't just stand there," I told them, looking anything but impressed, "get Mitlan, and get me and my friend some water."

They seemed unmoved by my orders.

CHAPTER TWELVE

MITLAN APPEARED AFTER all, dressed in the normal, boringly simple fashions of the Ascended: White collared shirt, black slacks, white tie, and grey jacket, cut to the length of mid-thigh. His flat-brown hair ran until it touched his shoulders, exactly. He remained the picture-perfect Ascended. Except for the expression on his face, hysterical to me, his surprise and confusion mixing to create a sort of frozen horror.

"Hey, Mitlan," I said, still not getting up off the floor, "work on your Welcome Wagon."

"Paige," he said. Recovering quickly, he turned to the guards. "Help them up," he ordered, "get them something else to wear, and bring them to the Chamber."

"Really, Mitlan? The Chamber? I come all this way and," the guards started to help us stand, and I swatted lightly at them to back off, "the best you can do is toss me right at her? I thought we were friends."

"If we were, it was a lifetime ago, Paige," he said, turning away and leaving the room. "One that should have stayed in the past."

The guards wrangled us to standing, finally, despite my annoyance, and took us to a small changing room off the main intake room. Separating us, they tossed a jumpsuit at me, flat-steel grey, and I assumed they gave Anders the same amazing option. I changed into it, making sure to put my WarBoots back on — good luck getting those off me, plate-faces — and stepped back out.

Anders looked at me.

"I did tell you to go with Shea," I said, as lightly as I could manage.

He laughed, and that started me laughing, and the guards just stood there, unsure why we were suddenly having a fit of the giggles. I pressed down on the inside of my WarBoot and charged it lightly.

Still laughing, not faking it — just one of those moments — I kicked a guard in the hip. Guard fell backwards, spinning. The other three all closed in on me, brandishing their batons. I held up my hands. "Sorry," I said, "reflex. Won't happen again."

They wanted to beat me senseless. We all knew it. The guard who slowly stood, armor blackened and cracked around the right hip, doubly so. But they couldn't. Not yet. Not if they intended to take me to the Chamber. Mitlan had seen my condition before he left— beating me senseless now would only cause the guards trouble later.

So they marched us down a series of hallways and staircases. But I wouldn't go quietly. "See, Anders," I said as we went, "this is why I didn't want to come back here. They have no *style*. Look at these dull hallways. Not a single tapestry. Me? I'd hang tapestries."

"Tapestries? Really, Paige?" he asked.

"Tapestries, Anders. But not here, no — everything needs to be in order, pristine. Boring. Like these assholes behind us," I jerked a thumb over my shoulder toward the guards. "You know what they do during their time off? They fuck woodchucks. And that isn't easy, considering this place doesn't even have woodchucks, naturally. They have to *import* fuckable woodchucks. At great expense, too, I hear."

Anders laughed, shaking his head.

"No, I'm kidding," I told him, "they probably don't practice bestiality. Partly because they couldn't afford the woodchucks, but mostly because they aren't that creative. I mean, here you are, in what is supposed to be the creative hub of the universe — that's what the Ascension is, you know, or what it styles itself as — but they just work as guards. No creativity there, it's frowned upon. Think of that. You live in a place that prides itself on the thing you don't have." I knew the guards were too well trained to give me the satisfaction of losing their temper, but I also wanted to keep Anders from getting worried. I'd taken him to a strange new world, and instantly gotten him in the thick of a huge mess. Couldn't be easy on him, but keeping him laughing and feeling like I remained in control would help. Knock-on effect — it might convince him I actually was in control. I wasn't.

Yet.

The doors to the Chamber were still the way I remembered them: overly large, made of warm wood carved subtly with whorls and patterns both floral and fractal. They didn't fit the rest of the space. I'd grown up sure the doors were part of some past that everyone wanted to forget, but no one would tell me the truth. I knew now.

Two guards stood in front of the doors and opened them for us, Mitlan standing just inside, the doors swinging, clearing him by inches. The man knew where to stand to make an entrance about him instead of the person entering, I'll give him that.

He leaned in close. "Behave yourself," he whispered. Then he turned his back to us and walked forward into the wider room. The doors closed behind us, with the always-satisfying sound of large, heavy doors doing their job. The guards who'd ushered us here stayed where they were, though it felt clear we were supposed to follow Mitlan. So we did.

The Chamber stood vast and mighty before us. Walls that seemed to bow out slightly in the middle met at a high-arching ceiling, forcing the entire room to feel like a protective bubble. As always, the room stood empty except for the chairs at the far front, a good sixty feet from the doors.

I say chairs, but thrones would probably be the normal way anyone would describe them. Big and lush, two matching seats sat at the front of the room so that supplicants, criminals, or ass-kissers could come and be dealt with. I knew which we were being pegged for, currently.

"Just keep quiet," I told Anders in a hushed tone.

"Yeah, I don't even *know* these people," he said, "I wouldn't even know what to say."

He wasn't wrong. Sadly for me, I knew exactly what to say — and what not to say. Back before I left, I might've considered choosing the safer path, there. But now, even though I knew I needed to be here, I couldn't give them a free pass. Yeah, I'd have to make nice, but if I did that too fast they would never believe I was me.

"All hail, the Mighty Queen of Nothing," I said as I approached. She glared at me from her throne, her cushy chair. I smiled in return. The Queen, as it were, wore no crown, dressed much like Mitlan. Supposedly she merely stood as first among equals, which is old-world bullshit for dressing like your subjects but making sure they know they're still your subjects.

"Neverchild," came her response, tone dismissive and bored.

"Don't call me—"

"Neverchild?" she finished for me. "But that's what you are. One of the ten. The last, wayward Neverchild, in fact, returned to the fold. But then," she smiled the sort of smile that has knives to it, "I have to ask — why?"

"I need your help. Earth is—"

"None of our concern," she said, shaking her head. "But then, you knew that. The goings on down there, on that little orb, they don't concern us. We are the Ascended. We are above them. They do not matter. I know, little Neverchild, you have always had trouble understanding that. But now you are home, and we can remind you."

"All right," I started, "I think you can dial back the—"

"Neverchild, if you—"

"You need to stop fucking cutting me off, before I come up there and remind you why you couldn't *stop* me from leaving," I said. I spat the words out quickly, feeling my anger rise. "And furthermore, if you call me Neverchild one more time, so help me..." I trailed off and took a deep breath. "But this is my fault. I came in here on the wrong foot first," I told her, forcing an air of calmness to infect my speech, "and set you off when there was no cause. So let me try again, if you will?"

She nodded at me, and I could read the amusement in her eyes. She was *loving* this, which made it all the harder. All I wanted to do was wipe the look off her face with my boot, but that wasn't why we were here.

"Queen Leoras," I said slowly, making each syllable distinct and clear, "I come before you to request — as one of your former, and therefore eternal, subjects — help."

"Much better, Neverchild. Do you recant your previous crimes?" she asked, smiling again.

I made a show of considering her words, knowing I had no choice in my response. "I do."

"Then to prison with you, and your companion, who, I might add, you dared bring to the Ascension without permission. Your return is also prohibited, but since you are recanting, I should overlook that particular charge in respect to your person."

"I need help, Majesty," I said, feeling caught. If I stayed a supplicant, this all fell apart, but if I didn't the same would result. Time for a new plan — but that meant buying myself some time. Supplicant it was. If I pushed my luck, we might skip right over prison and go to execution. Though — the thought nagged at me — why hadn't we *started* there? Something else was going on, and until I knew what it was, I couldn't work on a path clear.

"And, after your sentence is served, I am sure something can be worked out," she told me. "Make sure these two are housed together, I do not want the...human...left alone." With that, she turned to Mitlan and gestured him closer, whispering to him a while. He nodded, glancing at me off and on, while they talked. Great.

Mitlan left the Queen's side, gestured at us to follow him, and led us out of the Chamber. The doors closed again, letting the Queen do things that, I'm sure, included using the rear door of the place to go back to her private quarters and lounge, uselessly. As the sound of the shutting doors rang out once more, we were led away by the same four guards — well, by four guards... who knew if they were the same ones.

Our prison cell proved comfortable enough. I remembered the cells, if not fondly, at least well. Political prisoners tended to be treated decently. If they intended us to rot here for a few years, we would at least have comfortable beds, desks, reading material, and a screen blocking the toilets. The front of the cell stood a large, see-through layer of material with some sound holes, too small to fit anything other than a few loose hairs through, dotted along the top. A door, cut into the material but sealed up with atomic locks and hinges, proved almost impossible to discern. The atomic crap worked on a molecular-bond level — if you had a key, you could force the bits needed to separate and function as hinges and such. Without that, the material stood solid on a molecular level. Nice for an unpickable lock, really.

I surveyed the whole thing a few times as the guards milled around outside.

"Hey, we had an accident before we got here,

never mind the walk here," I said to the guards. "He lost a toe," I added. "Could we maybe get some medical attention?" Now that we were officially prisoners, they would have to treat us. Small favors.

A doctor showed up within the hour to look us both over and treat our various bruises, wounds, light burns, and so on. She also covered Ander's stump with a cream and bandaged it lightly. As she left, they brought us food. We ate, still in silence, and I realized we hadn't actually talked since before the Queen. Not more than a word or two. We finished eating and he got up from the table.

"Hey, Anders," I said, "sorry I got you tangled in this."

"I asked to come along," he said. He sat on a bed, writing in his journal. Of course they hadn't taken his bag from him, once they'd looked through it. Nothing close to a weapon in there. And none of them cared if he wrote down a log of his days in prison. It could rot in here with us.

"True, but you didn't ask to be set on fire, or tossed in a jail, or..."

"How are we getting out?" he asked. Yeah, neither of us planned on staying longer than necessary.

"Maybe I should tell you a story, first, and then you'll see it," I said, leaning back in my chair. "A story I should've told you before, maybe, but it isn't one I like to tell."

Anders closed his journal and shoved it back in his bag. I nodded at the gesture. "Is this going to explain why that woman called you Neverchild?"

"The Queen? It will, actually," I told him.

"Originally there were ten of us. Neverchildren. They called us that because we were all born on the same second, the exact second of the clock turning over into the two-thousandth anniversary of the founding of the Ascension itself. That, supposedly, made us special. I think it damned us, but only because the people here decided it meant we were special."

"Wait, Paige," Anders said, "why are you telling me all this now? Seriously. You never want to talk about anything — not how you do this stuff, or about you — but now, suddenly?"

I stood and stretched, actual Ascension medical attention making me feel worlds better already. "Jail makes me maudlin," I said. "No, but I do think this will explain a few things you will need, and show you what we're really up against here, and why." I shrugged at him. "Or maybe I'm just maudlin. Anyway, we were taken from our families and raised together. The Ascension decided we simply had to be super special and so they would raise us, and one of us would, in the end, be chosen to rule the Ascension when we came of age."

"Wait, really? But the Queen looks older than you," Anders said.

"She is. She's also not one of us. No, that whole idea twisted in on itself. They trained us — they wanted us to know more, to be better than anyone else around. We were to master all the things that a good leader should know: combat, strategy, politics, and cruelty. Not how I would have built the list but no one asked us, of course. Part of our training then became a way to choose who would be leader."

"Cruelty as a—"

"I know. But this place isn't...you can't take a bunch of powerful people, tell them they should rule their own island, and expect sanity in large doses, Anders. You just can't. So they wanted us to fight, to prove which of us should rule. Again, if they'd asked us, back then, we would've told them that a ten-person ruling body had a much higher sanity rate, and fairness allotment, than any one single ruler could. They didn't care. I don't think the Queen ever intended us to take over, anyway. But by setting us against each other, she could eliminate us and keep her hands clean. Nice move — if, possibly, easily considered to be evil.

"The games were simple, at first, and not lethal. Basic stuff, almost fun, you know — competing against people you were raised with, there's always competition anyway. When you take a bunch of kids all told they're super special from the start, they get *really* competitive, and it's not exactly hard to turn that into games that end in death.

"Nester and I—"

"Nester Never?" Anders put in quickly. "Really?"

"No," I said, laughing, "We didn't have surnames, then. But Nester and I agreed the whole thing was bullshit. We watched out for each other. We also refused to do anything fatal toward the others. But we were alone there. Five of us died over the next few years. Imagine it, being so warped by the people around you that you're willing to kill the people you consider family, just for a shot at theoretical power."

"Perfectly, sadly, human," Anders said, looking at me.

"You are not wrong, but the Ascended claimed to be better than human, remember. And yet they proved only that they could be as bad, if not worse. But that fifth death — there was no good reason except fear, I guess, why it took until five — but that last one made Nester snap. He decided to leave the Ascension for good. Forfeit."

"And you went with him," Anders said, nodding.

"I did no such thing, not then. I thought he was being ridiculous. Go to Earth? And do what? But his head was full of romantic notions about the planet, and he made up his mind, opened a breach as quietly as he could, and left. We all knew about the hallway and the shunting, but then the whole thing stood open to us. We were forbidden, but people *did* go to Earth for a time, and come back, with permission. But even so—" I cut myself short as I saw Mitlan come into view.

He stopped in front of the cell and smiled at me. "Oh, no, Paige, do continue. I'd love to hear this."

"Fuck off, Mitlan," I said, sitting back down and reaching for a book.

"Is that it then?" he asked, "I'm just Mitlan, your enemy, like everyone else?"

"Fine," I snarled a bit, "hey, Anders, meet my uncle. One of the few people I thought might be on my side through all of this. But who proved to be nothing more than a player for the throne himself." I turned to Mitlan. "That better, Uncle dear?"

"Damn it, Paige, trust me," he said. "You used to — or does that not make into your story?"

"See, Anders, here we go. Mitlan here — oh, sorry, my uncle here — said he would watch over me and protect me. Which he did — just enough to keep me alive, possibly, but never so much as to even attempt to stop a system we all knew was dangerous, corrupt, and frankly abusing children straight through to adulthood. I used to trust him, right up to when Nester left. Then, given the reaction, I saw through the shiny family ties right to the core. A rotten, blackened thing, like most of the jerks around here."

"He had to be held accountable," Mitlan said.

"For leaving a fucked-up system? For removing himself from the game? For that he needed to be punished?"

"Yes," Mitlan insisted. "And look what happened next. We lost you, too."

"I looked at Anders and shrugged. "When they decided they needed a hunting party to get Nester back, I volunteered to go with them. I told everyone how it would prove that I should be the chosen one. They all bought it. Idiots, the lot of them. Of course, I mean, of *course* I turned and helped Nester, and stayed after we drove off the hunting party."

"Yes, of course," Mitlan said, sounding weary. "Didn't you ever wonder why we didn't come back?"

"I assumed it was because you knew we would kick all of your asses. Nester had the best hands in the business for energy workings — and me, I was, and still am, the best problem solver you've ever seen here. The two of us, against everyone else? I knew who I would bet on. I did, in fact. And I was right."

"You were a stupid child wrapped up in thoughts of justice, without knowing what that meant," Mitlan said, adopting an almost chiding tone that made me want to tear his face clean off. "We came back and locked the passages to Earth," he continued. "While you and Nester ran amok on Earth we continued here, and the three remaining fought, growing deadlier and deadlier."

"As. You. Planned."

"Not as we planned," he said, "everything escalated. Quince tried to stop it, and was killed for his trouble. He wanted peace, to find a reasonable solution to who should rule."

"Which is all Nester and I wanted, but when we put forth the idea we were told we were being childish."

"And when everything started up here in earnest, we saw perhaps you were right. But Kental and Jursica rose up armies, intending to fight each other and then invade to secure the throne, to secure their takeover."

I laughed. An honest, gut-level laugh that went on and confused both Anders and Mitlan, I'm sure. When I recovered enough to speak I wiped my eyes, making a show of it, and told Mitlan, "Which is what we were promised. One of us would rule when the others were put down. You created the system, you get to die from it."

"Paige," Anders said, "letting them all die?"

"They earned it," I snapped at him. "They abused us, then told us it would all be worth it, with empty promises of power. I should feel bad because they got what they asked for?" I smiled at Mitlan. "So who won, and what did you do to stop them?"

"No one has won yet," he said, "both armies are still outside the city, waging war. But they make it clear, whoever wins, they will raze the city in the end. They don't wish to rule, either of them, they wish to destroy us."

"Good for them," I said.

"You don't mean that," Anders said.

"You can't be serious," Mitlan added.

"Oh, I do and I can. So Quince turned against the system as well and died for it? Shame. Shame he didn't come around sooner — I know it was him who gave Nester away when he left."

"It was," Mitlan admitted, "and speaking of, where is Nester? I think, in my gut, I expected you to come back, one day, but not alone — or at least," he said, looking at Anders, "with Nester, and not some random human."

"Nester is dead," I said, trying to keep my voice flat. "We spent decades helping people on Earth, forming ties, doing our best. Teaching," I looked at Anders. "And then I failed and he died. So I stopped. He was the last link back here for me, the only one who understood, fully, who I was. Without that, I couldn't...he was my best friend," I told Anders, speaking directly to him and ignoring Mitlan, "so, yeah, I stopped, and I 'retired,' and hid out, and tried to give up. Until someone wouldn't let me." I shrugged.

"I'm sorry," Mitlan and Anders said simultaneously.

"Thank you," I told Anders, before turning to Mitlan, "but *you* don't get to feel anything, you don't get to say anything."

"Is this what you needed help with?" Mitlan asked, pushing.

"With what? No, not with...The Subtle Knives of the Endless Blossom — I know you, Mitlan, you keep tabs on groups like this — they've gotten strangely deadly, upped their game. Enough that I needed help. I thought maybe Quince, or Jursica, would help me. I knew you wouldn't. But the throne owes me, as one of the chosen heirs, a voice. Hell, it owes me an army of my own, but I wouldn't want one. I just need some time in the back halls — and I'd been hoping for one of the others to join me, just for a while — to deal with this."

"Well then I am sorry," Mitlan said, as I knew he would.

"Of course you are—" I started.

"But I'll also have to take *those*," he added, looking down.

"Oh, no, you don't get the WarBoots," I told him, getting ready to charge them.

"Paige," he told me, "you have to know we can't leave them with you, not if we expect you to stay a prisoner. You can hand them over to me now, and you know I will take care of them, or we can do this the hard way. I believe the doctor has already been here once, so she'll know the way when you need her again."

I shook my head and turned to Anders. "Nice threat, no?" I pressed down with my heels, making the WarBoots release, and stepped out of them. I left them where they were and took a few steps away from them. "Fine, then, come take them."

"I'm not *stupid*, Paige, regardless of your attempt to prove me so," Mitlan said.

I shrugged and sat back down at the table. Mitlan stared for a few seconds, then called over a guard. They opened the cell door, grabbed the WarBoots, and hurried out, securing the door behind them.

Mitlan left, carrying the WarBoots, and the guards moved away to their posts nearby. Everyone, it seemed, felt they were done with me. I'd not be allowed to rot. Except none of that explained why I'd been left alive — hell, or why they'd left Anders alive, and let us both be in the same cell. It spoke of a mercy, or at least a niceness, that the Ascended didn't posses. Which meant I was right.

"So, Paige," Anders said after a few, "what was I supposed to get from your story?"

"Funnily enough," I replied, drumming fingers on the table, "I thought it'd stick out before Mitlan showed up, but with what he added — well now I'm certain I'm right."

"They want you to help *them*," he said, smiling slowly.

"Exactly," I told him. "So let's get some sleep and heal up some more. They'll come back with an offer soon."

CHAPTER THIRTEEN

A FEW DAYS later, my resolve started to waver a bit. Well, not really — but it got old, fast, just sitting in a cell. We could wait for them to come make an offer, one I knew now would be tempered with attempts at making me stir crazy so I'd say yes faster, or we could force their hand a bit.

I knew which I preferred. "Anders," I said, straightening that day's ugly jumpsuit, "get up, we're leaving."

"Oh, I didn't know they let us decide," he said, picking up his bag and joining me near the clear front of the cell. "Why did we wait so long, if we could just go?"

"I thought they'd come back faster," I said, "but if they won't, then we're gonna just go."

He nodded and waited for me to do something. I looked at him. "No, Anders, this needs you to work."

"I don't know how to pick *normal* locks, Paige," he said, running a hand down the almost invisible seam where the door would open.

"There's a device they carry that forces the atoms of the door to realign," I said, "preprogrammed atomic restructure. Nice little thing. But I don't have one. I do, however, have you."

"So you want me to rewrite the door's atomic structure, you're saying?" he asked, giving me the sort of look a chicken gives the rain. Utter confusion as to why this would happen to *him*.

"Honestly, a badger might be better, if I had one. Oh, a flamingo. That would be perfect. Is there a flamingo in the cell with us?" I asked, looking around for effect. "No, all right, so we're down a flamingo, and I never thought we'd actually have a badger. They don't get caught often. Now flamingos," I said, taking Anders's hand and pressing it hard against the cell where the door seam would be, "they're giant fuck-ups. They get caught all the time, if you didn't know. They also, I've found, don't mind jail much. They just sort of go along with things, flamingos. Still, pretty things, and good for lawns."

"I think the ones on lawns are fake," Anders said, his eyebrows knit together in confusion.

"That's what they *want* you to think," I told him, smiling. "Now hold still." I slid Anders's hand down the seam a ways and then back up. "Funny thing, Ascension technology. They are *very* careful, and gear everything toward fail-safes and redundancies. They love this sort of atomic locking because you can't pick it, there's nothing to do without the knowing the proper sequence and replicating it. Now, if you can get your hands on that sequence, fine. But they change it every few days at most, and encode it on the guard's lock boxes, so grabbing the right one is even harder."

The seam opened, and I pushed the door wide, waving Anders through. He looked at me, then at the door, then finally walked through it. I followed and let the door close, and reseal, behind us.

"The thing is," I said softly, even as I looked around for where the guards were, "it's all crap aimed at keeping their people in or out. They don't code for normal-from-Earth human at all. So if you happen to have Ascended medicine in your bloodstream, and, say, slightly nervous sweat on your hands, the mix makes the door think something has gone *very* wrong and it opens for you, in a safety protocol."

"Why do you even know that?" he asked in a whisper.

"Oh the things I know," I told him, "but, well, in this case, it helps to be a curious kid and ask a whole lot of questions of adults who just think you're stretching your brain, not already planning a possible rebellion. Silly, that." The guards were all down a hall to our left, so we went right, and once we did that, no one thought to stop us. After all, they reasoned, you can't get past the locks, so if you walked around, even if you were in a jumpsuit and had no shoes, like me, you must be allowed to.

We left the prison and worked our way out of the North Tower completely, walking off into the main part of town. I stretched my arms out and smiled at Anders. "Anders, meet the Ascension."

He looked at the tall, gleaming towers, made of glass-like material and metal. Everything felt sterile, in the way a collective cult will — and to some degree, I mean, well, here we were, right? For all their pretension to being above and beyond humanity, and to knowing secrets of the universe that could be plied for power, the Ascension had never got the hang of art for art's sake, choosing instead to push for a level of conformity on the outside. In their homes I knew they cut loose and, like any repressed society, were far more colorful than they let on. But outside? A shitshow of drab proportions.

Anders took it all in, though. From the decently spaced-out buildings to the wide-open sidewalks full of people, most of them in fairly normal, drab clothing, a lot of greys, blacks, and whites. People of all shapes, sizes, and colors, at least, walked around. The way they regulated everything else, I admit I half-expected some fucked-up eugenics program to kick in one day. But so far they'd proven themselves above that. Turns out an extreme othering of the rest of humanity to the degree of forming an entire pocket universe had opened them up for a drop in racism and misogyny. Not that it took care of the issue entirely, of course — no matter how far above humanity the Ascended decided they were, they could still find a way to blame people based on skin and genitals if they wanted.

But they built a pretty town. There were, maybe, a million and a half total people in the entirety of the Ascension. Most of them lived here, in this one city. The rest dotted the countryside they'd built outside of it, stretching for acres upon acres just to be pretty.

"Now let's see if I remember the way..." I muttered as we walked.

"Going to a breach back to Earth?" Anders asked. "Or are we holing up in a safe house?"

"Points for ideas, Anders, but no." I gestured to a large tower. "We're going shopping."

"Paige—"

"We need new clothes," I pointed out. "We're going to eventually be questioned wearing these jumpsuits, and right now our only other options are mugging a stranger or going naked. Neither feels like a *great* move, to me."

We wandered into the shopping complex, just strolling in like I owned the place. A mall by any other name smells just as desperate. No matter what you did to them, malls all looked the same — a universal constant, perhaps. I wondered what caused it, then stopped, because I really didn't give a shit. I made a straight-as-could-be line for my old favorite clothing store.

I fussed about the place, looking at fabrics, and found what I'd been looking for: The exact suits I'd pulled out of the box back in that motel. I bought two of each, on an old credit account, and extra shoes for Anders, leaving myself in socks. After we changed into one set, I discreetly waited until we left the shop to hit a bathroom and fold the universe around the other set, sending them back to me then. Nice, closed loop. Good. Only a handful more to go, really. But you took care of what you could, when you could, I felt.

Then we headed back to the store. "I need to return this cravat," I told Anders, undoing the dark red of the ascot from the collar of my suit and smoothing the burnt orange lapel of my jacket. "I've changed my mind."

"Paige, what are you playing at?" he asked. "Seriously, are you trying to get caught? Won't they be looking for you?"

"Now you get it," I told him, "but they've been really slow to figure it out, so I guess I have to give them another chance. Though, really, I do think something else might look better?" I held out the ascot to him, but he just shook his head, refusing to join in.

We loitered around the store a few while I fussed with a slightly lighter dark-red ascot around my neck. Anders kept growing more uneasy by the minute. "Anders," I said, lightly smacking his shoulder, "remember, they *need* me. Worse yet, they know it. We're fine. I just got bored and hated those jumpsuits. So I thought I'd make them work for their supper, as it were."

Anders started to protest, even as a swarm of guards rushed into the shop. I laughed and nudged him with an elbow. He sighed. I held out my hands in the classic "take me away" pose and Anders followed suit. The guards were perfectly nice about it, by which I mean they neither bothered to speak to us nor contrived to hit our heads, trip us, or otherwise use all the normal sly tricks for making someone regret knowing what a cop was.

I realized, as we were walked back to the North Tower, that my mood had shifted, even just smelling the air of the Ascension. I hated having to admit that, even to myself. I hated the truth of it. Home remained home, even when you hated it. Well, even when you had no use for the people there.

Maybe that could be why. The people here could go hang, but the place itself retained magic for me. The secret spots, hidden away from where everyone thought to look, where Nester, Jursica, and I could hide. The spaces where we watched the first five get killed, one after another, in a horrible escalation.

That one night was bad enough we vowed

never to speak their names again. I don't mean all of us dubbed Neverchildren, no — I mean the Ascension just decided that when you have five people, all early teens, end up turned inside out, you act like that simply *did not happen*. I'm normally one to face my demons — well, all right, I pretend I am a bit more often than I actually am — but that one is a red-and-black blur across my memory. The details don't hold.

Yet even that, a horrible lack of detailed memory of an event, made me feel more whole, just being back near where it happened. Which remained ridiculous to my brain, that things worked like that, but I couldn't escape it. This place had shaped me. I would always be connected to it. And I hadn't been back in far too long. I could feel my own abilities heighten just walking the streets, even with my wrists tied together.

Fuck, the handcuffs themselves felt different. Different alloys, slightly, than were used on Earth. The air carried that tinge of lemon it always did, and the clouds hung exactly right, for a definition of right I couldn't articulate but knew in my bones.

I'd felt removed from life for years, giving up and giving in. It happens, and I couldn't think of a reason to realistically regret that choice. Regret just felt like a waste of time. I could choose to be back — not in the way I'd told Anders, going from one moment to the next and existing — but to really be myself again.

The only bit that rankled at me was my shift, this emotional sea change being set off by being back with the Ascended. The simple fact — I could place it for location over people, for a sense of home, sure, but even then — there remained exasperation. With myself, of course, that I could be so simply redone by a mundane thing like 'going home.'

Shoving it aside, as we were dragged back a cell, Mitlan waiting for us, I did decide then and there that I could be the person I'd wanted to be when I left. The difference would be in how. I couldn't be, quite, the person Anders thought I should be, but I could use that shadow of self for inspiration at times. I also refused to be what Mitlan, what the Queen, wanted from me, but again I could take pieces from that, too.

On the other side, I realized I couldn't have been more annoyed at myself for stopping to feel things like that, or explore them. Reconciliation with my past selves and my hopefully future self would take some time, I supposed.

Mitlan turned and followed us as we were led back into a cell. The door closed and he tapped the clear barrier with a finger. "Smartly done — once we worked out what, exactly, you'd done."

"I needed a new suit," I told him, straightening my ascot.

"What you need is—"

"No," I said, turning away and walking over to the table in the cell. Anders sat on a chair there, watching this all unfold. I sat on the edge of the table, quickly crossing my legs to sit on top of it fully. "Anders and I are going to do whatever we want, while you provide this nice resting area for when we're bored."

"Paige—"

"Mitlan," I said, cutting him off, "you need

me. I need you. The interesting part of that is, of course, that you need me. You guys should be good enough to stop two little protégés by now. You clearly thought you could stop people coming back here, with that fire trick in the shunt hall. So what's different?"

"Paige," he started up again, "if you are truly willing to listen, and to help, I can release you and explain all."

"I tell you what," I said, "get the Queen in on this plan. I will end your problematic little tiff if you, in turn, will help me with my problem. All I need is some access to the armory and labs, not even a single person. But only if we discuss this all in front of her."

"I can't promise—"

"Then try." I closed my eyes and rested my hands on my knees, making a show of meditation. "Because," I said softly, eyes still closed, "we both know I can be a bigger problem than I have been so far." I allowed my hands to start glowing, knowing that even Mitlan could tell the light show stood harmless, but sending a message.

I sat like that, waiting in silence, until I heard footsteps moving away. I remained unmoving until Anders whispered, "They left." Unfolding and sliding off the table into a chair across from him, I smiled.

"So, Anders, you do *not* look happy. I'm getting us everything we wanted."

"But when?" he asked. "You just signed up to fight a war before they even think of helping us. That can't be quick."

"A week, maybe two," I said, "it's just a war

between two very angry, fairly powerful idiots," I told him. "Even if it takes longer, it's what we need to do."

"What we need to do is get back to Earth and solve the Subtle Knives problem," he said, "before it gets worse. You still don't even know what they're planning. Shealano is off by herself, on the run from them, and we're not sure if they decided to follow her after all. Paige, we have no idea what's going on, how bad it is, or anything. How can we just ignore that and decide to fight an entire war here?"

"You don't get to fight the fight you want, Anders. Not always. Right now we have to deal with what's ahead of us. Could we escape again? Sure. And if we go back, if we were to head back right this second, what would we have? Not much more than we had before, so what changes? Nothing. Shea had the right idea. I needed to come back here, but that isn't just to say hi."

"She said something about your mantle, and that you gave it up? But talking about it, I don't see what it could have been. You'd only have a mantle — I mean, you'd rule this place if you had stayed and won, right? But you didn't. So what mantle..."

"Well, they liked to tell us we'd rule, but I always had doubts. Either way, what Shea meant wasn't...she meant more remembering who I was. Before. And she was right! I hate that she was right, but she was."

"So that's it? You had to step back here and get arrested and now you're all better?" He shook his head at the ridiculousness of the universe.

"Now you're getting it," I told him, "but once

here, I also realized what I'm telling you now: we need some tools to do the job right. Because we simply do *not* have the information yet. We'd be going back in blind, and not much better off than before."

"Then why did coming back here at all help?" He stood and paced in the cell.

"Anders," I said sharply. "When you found me I was at my lowest, we both know this. Shea knew I needed to remember who I was, in a way I simply couldn't on Earth — but she also didn't really know what she was talking about. She'd heard some stories, late night drinks and tales around a table, sure, but that was all. You know more about my past than she does, currently."

"But you two—"

"Had a fling, and a friendship, and more fights than either should be able to withstand. Sure. You've trusted me up until now — can I ask that you keep doing that, for a bit longer? We need to play the long game here. We need information, tools, and a plan."

"But outside of the tools, how can you get the other two from here?"

"The tools get us the other two, Anders. I know what I'm doing. And I want to show you, just like you want. But all of this, it starts with playing the long game, not the short, not anymore." I walked up to the wall of the cell. "Remember," I asked him, "when we spent a few days here, and I—"

"I was here, Paige," he said so dryly I laughed.

"See, since then, I remembered who I was. I know that sounds stupid, but..." I pressed my hand to the cell front and focused on the energy the clear surface gave off. When I'd been here as a kid, I could never mess with it. I'd learned a lot since then. "Sometimes, Anders, you just need to accept yourself, shortcomings and all." I pulled the wall apart, slowly, watching the surface of it cloud up and then dissipate as the energy holding it together ate it alive.

"So why did we spend days—"

"No, Anders," I told him as I started to walk down the hall where the guards were, "I couldn't have done that before. I mean, I probably could've, but I wouldn't have tried. That's what I'm trying to tell you. Anyway," I said as we reached the guards, "I'm sick of waiting for Mitlan. Let's go see the Queen."

The guards heard that, of course, even as they drew their batons and squared off with us. I shook my head at them. "Folks, I just walked out of that cell, for the second time, and you think you can *stop* me? Do the right thing, go announce us to the Queen. Make it look like a communications screw-up. Blame Mitlan. Otherwise," I shrugged, "I'll go in there myself and you'll look *really* incompetent." The guards didn't even seem to consult each other, rude if you ask me, before one of them took a swing at me.

Anders stepped in and punched the guard in the side of the neck, just under the helmet. As he fell to the side, I grabbed his baton and gave it a quick slash in the air. "Thanks, Anders — now, can we *please* just do this my way? Because I can feel the energy in your suits, and that means I can use it. And if I use it... have you guys ever seen a flamingo—"

"Paige," Anders said with the exasperation of a parent.

"Oh fine," I said, dropping the baton on the floor and letting the noise ring out down the hall. "Last. Chance."

The three standing guards considered their options, silently. Always so silent. Annoying. One of them started to move, and as they did I ran right at them, laying hands on the two helmets I could reach. Both guards screamed tiny, high-pitch screams and then dropped the floor. The last guard got a swing in, and I found out the hard way that the batons were charged nicely. The zap drove me to my knees, but that just let me grab the guard's legs and concentrate. I did the same thing I'd done to the other two — turned the energy in the suit inward, releasing it all as one large charge to the occupant.

Standing, I looked at Anders. "I need to teach you that trick. Soon, I think."

"Are they still alive?"

"Of course," I said, "no reason to kill them. They aren't bad people, really, but they'll remember the pain. Once they get someone to help them out of those suits they'll be fine. But also I'm kidding, mostly, about teaching you that one. Reversing the energy of a suit like that, it isn't something to just teach you. I didn't know I could do it — those things are shielded to hell and back against exactly that trick."

"So how did you?" Anders asked I started to continue down the hall.

"You ever just feel like yourself one day?" I asked him.

"I have," he answered with a smile. "I'm glad you found that thing."

"Don't," I told him. "I'm not happy with what... no, that's not it. I'm not happy *where* I found it. So let's just leave it alone and not pick at yet another wound."

We walked back to the Chamber in peace, which confused me, but I kept quiet about it. We should've been swarmed by guards. There should've been panic in the building by now. The guards I'd dropped wouldn't stay that way for too long — certainly they could've called for help by the time we got to...and it dropped into place. When we got to the door guards I bowed, and Anders followed my lead.

The guards opened the doors, and I caught Anders's confusion as we walked past them. "The Queen," I said loud enough that I could be heard at the front of the room, "has allowed us this audience."

"Indeed I have, Neverchild," she said. "Now, tell me why I should not have you executed for your *continued* crimes?"

"This war you want me to fight for you," I told her, shaking my head as if this was simply the saddest news around town, "is what keeps me alive. And about that war — I noticed how empty this place is." I looked around. "Mitlan is still here, sure, but the others — where is the rest of the court? Seems to be just you two and a bunch of guards, all of whom seem even less inclined to pretend to be living people than usual."

"The makeup of the Court is of no concern to you. What you need is to—"

"It is my concern, though, because if I'm right, then the missing here have joined the war and abandoned your rule, haven't they? You're hanging on by a thread. You don't want to stop the war, per se, so much as you want to stop the threat to your control."

"It is not that simple, Paige," Mitlan's voice rang out behind me. He strode across the room with purpose, trying to look every inch a member of the Court. It made me want to laugh.

"Can I just ask—" Anders started.

"No," the Queen said quickly, shutting him down.

"Anders, let's hear it," I countered.

He listened to me. "Which side do you want to win?" Looking around the mostly empty room, he continued, "I mean, which side is in your pocket, or has told you they will be?"

"Oh, good one, Anders," I smiled, "perfect. He's right. You've told me about this so-called war, and how both sides want only destruction, but you wouldn't send me out to fight two armies, would you? You have something else in mind. A winner."

"It's not that simple, Paige," Mitlan insisted. "The Weird War won't—"

"The what now?"

"Weird War," he repeated. "While at first the fighting remained mostly the sort of battle plan you might think, as they escalated they both started bending the rules of physics, more and more, until they were attacking each other with reality itself. It has gone much farther now, and the Weird War threatens the stability of the Ascension itself."

"But you stopped to give it a cute name. You

guys really do just suck." I shook my head, shaking off the annoyance like a dog shedding water. "I still think Anders is right: you want one side to win."

"Kental," the Queen said. "He has sworn by everything, bound himself by whatever promises we could find, that he would work with us, if he were to win, and would be able to restore the Ascension to what it was."

"I'm not sure which is dumber," I said, looking directly at Mitlan, "you all for believing him, or him for thinking that would be believable. I mean I suppose it's you since apparently he's *being* believed, but fine."

"Be careful, Neverchild," the Queen said, "you have some leeway because we do need you, for now, but we were solving this without you before. We could again."

"Then why do you need me at all?" I asked. "Honestly, I'm curious."

"You were trained for this," she said simply.

"And if I die doing it, especially if I make it a little better, you guys are far better off, isn't that right?"

"Paige, it isn't—" Mitlan began.

"Yes, exactly," the Queen said.

"I appreciate the honesty," I told her, "though I am still not sure why you aren't actively just letting them tire themselves out and then dealing with this."

Mitlan coughed lightly. "When we say the Weird War threatens the Ascension itself, Paige, do not take that as anything other than literal."

"Listen to him, Neverchild, and consider this," the Queen said, "as incentive if you must. If this

Weird War continues at the pace it is going, it shall destabilize the very dimensional cradle that the Ascension sits upon. And if that happens?"

"This place returns to Earth," I said, my voice soft with a sense of amazement. I'd never thought that would be possible.

"And if this land, this whole land, did that, not only would it have nowhere to be, it would not necessarily appear at sea level. We would all be destroyed, probably, but also cause the death of millions of humans alongside us." She looked around the room slowly before continuing. "The laws of physics in this place..."

"Oh no," I said, looking at Anders. "They're *mostly* the same as on Earth, but little differences. If you toss those two together with no warning, I mean it wouldn't destroy the world or anything, but it could...I have no idea what it could do."

"Neither do we," Mitlan said. "Obviously if you had not come along we would go a different route, but with you here, this is the best course."

"So, stop the war, and then you'll gear me up with information and whatever else I need to stop the Subtle Knives?"

"That is the deal," the Queen said.

"Well, Anders," I told him, "I guess we do this."

CHAPTER FOURTEEN

WE WERE TAKEN to the edge of the city and offered an escort to Kental's camp. We turned that idea down quick. Not that we planned on pulling a fast one, but seeing Kental again, at all, and convincing him I wasn't there to ruin his fun but help him win, would be awkward enough without showing up looking like either a prisoner or a new insurgent force working for the throne. Which, I suppose, is what we were, really, just Anders and I. Really no point in advertising that more than necessary right off the bat, though.

The wild woods and open pastures outside the city still stood, looking normal to my eye. At first. Anders and I walked along the route Mitlan had given us in silence, for at least an hour. Part of me wanted to talk to him, to tell him how I understood better now where he came from, emotionally. I wanted that specific release that comes from telling someone they were right, and you could realign with them now, and see their point of view, but I didn't give in.

Because I also knew I wanted the emotional release, that cheap little dopamine hit, for purely selfish reasons. Anders would get it through how I treated him, how I behaved and taught him, rather than me just saying a bunch of words the way I tended to.

Even as my will started to fade a little, and I thought about opening a discussion — possibly, if not hopefully, a healthy one — the scenery started to change in ways that kept the silence. The trees twisted in on themselves, leaves strange hues of blues and blacks with the occasional purple. The moss and ground underfoot felt wrong as well. Spiky against the soles of my WarBoots. Yeah, the WarBoots — they'd been forced to give those back to me. I needed them, and the Queen knew it. She knew, as did I, that the stakes in this war were now firm enough in my mind that I had no intention of ditching everything again.

Not that I knew how to get back to Earth just yet, anyway, but they didn't know that. The fire trick would still be going in the shunt hallway and opening the door alone would cost me more energy than I had to spare. We were stuck, even if I felt positive no one else actually knew that. Score a totally useless point for us, I suppose.

The landscape kept changing, the trees now looking like they were made of glass, or some type of crystal. The ground underfoot kept crunching, as well. The air tasted of...

"Is that fennel?" I asked Anders, breaking our hours-long silence.

"In the," he sniffed, "air? I think so. Is there fennel growing around here, maybe?"

"No," I ran a hand along some bright-pink crystal leaves, feeling them shudder on the branch, threatening to drop, "this is all just accidental side damage, I think. I get the Weird War name now if we're still a while out from Kental's camp, much less the front lines of a war, and everything is already this utterly fucked."

"They did this by accident? Changed," he

looked around as we kept walking, "everything, simply by accident?"

"I could tell you how we were taught to not let things get out of control like that, how there are safeguards and exactly how this should never happen. I could bore you for hours, like a sloth learning about slow-motion filming. Useless. Since it obviously has, and is continuing, to happen. They're out of control. And if a bunch of the court is with them, on either side, they have a lot of power to throw around. Not enough control, not enough care, but more than enough power."

"The guards," Anders said, making me blink, "I meant to ask."

"What about them?" I plucked a leaf from a tree and threw it at the ground, watching it shatter.

"You made the Ascension sound like all these people who had learned, for lack of a better term, magic—"

"Lots of better terms, Anders. Energy manipulation, reality bending, building-block shuffles—"

"Fine, but if they all know that stuff, what about the guards? Or the guy who sold us these suits? I thought this would be a paradise of enlightened being, even if they were the assholes you claimed. Instead it's what, a few powerful people at the top and then just Earth?"

The woods opened up into a wide clearing, exactly like we'd been told they would. We were getting close. The grass underfoot seemed softer, if also now bone white. Shrubs sprang up, here and there, dotting the fields with leaves both crystal and metal.

"Anywhere there's power there's inequality," I said, "the Ascension is no different. But even the guards, the people washing the floors, live longer, healthier lives here. They know tricks — some of them small, to be sure, but they know ways to make the universe work for them. And realistically, Anders, not everyone wants to run the big show. Some people are really and truly happy just serving pie, or hugging otters."

"Otter hugging is a job around here?" he asked, looking around the clearing as we walked. Like him, I grew more wary. A grove of trees is excellent cover, but out here we were so exposed it made the hair along the nape of my neck stand up.

"I don't know," I told him. "I wouldn't put it past someone, though, to find a way to monetize that sort of thing. You know, I once knew a guy back on Earth, I have to be honest here, who made his living shaving inspirational messages into camels' fur for their owners. So let's not judge the side jobs in either place. Just respect the hustle involved. But seriously," I said, pressing down my heels inside the WarBoots to start to charge them while we kept walking, "there is a, normally, a far larger luxury class here then in most places on Earth. Even then, someone has to clean the floors. People will pay for that service, even if the work involved is miniscule given the talents involved around these parts."

Any reply Anders might have wanted to make got lost in a crack of gunfire. We both dove for the ground, as if it would provide any real cover. I also started pulling energy in and sorting it, trying to see how many people were out there.

"We're here to talk to Kental, on behalf of the Queen," I said loudly. I had a hazy sense of at least thirty people but, looking around, could see none of them. I let my eyes drift focus and looked for energy fields instead — stupid stupid stupid, why hadn't I been doing that all along? Lazy and out-of-practice hunting. Almost got us killed there.

"I assume," a voice said, "you have proof?"

Luckily I did. I stood, slowly, and gestured to Anders to do the same. "Of course," I said, seeing indistinct shapes around me now. They'd been with us a while, I guessed, though why they'd chose then to reveal themselves I didn't get. Yet.

"Show it to me," the voice said, as the woman it belonged to filtered into normal view. She stood a good five-foot-five, short hair brushed back, wearing what I assumed were hunting clothes: loose fitting but not baggy, tucked in and secured against anything being able to crawl up a pant leg or sleeve, and patterned in lightly glowing swirls that would help store energy to cloak them.

I fished out, again as slowly as possible, a sealed letter from the Queen. I hoped it didn't actually instruct the reader to kill us, but I doubted she'd bother going that route. Chances were we wouldn't survive regardless. I hadn't told Anders that because I knew he counted on us getting back to Earth, but the reality remained that, for us, fighting this war left us a much smaller chance of reaching our goal. But Earth had other people who could fight for it. I trusted Shealano to rally the troops, if need be.

Plus, it came down to the risk in front of us versus an unknown blob of maybe we still needed to work out. This was the right — the only real — choice for us. Anders needed to keep that hope burning, though, for both of us, so I left him to that.

I busied my brain with these stupid thoughts while the woman cracked the seal and read the letter. She looked at me over the top of it, and then at Anders, a few times as she read, in apparent disbelief. "Come with me," she said, and turned away from us. Well, better than shooting us, really.

"Troop," she said to the mass of people still camouflaged around us, "go visible spectrum." I counted thirty-six people swimming into view en masse. Anders hissed as he sucked in a quick breath out of surprise but didn't say anything. I leaned in and whispered close to him, "Don't feel bad, I didn't think to look for them either — but try to see, like with the barriers — now you'll see their trails, they're still pulling in energy to recharge those outfits they're wearing."

He nodded. I hoped the exercise would mean he wouldn't have time to worry. I knew I worried, though, so he probably did as well. We were marched through the field, people buffering around us on all sides, the woman in charge glancing back more often than necessary by anyone's count. I suspected the Queen dropped my name, and this woman kept checking to see if I was really there. Reputations can work for and against you. I forgot that last half, every now and then.

I caught her making a few recognizable hand motions as we walked. Kental was using our old silent communication game to talk to his people in the field. Smart play. The range on the trick wasn't huge but you could, theoretically, replay through people, using them as stations if need be, I supposed.

We walked for a good fifteen minutes, and a camp flickered into sight. Fuck the amount of energy it would cost to hide everyone from all view — but they weren't quite doing that, were they?

Risking my neck a bit — there remained a good chance someone in the troop was watching me closely for anything sneaky — I reached out with a bit of my own mind and read the fields around the camp. Yeah, they'd saved energy by only making it hard to see if you didn't already know where it stood. Once you knew where they were and what the area really looked like, you could always see it. Good way to save on expenditures — this way there would need to be ten people, not forty, dedicated to keeping that sort of swirl going in the area.

The camp itself impressed me in a whole different way. The buildings would only be called tents on a technicality. The place felt huge. To be fair, it felt huge because the grounds covered an area that fit the definition of the concept of 'really big.' People wandered back and forth, all looking that specific brand of overtired alongside overworried that accompanies a war.

Kental had certainly rallied supporters, outside of the Throne. I wondered how empty the city must be, assuming Jursica commanded the same-size army. I'd chalked up any emptiness to the time of day — busy people, the usual excuses — but no, they'd marched to war. The Queen couldn't expect this all to die down simply, could she? Of course that would be her plan: toss me into things, hope everything turned sideways in a manner she could exploit, and build something stable out of the rubble that left her in charge. Not a bad plan, if no one knows you're doing it.

Anders and I were walked over to a stupidly big tent and taken inside. Lush, in a way tents tended not to be, with rugs and furniture filling the space beautifully. We stood there while one of our guards whispered to someone obviously further up the chain of command. Nodding commenced, and that person went off to find another person in the tent and so on. I stood, shrugging at Anders, who shrugged back.

"You know," I said to him, "this tent is too big. That person there," I pointed at the whispered-to person heading deeper into the back, "is going into another room. This tent has *rooms*, Anders. That's too big for a tent."

"Hospital tents have rooms, Paige," he told me.

"I know *that*," I replied, "but even so, too big for a tent — just make a building out of something other than fabric and call it a day. 'Tent' just doesn't encompass the largeness needed to do this sort of structure, or at least it shouldn't. If you saw a giraffe but the neck went on for twenty feet instead of six, you'd think 'Holy shit, that isn't a giraffe, not with that neck!' and you'd have a point."

"I—"

"I'm not sure how you could structure neck bones to allow for full flexibility and movement but also hold up a neck that long — the musculature alongside it would probably mean a neck six times as thick, which would have to bring the whole animal up to proportion, and that, Anders, is my *entire point*."

"I thought your point was that this tent is too big."

"Exactly. Now hush," I told him, seeing movement from the back room of the tent, "Kental is about to come out and act surprised to see me when we both know the Queen told him I was on my way."

Sure enough, Kental emerged from the back room and strode forward, fully playing the part of a would-be King. "Paige!" he exclaimed, holding his arms out wide as if to embrace me. Bald, with a long, black handlebar mustache, Kental had been built for grace by whatever roulette wheel spins these things. His arms and legs were slightly too long, and his torso seemed almost fluid at times. He didn't move so much as glide, mostly. He did it now, seemingly floating over to me and Anders.

I took in his solid brick-red jumpsuit, adorned with epaulettes as well as knee and elbow pads, plus of course bracers, all in the same soft metallic blue. His boots were a nice mud-covered black, real boots of the people.

"Fuck, you're an asshole," I said by way of greeting. "We both know why I'm here, and what my job is. But come on, Kental, look at how you're dressed. Look at," I pointed around the giant tent, "this stupid place. You built tents too big. You wear shitty cartoon outfits. You want this *so bad* you're willing to kill everyone to get your way. You're a shit."

"It's good to see you, too, Paige," he said, smirking in a bad attempt to hide how much he hated me. He let his arms drop to his sides and made small, not-even-really-trying-to-hide-them gestures at hip level to the guards around us to stay where they were.

"Shut up, I'm talking," I told him. "Now, I'll go win your petty-ass war, since *you can't*, and hand you the whole big prize of being the bestest to ever live so you can get screwed over by Her Majesty. It's what you want, after all, and who would I be if I couldn't give you exactly that?"

"Certainly not a friend," he said, voice growing colder.

"Exactly!" I said. "But here's the thing. You guys have that letter — and I know you were informed before that, even — and I'm sure the Queen, in her infinite wisdom, saw fit to command you to give me whatever I needed."

"Words closer to that effect than I might like," he admitted.

"Good. Well, good for you. Because I want none of it. Well," I said. "Well, I mean. Almost none of it. We'll need some equipment, bags of food and water, I guess, and then I want you to stay put. I don't mean pull back your forces or anything obvious, but it'd be nice to not have to worry about you attacking from the rear while I settle this."

"You're trying to make sure I don't attack so that you can go and warn *her* to—"

I laughed at him and turned to Anders. "Do you believe this guy? He thinks if I wanted to sell him out I would do it this badly. I can't deal with him."

"And yet you *must*," Kental said, before Anders could open his mouth to reply to me. "I will give you your equipment and supplies, but Paige, if you even *hint* toward betraying me..." He tried to give me a menacing grin. It ended up with him just looking kind of hungry, but I suppose the effect remained the same.

Kental turned and left as I started to reply. Fine. We would've just sniped at each other all day, anyway, and best to get this stupidity over with. I shrugged at a guard standing nearby and gave him a list of things I needed, asking for a place to sit and wait and prepare.

CHAPTER FIFTEEN

ANDERS AND I ended up setting up temporary shop in a small tent whose luxury consisted of exactly two chairs and nothing else, which suited me fine. As soon as we were alone, Anders spoke up.

"Paige," he said in a tone that let me know everything, "are you sure this is the right move?"

"It's the only move," I told him. I unbuttoned my jacket and sat in one of the chairs. "And we'll get this done as fast as possible. I don't want to be here, either."

"Don't you?" he asked, sitting down as well. "You seem more..." he trailed off to silence as he tried to find the right words, "present, I suppose. Like this is where you want to be."

"Ahh shit, Anders," I told him, fussing with my ascot, "of course it looks that way. I *feel* more like myself than I have. But that's not this place — well, it kind of is, and I think you understand that. It's home even if I hate it. It's a comfort thing. But it's also just the effect of you being around — and don't let that go to your head."

He perked up at that but remained silent.

"You kept pushing, you kept trying to drag me toward the person you thought I should be — and yeah, you annoy the shit out of me with it, or did, but you're also not wrong. The two combined, and that happened here, because half of it couldn't happen anywhere else. But don't think that means

I want to be here, or that I enjoy it." I clapped my hands suddenly, and they started to glow. "The thing of it is, Anders — I'm good at very specific things, but normally, none of them is damaging." I traced patterns in the air, leaving tiny light trails from my fingertips. "You've seen how I do things. But this will take something different, something I haven't really let myself do for a *very* long time."

I traced a pattern of light across part the arm of the chair I sat in and watched as it left a burn mark. Anders watched, eyes growing a bit wider, and I smiled at him. "But maybe doing things differently is the order of the day," I said, stopping the glow across my hands. "As for you, we should get you a bit more up to speed so you can help. The supplies I asked for will be good for that."

He nodded, obviously not sure what I meant. "So this really will be combat?" he asked after a minute. I felt grateful he looked disquieted about the idea. Sure he'd jumped right in with the Subtle Knives outside Shaelano's place, but that didn't mean he'd enjoyed it. His distaste matched my own.

"Not if I can help it," I said, "I mean, you've seen me work now, right?"

"Some?" he half shrugged. "You seem to…I don't know if I'd call it work…"

"Hey now," I laughed, "it would be way easier to blow shit up and go through problems than it is to talk around them. So yeah, to be clear, I hope to not have to actually fight. If I do, though, I would also like us both to get out of it alive, and in the same general condition we're in now."

"So what do you want me to—" he fell silent

as someone entered the tent carrying two large backpacks.

Setting them down, they looked at me, ignoring Anders utterly. "Kental says your supplies are here, and as such you should have left camp inside the next hour," they said flatly, then turned and went before I could thank them.

"What I want you to do," I told Anders, opening one bag and seeing a bunch of water bottles and wrapped things that smelled faintly like food, "is learn quicker than is honestly comfortable. What I honestly expect is for you to do what you can and hang in there. You're good at that."

"Oh, uhm, thanks," he said, trying to hide his pride. I opened the second bag and smiled at the contents. Anders stood there, dealing internally with his own feelings. I gave him the space, partly out of kindness, and, admittedly, partly out of greed seeing the supplies we'd been given.

When I'd first been on Earth, with Nester, we'd not been heavily armed or anything, but we'd managed to bring over a few goodies with us. We also knew how to make more. But that cost, and the longer we stayed, the more haphazard our prep work got, making do with whatever laid around. You ended up with potato bombs — but they worked, so who cared? Also they were easy to find and make.

So it'd been a damn long time since I'd seen some of the stuff in the bag. I started to unpack it, to show Anders what most of the things in there could do. Well, I held each up, explained it, and replaced the item in the bag. In no way would I actually set any of the stash off for no good reason.

To be clear, nothing in the bag would be lethal, really. In the way that a butter knife isn't lethal unless you mean it, at least. Regardless, we had some Howlers, Reflectors, Gatherers, a few Store Bottles, your basic Blinder set — all the simple stuff.

There were ways to stack effects, but I never went for them. I didn't go for a lot of the complex stuff — not out of a lack of skill or hatred of learning, I just tended to honestly like the simple ways better. They let me get creative.

Anders and I left the tent not too much later, heading out toward enemy camp. Sort of. I mean we headed for the real front line, and from there I hoped to get us through without incident. But that sort of hope is almost never actually rewarded.

"So what you need to remember," I told Anders in a soft voice as we walked through Kental's end of the war, now quiet, "this is all just an innate human ability. That's where we get it from. You can feel patterns already, it's a sense you have. Everything comes from there. If you can feel it, you can shape it, if that makes sense."

"It doesn't," he replied, "at all. I mean, it's a sense? Fine, I can smell a French fry, but I can't make my ability to smell it turn into a way to get a French fry."

I laughed a bit, "That's true, I suppose," I said, "but Anders, when you felt for seams in the world, you *felt* them."

He hmm'd a bit as we continued to walk, and nodded eventually. "As if more than one sense was at work, in a way."

"Exactly. Trust me, with practice you can move

the stuff around. You just have to learn to know yourself hard enough that the doubt washes away in the moment."

"Then how can you do it?" he asked.

That rocked me back on my heels, almost literally. It stung. Hard. Anders wasn't wrong, which is why it hit me the way it did. Back in the day, before everything went to shit and Nester died, I had known myself. I could turn on a dime with what I knew about myself. At least, when I needed to work. The doubts fell away and there would only be the moment. After that — well, of course I doubted, and that doubt made me retreat, and this is all well-worn territory, but that Anders still saw me that way even as I felt I'd come out of the hole and recovered more and more of myself as we'd been going — that scared me. Mostly because he could be right.

"That's unfair," I lied.

Anders sighed and shrugged, "It came out meaner than I meant," he said, "but it is a valid question."

"Let's just say," I said, "I can do more than you've seen, especially now." I told him the truth and hoped we could leave it there. Thankfully, he did let it lie, and we walked a bit further. I reached out, trying to feel anything odd up ahead, but the feedback felt like someone had cross wired a truck full of amps together and hit the on switch, laughing as they ran.

I shook the pain off and warned Anders away from trying the same thing. The further we got from the pure safety of Kental's camp, and the closer we came to disputed territory, the worse the landscape got as well.

Trees and grass changed into impossible things, as they had when we first approached Kental's camp. Glass, metal, whatever else infected the close reality around us, changed them.

"Sloppy," I said, "but even so, we should get out of sight. We're getting closer to truly unfriendly areas, not just the unfriendly we know."

Anders nodded, trailing a hand along a purple crystal branch. He pointed, having seen a much denser path that would do for a while. I followed him as he made his way through it. "If only the ground didn't make so much noise," he said, glaring down at the assorted fucked-up landscape underfoot.

"That I can do something about," I said. I stopped walking — Anders noticed a step or two later, if only due to the lack of noise from footsteps. Closing my eyes, I focused on the ground cover, feeling the swirl of rampant loose energy. "Actually," I said, as I started to untangle the chaos carefully, "you should try this."

Anders, I opened an eye a bit to see, closed his eyes, and I heard his breathing slow. Good. "I can see the — ow, this is a lot."

"It is," I agreed, "but try to straighten it out some. You know what grass is, what moss is — mess with the energy until they feel like what you think those things actually might feel like."

"How do I know if I'm right?"

"That doesn't matter — if you get close enough it'll suffice and quiet things down. But, for an example, keep feeling and seeing this." I let the energy coil around my hands, tugging and separating out strands of it. I thought about grass, moss, dirt — the smell and feel of them — and let that guide me. I worked quicker than I would have if I'd really wanted to get it exact, but slow enough to not break a chain and set off more trouble.

"Now you try," I said. "Just feel the energy, use your hands, treat it as a physical thing. Don't overthink the process, just let it happen and adjust how you move and interact with it until it feels right to you. Once you have that, start to do what you felt me do, as close as you can, but also quick. Don't worry, there's no wrong here. If something starts to snap, ease off, but I'll catch it if you don't. Promise."

He worked, very slowly and clumsy, but he worked. Strands started to move, and I felt the urge to say something but stayed quiet to let Anders explore his own senses for the first real time in his life. I considered putting him in charge of quieting our path, even if that choice could only slow us down. Truthfully, I couldn't find any rush in me, not when all I got closer to would be seeing Jursica, and probably fighting to get there regardless.

But whatever ability I'd found to shut up and be silent as Anders learned gave out, and I started to give him advice when the tree near me exploded into tentacles.

I don't mean the branches came to life and reached for me.

I mean: Tree. Exploded. Into. Tentacles.

They didn't reach for me, or Anders — they simply flopped on the ground wetly.

Still had the desired effect, or at least an

effect. Anders and I both hit the ground, not sure what'd happened for a second. I caught sight of the tentacles and the incident unfolded in my mind. "Anders, we have incoming, ands this is going to be strange — they're fighting on my level. But I need you to help."

"I can't do that stuff," he said, pointing at a nearby tentacle.

"And I wouldn't want you to if you could," I told him. "Really who ever *would* want to? No, just focus and feel the energy from the ground like you were, but instead of untangling it and setting things right, I want to you feed it to me — can you do that?"

"I don't know."

"Good enough," I said, standing up. As I did, I gathered energy from the noise all around me. A feast at my fingertips. I drew it into me as an untangled mess of raw potential and considered the situation. Anders stood up, behind me, and started to work. What he did would be key for me, as just taking in this much garbage — energy spoiled and left to destroy the natural state of things — could be harder to work with.

Yes, a metric ton of it laid across the land, but I would have to sort it some in my mind to get the results I wanted. Anders could feed me the good stuff — more natural, easier to reshape into the strange for protection.

Make no mistake, the game remained protection, not attacking. But they didn't have to know that. Although…who were they? I smiled and twirled energy until it shaped the way I needed.

"All right," I said loudly enough to scare any

birds in the area, except of course there were none. Birds knew better than to hang around when the trees turned to iron. "There's no reason to attack anyone. We just came to—"

Getting cut off by a flying spoon coming for my head stood up there in new, unexpected experiences. Instead of ducking I threw my hands up. Energy spun to form a shield, of sorts, and the spoon dropped to the ground, making a crunch as it did.

Whoever they were, they were terrible at attacking. Taking the raw messed-and-coiled energy and just throwing it, no plan or formation. Not a mistake I intended to make. I kept the shield theory up and wove a shell over Anders and myself. The light glittered a bit as it passed through my barrier, and I called out to the forest again.

"You're new at this, I get it," I said to the air. "Please understand I am very much not. For every spoon you throw at us, I *could* return fire with a horde of elephants, fifty feet up. I wouldn't, because why would you hurt elephants, but the concept remains — and now you're all looking up wondering *exactly* how mean I'm feeling. Because who," I asked the unseen soldiers, "even thinks of that, unless they're willing to do something at least *close* to it, right? Welcome to the party. Let's stand down and talk."

While I went on, Anders started feeding me untangled energy. Not much, but it would certainly help. On Earth I could work energy, but this place, the Ascension, had been designed with energy work in mind. The laws here were different, in very subtle ways, and they enabled some truly startling levels of results.

No more attacks came, but also no answering cries, so I decided to use the energy Anders was feeding me to build up our defense. The shielding I'd laid down wouldn't travel well, honestly. It didn't reform around objects, so moving it would either break it or knock down a bunch of the forest, and I didn't want either result.

Between the amount and strength of the energy, and the different rules, I decided to go big. Dropping the shield, I poured that working back into my current idea and smiled as a ring of waist-high sloths ran around us at a decidedly unslothlike speed.

"That should be good to travel with," I told Anders. "So let's keep moving."

"Wait, but won't the sloths get hurt?"

I smiled at him and clapped his shoulder for extra credit. "Good on you for watching out for them. But no. They're each roughly as hard to hurt as a tank. They're also not, I mean come on, they're not alive. They're basically really cool-looking robots, without being mechanical or anything. But they have no insides, literally. Hollow, to help them absorb damage. They're..." I laughed as we started to walk, "a screensaver, of sorts, I guess. Just repeated code that looks cool."

We took to walking slowly, circling each other as we went, so we were always able to see in multiple directions. No more attacks came for a few minutes, and I thought maybe they'd learned their lesson. No such luck.

The sky darkened quickly, too quickly, and we both looked up to see some shapes falling toward us. Oh, those *assholes*. We ran for cover, and to get out of striking range. The sloth circle couldn't keep up, and I watched some of them pop like the balloons they sort-of were under the weight of the attack. I had no idea what the things from the sky were supposed to be, but they worked. Large, amorphous blobs from the sky. Jerks stole my idea.

Of course we needed to keep going, which would bring us closer to the people attacking us. Small favors, I suppose — the attackers clearly weren't working for Kental. Even so, I needed to stop this.

"Paige," Anders said as we crouched behind a rock, "can you use the WarBoots? I mean the name alone..."

I laughed — he was not wrong. On Earth, the state of energy meant they were great for FastWalks or a bit of kicking down walls and such, but most of their larger functions just needed too much raw input. A problem easily taken care of here.

I pressed down inside the WarBoots and started to feed them more and more energy. They started to glow, and I smiled at Anders. "Good idea," I told him, and stood up. All we needed, realistically, was to chase them off and get some clearance. Any real, straight working would end up warped if I didn't remain very careful, and the enemy, as such, looked to be totally unconcerned with fallout.

The air got thicker as I worked. It became soupier, like a dense fog made of...I tasted the air... butter? "Anders, does—"

"Butter," he confirmed. "Paige, we can't

breathe butter."

"Such a fallen world we live in to have that be true, and yet here we are," I said, struggling to get words out. We both fell silent then, knowing we would soon drown in butter. Inventive, if only I could be sure the effect had been intended.

WarBoots charged, I stomped down *hard* with my right foot and focused out as I did. The air cleared instantly. The ground shook. A few trees toppled, radiating away from us. I motioned for Anders to stand. "We just have to make it a bit further then shelter for the night, I think," I told him.

"Can't we FastWalk the rest of the way?"

Full of ideas, this one. "No," I told him, "I'm not sure how far, or in exactly what direction, we need to go. We'd waste more time and far more energy. But it's a good idea, if we could."

We started to move again, pausing every ten or so steps — never quite the same timing to keep things fresh and unpredictable — so I could stomp the ground. The occasional toppled tree and associated ground shake wouldn't stop anyone, probably, but they wouldn't be quite as quick to throw down, I hoped.

I gave up on that hope when I saw a barrage of incoming trees. Trunks and all, just flying at us. I kicked out with the WarBoot, and at the stop of the kick released the energy. Worked as well as kicking a wall, even though all I hit was air. The force shattered the trees and deflected the debris.

"I'm getting sick of this, Anders," I said. "But," I continued, raising my voice, "I really don't want to attack anyone if I can help it."

We grew quiet, taking a few steps as softly as we could manage. Anders kept working on untangling energy and feeding it to me, and I wove it and trailed it along in case of need. He got steadily faster and more able to do a working while walking. I wanted to tell him how much better he'd already gotten, impressive while in the middle of this madness, but worried it could make him self-conscious and trip him up some, so I kept my mouth shut.

Another few feet and another stomp. The WarBoots could keep this up all night if needed, but protection while we slept would be crucial. I could take first watch, no worry, but eventually I'd need to sleep and Anders would be up at bat. He could, now, spin some energy, but he still didn't know what to do with it, certainly not enough to uphold anything strong enough to keep us safe. Unless...

I kept playing with the idea as we made uncertain progress. The light was fading. We'd have to find shelter for the night or risk bigger problems, and soon. We still had to flush whomever hid in the tree line, or at least make them go away. Against my own better judgement, I reached into our bag of goods and grabbed a few things.

"Ears and eyes," I said softly to Anders, and I tossed three metal spheres straight up. As soon as they left my hand I covered my ears and closed my eyes tightly, ducking my head.

The two Howlers went off first. Even with my ears covered and being directly below them, the safest spot to be, I could *feel* the sound they produced.

Then the Reflector went off. I only knew because even with my eyes closed, the light hurt. I gave it a few seconds and opened my eyes. Tapping Anders on the shoulder to give him an all clear, we both looked around.

"Hear that?" he asked softly. I listened and, sure enough, I could hear human voices, not too far away. Whimpering. "Did you just permanently deafen and blind them?"

"Reflectors don't blind — well they do, they absorb and reflect all the light and...that doesn't matter, but the answer is no, not really."

"Not really?" Anders asked as we went in search of the fallen enemy.

"Healing around these parts is spectacular, remember," I said. "They'll be fine." We came across the six of them, on the ground and looking far worse for wear. I had to reassure Anders a second time, and appreciated that, actually. Compassion was a strength, and one I didn't want to find lacking in someone I traveled with, much less taught how to be dangerous.

I sighed and changed a few fallen branches into a good hefty twine, not enjoying messing with the local flora any more than it had been but having no good choice. Anders watched me, and I could feel him sliding into mental view to see how I'd manipulated the energy to affect the change. Nice.

We left them there and struck out again. Once they'd been disabled, Jursica's fighters, all of the obfuscation they'd relied on evaporated. That's how we could find them, sure, but it also let us see some of their tracks. They'd been following us from a distance, of course, but we could see what direction they'd started from. Good chance that would be the direction of their camp.

So we went left, literally, striking out in a different direction. I wanted to put some radial distance between us and the actual front line of the fight. We cut through more trees, crunching on whatever the ground cover ended up made from now, and, after about thirty minutes, I stopped us, dropping my bag. Anders dropped his and opened it, getting us each some water.

I set up a shield, showing Anders how I did, that would hide us, and protect us, for a while. It wouldn't do to sleep under, but it would be fine to sit a while.

"The more of this I see, the madder I get," I said.

"The fighting? We haven't seen much of it—"

"The land, Anders. This is bullshit."

"They'll reset it, though, right? Fix it all back to normal?" He handed me some cured meat stick thing.

"No," I said, sneering at the world. "That's the thing. They're not changes done on purpose, it's all slop and leftover effect from badly trained people playing with large firehoses. And then, even then, sure I could turn a bit of it back — you could, they could if they *wanted*, but that's *for now*. The longer this sort of change sits, the deeper it roots. Eventually it just is the forest, this mess of glass and metal and fuckery. Dead trees, dead ground, the lot of it. You'd have to clear it all and replant, and even then you'd have to untangle the knots they left so the weird stopped sprouting alongside the correct."

Anders just looked around, seeing everything as if all new. "So this is all dead?"

"You think a glass tree is going to grow? They killed a forest by being lazy."

After that we ate in silence for a while. We stored our trash back in the bag and Anders unslung his shoulder bag to take out his journal and write a bunch down. I wanted to set up camp first, or move again, but I'd let him take the time. He had a lot to digest, if not a great meal to go with it, and though the journal still annoyed me to no end, I couldn't bring myself to nudge him about it.

We moved camp again, though not too far, for better shelter. I wove a shield around us again and made Anders do some of the work, to get him used to it. The shield would hold, mostly, but, more importantly, it would ensure we couldn't be seen. I hoped. Either way, the thing would alert me the second enough pressure to come close to breaking through hit the energy. I took the first watch, letting Anders get some sleep.

Hours pass slowly when you're staring into the darkness and trying to stay alert. Thankfully the weather held out nicely, so our lack of fire didn't matter. A dead forest loomed around me, the moon casting shadows that hardly shifted.

Growing up, I hadn't considered the moon, stars, or sun at the Ascension. Why would I? They were there, the way they were supposed to be. Now, however, I stole glances at the moon, wondering what it actually could have been. Ages ago, when the bubble reality the Ascension occupied was first formed, they installed all of the sky and set the whole shebang to run by itself for eternity, I guess.

That working by itself could stand as the most impressive thing created by humanity, or post-humanity, I suppose, if you listened to their ideas. Still, they went on to create the rest of the land and physical rules, tweaking as they went but keeping things in balance. The sheer math involved in making this whole place tick over for countless centuries...I doubt I would have liked the assholes who built it. They could have built anything and they basically built Earth, but ever-so-slightly geared toward them.

Just imagine you could build a world of your own, for your friends and family. Picture it — what you could do with a space like that, left to your own imagination. Imagination that you prided yourself on — that was, in fact, the root of why you were doing any of this to begin with. To prove how great you could be, how powerful and above humanity you were.

With all that in the mix, you basically just copied what you'd seen and called it special.

The Ascension itself stood as proof of why I felt justified in my annoyance and dislike of the Ascension.

The hell with it. Hours had passed with me just losing my head, greying out into space, and keeping watch in varying measure. Time to wake Anders. I did, and we went through how the shield worked, both of us sleepy at the opposite ends of the spectrum.

I bedded down, wrapping myself in the one thin blanket we had in the bag, and tried to sleep.

I didn't get far. The alarm I tied to the shield woke me within a few...minutes, I'd guess?

I got up and stood by Anders.

The wind had picked up, causing a tinkling, instead of a rustle, from the area. I ignored it at first, until I noticed that the gusts would come in strong, then change their direction by exactly ninety degrees and pick up again.

The winds were being used as a probe. I asked Anders if he saw what set the alarm off in the first place, and he pointed to a large metal branch a few feet away. Blown here by the wind, which had then eased off a bit and started doing this cardinal points nonsense.

Anders, at my request, shrank the shield down to a minimal state, which would strengthen it — the inverse square law still held here, at least. Well, mostly. Enough. I watched him work, ready to back him up though I didn't need to. In a few years, he could be really good at this, if he wanted. Of course, back on Earth it'd be harder, but even so. He had the will to push through and do this stuff.

None of which told me anything about whoever sat around feeling out our defenses. I could be getting sleep instead of this bullshit. If for nothing else than that, I would make sure these fools regretted their move.

"To all and sundry annoying people out there in the darkness," I said loudly, "who have, obviously, made hiding useless, *can we help you*?" I pointed Anders to the gear bag, and he dragged it over. "You know, by now, who I am. Do you really think this is a good idea? Pissing me off?"

It probably was, realistically. Getting me tired was strategically sound, really, but they might not know that.

"Yes," a voice from the shadows replied. A voice I hadn't heard in ages.

"Jursica," I called out, "leave your raiding party and let's talk."

She stepped into view, only inches away from the shield. Shaking her head, she reached a hand out to feel the shield itself. "What raiding party? Fuck, Paige, why would I need one, any more than you would?"

"One of us is waging a war here, and it ain't me," I said.

"Let me in, we'll talk. We both know, though maybe your little lamb here doesn't, this shield wouldn't hold three seconds if I felt like ripping it apart. So make things easy." She thought and looked around. "Wait, shouldn't Nester be here? Are you two trying to—"

"Nester died, Jurs. Don't pretend you care, " I said, sitting on the ground casually, "and anyway, the shield passes sound just fine. And I'm glad you think my work is that shoddy. It'll make watching you try that much more satisfying." She actually wasn't wrong, but not for a reason she'd hit on. Was the shield going to be easy to break? Sure. But when she broke it — if she did — it would happily shatter, then reform around her and choke all light and air from her until she passed out. It'd also absorb whatever she threw at it and use that in its own attack. So yeah, goading her a bit? Why not? I'm not *stupid*.

"Have it your way, chicken," she said, sitting

on the ground as well. Anders remained standing until I glanced up at him.

As he sat, he asked, "Why would you come out here by yourself?"

"Oh, Jursica thinks she's invulnerable," I said.

"I could say the same, Paige," she countered.

"She also *finally* got word I was in play and came to see for herself. So what can I do for you, Jurs?"

"Turn around and don't try to kill me?" she asked. "You couldn't by yourself, anyway, never could."

"I'm not alone — I have Anders here," I said, "but regardless, who said I was here to kill you?"

"We both know you were sent here to end this," she said, running a hand along the sharp grass next to her.

"They never specified, and I wouldn't have agreed to killing being required. Honestly, Jurs, I don't even know that Kental should win, but that isn't my concern." I stood up and started to pace in a small circle. "My only concern here is that this war ends. It *needs* to end. Look what you two have done to the forest. I'm sure it just gets worse from there, and if I don't stop one of you, or someone doesn't, at least, the Ascension will fall."

"And that's bad?" she asked.

"Hah! Probably not, except for the bit where I mean the phrase fucking literally, Jurs. I have no love for this place," a lie, but a truthful one, "no more than you do, I'm sure, but if it falls — actually falls — it'll take a large chunk of Earth with it. And that's just not worth it. Not even to get even with them for what they did to us."

She grabbed a fistful of dirt and threw it against the shield, which hummed on impact. "To us?! You ran away! You weren't here when they took that out on the rest of us! When Quince led us, organized Kental and myself to help to end their stupid games, and when he died for that. After that...well...if we were going to play, we would play for keeps."

"That sounds...rational," Anders muttered sarcastically. I agreed — these were rantings, not explanations. Luckily, Jursica didn't seem to hear him, or considered him beneath her notice.

"Don't you get it, Paige? You can join us, we can bring this entire fake world to a halt, and—"

"Did you miss the part where I don't want the Ascension to crash into Earth or boil away into space? I'm pretty sure I was clear on that."

"So you side with Kental?" she asked.

"I don't side with either of you," I said. "I side with stopping the war. Right now, that means the lesser of two evils, regardless of what anyone else thinks my job is, what they expect — to hell with that, I just want to stop the whole stupid process." I shook my head sadly, seeing where this headed all too clearly. "Right now, that means stopping you. Come with us. Give up on this and I can promise you we will protect you."

"It's almost precious that you think I would agree to that," she said. "Or that I would let you leave here alive at all."

"Paige," Anders said, "time isn't on our side to keep this up."

I looked at him and thought about it. While we diddled about here, who knew what the Subtle

Knives were up to — for all I'd passed that off to Anders before, he was not wrong here. We needed to keep moving, to solve this, and get back. That didn't mean we should rush through stuff and put more lives at risk, but it also kind of did, which left me in a bad spot.

Plus, of course, Jursica was revealing herself to be off the deep end here. I could understand why — I sympathized, though telling her that would, of course, make everything worse. I'd originally agreed to back Kental simply to buy time while I worked out the right course in this war, but Jursica seemed to want to just destroy. If she had her way, it wouldn't matter what the Subtle Knives did back on Earth.

"I know," I told Anders.

Jursica laughed. "Running out of time? I promise, it won't be a problem much longer."

"Please," I asked her, "could you stop talking like some sort of volcano-base–owning lunatic?"

"Oh I'll stop talking," she said, standing and dusting herself off slowly. "Good-bye for real this time, Paige. Die well."

"Yeah, sure, Jurs, see you later." I watched her go and held a hand out to Anders to help him up. "This is going to get ugly, quick," I told him.

"What's the plan?" he asked, seeming to brush off the mortal danger. I couldn't be sure if that was due to a lack of understanding or an oversized amount of trust in my abilities, or even in his own. That sort of death-defying assurance would normally be a problem. Reality, even if we could bend it a bit here and there, still won out in the end, and knowing the stakes helped immensely.

But panic wouldn't help either. So be it.

"She's going to head back to her camp. We still need to get to her. So we go, and we get her. But she'll move faster than us, and ensure that everyone in the way is aimed directly at us. We're going to have to fight our way in this time. Nothing subtle or fancy about it, all right?"

"Tell me what I need to do," he said, before taking a deep breath.

"Get creative," I told him. "Look, you know how to move a lot of this stuff around. Past that it's simply finding the will — the personal fortitude to allow the creativity to guide you — and to know when to stop."

"Really?" he asked me. "That's…that's it? Once you can do any of this, any working with energy, you can do it all?"

"Sort of," I admitted. "No, of course it isn't quite that simple, but also it really and truly is."

"That makes even less sense, thanks," he said.

I shrank the shielding down from a big bubble to personal-umbrella sized. "Everything packed?" I asked.

Anders rolled up the sleeping mat and shoved it into one of the bags. He hoisted one on his shoulders and offered me the other. "Weapons," he said. I nodded.

"Can you see the shield still?" I asked. Securing the weapons bag on my back and smoothing out my jacket, I watched him flicker into being able to see this energy clearly. He nodded and I held out the new, much denser shield to him. "Good, take it. I'll be too busy to block anything."

"So I'll take the front," he asked, a bit of

nervousness in his tone.

"No, of course not, but you need to watch our rear. We have to get to Jursica's camp, and that'll be noisy for a while."

"Only a while?" he asked, moving his hand around and seeing how the shield followed perfectly.

"Trust me," I said, then started moving. We walked, following a path I could half-trace. Jursica, letting me know which way she went to send us directly into traps. It'd do for a while, until first contact. Which, of course, would come sooner than later.

As we walked, the fucked-up ground making too much noise, the dead forest continuing to make me angry, I wondered if Anders had been right. Obviously, he was and wasn't — the basic dual-problematic outcome still applied. Still, if I'd forced the issue earlier — and even now, to be fair — this could've been over faster, possibly.

What, after all, did I owe the Ascension? There stood my failing, in front of me. I tried too hard to give back, even in dumb resentful ways such as ending this war. Doubly so when the people I gave back to didn't deserve the work. Was that even a failing? I couldn't quite tell anymore.

I put out a callous air, partly as protection, of course, but honestly I didn't care as much as anyone might think. That, in and of itself, felt like what I was fighting against internally. I wanted to care more — I thought I should, in different ways — so I tried to prove, to myself, that I did. I pushed to show people that I would go to the end of the road for them, even when I didn't want to, and even when it worked against my purposes.

A lot of good got done, in the end, with that broken impetus, so I couldn't just toss everything out with the emotional bathwater, as it were.

No answer, no fully formed perfect resolution, came to me before the first attack hit.

I was walking in front, not caring about noise, knowing they were coming for us, knowing they'd been sent by Jursica in a rage. Happily lost in thought, I'll add, which might not have been the brightest move I'd ever made.

The ground exploded in front of me. I tried to spin a shield, but the debris hit me hard before I could fully react. I made sure to throw myself backward, to cover Anders, who screamed as I collided with him.

"Contact front," I said, dazed.

"You think?" he said, moving to hold the prepared shield up in front of us while I got to my feet.

The dirt and shards of trees whirled around and came together to form a golem, staring us down. That wouldn't do. I stood up and moved next to Anders, dusting my jacket off and resetting my bag on my back.

"Get behind the shield," Anders said, bracing himself for a wallop.

"Nope," I said, "no more hiding." I grabbed as much raw, dirty energy as I could, quickly, and clapped my hands together, letting them glow with aftereffect. I took that energy and let it spill out toward the golem, spinning the atoms of everything the energy touched as it did. A wind picked up, and as my working touched the mass of dirt lumbering at us, its very form started to spread out until a cloud of dust with the shape of a man threw a fist at us. The punch, from fist to arm, passed through us, the way a dust cloud will.

I shrugged and started to walk again. "They're not good at this," I said, raising my voice, "but they're starting to make me angry."

I considered waiting and seeing what their attack force looked like, but that would be my normal play. I still didn't want to kill anyone, but I needed to make it very clear that attacking us would be a bad idea. To that end, I continued to feed my cloud of separation, as I'd decided to call it, and let it grow and spin and eat away at the dead forest. Trees of whatever material got pulled down and their dust added to the cloud as I pumped more and more energy into the spin to keep it going. Separating material at an atomic level to reduce things to dust without using force took a lot of fuel.

Back on Earth I wouldn't even try it. But here, where the energy ran freely and the physics were easier to exploit, why not? They could stop it easily enough, if they knew how. I certainly knew how. I wondered how well Jursica trained her people. The initial cries of surprise told me she didn't really care, at least not this far out.

I let the cloud dissipate and nodded at Anders. "Now we can start walking again." We turned and walked back into the forest, since the wide-open path I'd cleared would still be a bit too easy. We didn't want to be spotted instantly — they had to work for it at least a little. It built character. Let them see the empty space and piece together who had done it. Let them worry.

Unslinging the bag from my back, I kept walking as I fished a box out of it. I handed the box to Anders while I got the bag back on. Reaching for it, I smiled at him. "I want to leave a surprise for them in case they try to take the clearing," I told him, then I opened the box and blew into it.

My impulse, my designs, imparted into the box — along with some energy and breath — and the thing primed itself for use. Then I closed it again and threw it into the clearing. The box landed and beeped once, loudly. Stupid design, really, but safety features will often go overboard.

"Is that a land mine?" Anders asked.

"Not really," I said, "but, well, a proximity alarm in the box will go off if they come anywhere close to it. And then the fun starts."

"Define fun," he said, glancing toward the clearing as we walked further from the edge of it.

"Ever been swarmed by a few hundred really angry flying bears the size of wasps?"

"Has anyone?" he asked.

"Not yet," I shrugged. "But they could still set the thing off, so who knows, really?"

We walked on.

CHAPTER SIXTEEN

ABOUT TEN MINUTES later we heard a growling buzz. Anders glanced back but I didn't bother. Instead, I kept us moving. We needed to keep going, and quick, so we could surprise Jursica. She wouldn't think her first wave, or even second, could take me out, but rather the combined weight of them.

About half an hour later, I felt the world ripple.

Kzzt.

My brain vibrated the way it will when you're about to fall asleep, or possibly just tipped over the edge ever-so slightly, and a noise startles you. That hindbrain shake. You can feel it in your spinal cord. I glanced back at Anders, who rubbed an arm with one hand absent-mindedly. Yeah. Not good.

Kzzt.

The world fizzed again. This time visually as well. A signal sliding in and out of tune with my eyes for less than a second. The sky sat pink now, the air heavy with a strange taste. I froze in my tracks and held a hand out to stop Anders.

Kzzt.

The now-purple sky grew darker by the second, but I didn't notice — I was too busy drowning. I tried gulping air, but my lungs simply filled the more I did. I spun around as I started to fall and saw Anders clutching his throat too. I clawed my way forward, kicking out toward Anders to get him to follow me if he could. Two feet, then five, then I sucked air in and rolled over on my back, hacking up what tasted like carbonated coffee.

I threw it up on the ground, and forced myself to sit up enough to reach back and grab Anders, dragging him forward enough to get his head out to safety. "We need to keep moving," I said weakly, when we'd both stopped coughing.

"What the shit is—" he asked.

"This is the war," I said, looking around. "Rewriting reality on the fly, in small columns, to kill, confuse, and otherwise get rid of the enemy. Those other folks were a stupid appetizer. This is the threat, which means we're close to the camp."

"How did we," he asked me as we started to move again, changing direction enough to never quite move in a straight line every ten or twenty feet, "bypass the front line and end up here? We never encountered actual fighting..."

"Later — I need to prepare a defense before they fold in on us again." I wove a few ideas and prepared some attacks. We kept walking, but I had to pay attention to my work, not the forest. I heard a small *ting* off to my side and saw Anders' arm, the shield having deflected something away from my head. "Shit, thanks," I said, trying to see what had even come out at us. Small stones, a storm of them.

We kept moving away from the storm, which didn't chase us at all.

"Paige, was it raining rocks?"

"Aftereffect," I said, "like what happened with the trees. You change reality in pockets the way they are back there, and nothing goes quite back to normal. It's why I try to not do it."

"How do we fight that?"

"We're not fighting it, that's the point. We fight the *people*, not the reality." Easier said than done, of course. We were nearer the camp than we should've been though, which helped. I'd have to explain to Anders, but the way they fought, the frontline itself would fold into a pocket dimension on and off, as reality couldn't take the strain. We'd walked over it without noticing some time ago — not sure exactly when. That wouldn't hold, but once he'd mentioned it, I started looking out for folds we might walk into by mistake and skirted us past two more.

The nice thing about them, really, was that if you side-stepped them, they would literally fold together some space around them. We benefitted, which felt dark to even say, considering the people inside them fighting and dying for bullshit.

Even with that bit of luck, we'd still have to get past the people warping reality in pockets around us. I had just the thing, I just didn't relish using it.

"Anders, I think we have one last push, so I want to make a lot of noise then sneak into the camp, OK? Get ready to move."

"How are we going to manage that?"

"Just trust me, and keep drawing energy into that shield. Get ready to expand it, too." I smiled at him and he nodded. "One other thing," I said.

"Yeah?" he asked, tensing.

"We're going to have to go right at the reality warping. Don't stop, just keep moving. Be prepared to hold your breath, or possibly walk with your eyes closed at times if need be. *Don't stop* unless I stop you, all right?"

"No other way?" he asked.

"Not if we want to get there and have a hope of getting back out," I told him truthfully.

He nodded again. I nodded back. Then I started to move. A brisk walk, my hands moving continually at my side, giving off trails of light. I felt the world sizzle around me and took a shallow breath to test the air. Breathable, but stale somehow. The light seemed fine. I didn't want to know what had changed here and didn't intend on sticking around to find out. We kept moving.

The same spine-creeping sensation and the air grew heavy, somehow literally. Damn it. We pushed forward, quicker, to get out of it and back into breathable country. As we did, I lifted my arms from my sides, my fingers still moving.

No speeches, no more chances, nothing.

This needed to end.

My arms raised higher.

My fingers twitched faster.

All around, the trees shattered.

I spun the debris, flattened it, polished it against itself. A cloud of razor-sharp spinning disks floated over our heads, moving with us.

The world shifted and the air felt caustic. The disks kept moving, some of them tarnishing quickly. I didn't like to think what our lungs looked like just then. We pressed on, barely making it, stumbling back over into another zone we could breathe in.

The air stunk of sulfur but still managed to be breathable. I used the blades to chip more material free and make even more blades for my cloud. I waited for the next shift to hit, focused hard on the feeling. It hit with a tingle, and I sent the blades flying in every direction. They hunted, each of them seeking out the source of the last few shifts. They would be drawn to the specific energy, hunting them down to rip through them.

Would they actually kill anyone? I didn't think so. Anyone good enough to warp the world like that should be able to defend themselves. Then again, if they didn't manage to and got cut to ribbons, the forest owed them one.

The blades whined and buzzed and cut through everything in their path as they sought out the folks behind the reality shifts. I just needed them to drop the shit for a few seconds, all of it, to feel our path clearly. With the folds, we were close, I knew, but also knew we could still fall in one if we weren't smart.

Anders's original suggestion would be our saving grace.

A few screams started and I focused down hard. "Grab my arm," I said to Anders, as we kept moving, "and get ready to FastWalk."

"I thought you said that was a *really* bad idea."

"I did," I agreed readily.

We moved together, as I listened to my evil little army do its job. I couldn't lose focus on them — they needed energy pumped into their system to keep moving and hunting. The hunting end of the work stood the hardest, and needed the most concentration.

"Anders," I said, losing my battle to split my focus. I didn't realize how well they would be able to hide themselves, even with the screams starting. "I need you to see the path. Feel the energy, let me know when the path is clear."

"Clear of what?" he asked, not looking at me.

"See how you can tell that reality is off, up ahead?" I asked as we passed into another zone, feeling the normal mild shock as we went blind. Light didn't work right here, even though we could see the area we were now in before we stepped into it. Damn it. "Like right now," I said, annoyed. "Keep going, but feel the energy up ahead. If I can distract or put down enough of these folks, the way forward should clear enough for us."

"Got it," he said, as we fizzed back into an area we could both see and breathe in, though it still wasn't quite *right*. Alongside the aftereffect problem, one of the dangers of this sort of warfare was utterly forgetting what normal reality felt like — and being so completely sure, even when you were back in it, that reality felt off you could go insane with time.

I narrowed down to putting one foot in front of the other and keeping the blades searching. I didn't let myself enjoy it, though. Not much. Not that I'd admit. The screams kept up, but not many and not often.

This had to work. If it didn't, and soon, I would run of stamina. Tons of energy around, but fighting through these disturbances wore on me. Anders, too — I noticed neither of us walked as fast as we had when we'd started pushing through.

It hadn't been weeks of fighting or anything, but not enough food and nearly no rest certainly didn't help. If this failed, I didn't think we would see the other side. And if we did fail, who knew what would happen with the Ascension, much less

Earth.

No, we had to make it. That was all there was to *that*. But it didn't feel like we would. I could feel myself start to lose the drive to push forward. I dug deep. I pushed. I heard Anders say "Now." I... wait, shit, that was a signal. Right.

I tapped my heels inside the WarBoots quick as I could manage and glanced at Anders. He looked as good as I felt. We took a step forward, together. I hoped I got this right. Should be a step and a half. The step went fine. The half — and I warned him quickly we would stop suddenly — ended in a sliding, ungraceful, dirt-throwing mess.

Luckily for us, a wall stopped our slide. We hit it hard, but at that point who cared? We were in the camp. The sneaking part remained questionable. Huddled up against the wall, I listened for anyone rushing to work out who had just appeared in the area, but no one did.

That's when my mind clicked over and I realized neither Jursica or Kental wore their WarBoots. Did they even have them? Assuming they did, why wouldn't they wear them to their own little Armageddon?

"Get up," I whispered, "someone heard that and we need to get moving before they come by."

"I don't hear anyone," Anders said. He stood with me, regardless.

"Me either, but right now, I don't trust either of us fully on that front."

He agreed non-verbally, the look on his face a mixture of shame and admittance of how out of it we both were. Too bad — we needed to keep pushing. Just a bit longer.

I spotted a large tent, thankfully not overly large, but it said 'Jursica' to me in large letters. The outside hung with the sort of frippery she thought leaders should hang, and so on. I pointed it out to Anders and he shrugged. We started to move.

Someone came out of, seemingly, nowhere as we did. "Hey—"

Anders' fist cut them off, and he grappled them to the ground. Well, maybe he just sort of fell on them, but it worked. I had a clear shot so I took it and kicked them in the head, hard enough to put them out.

Anders stood up and shrugged. I shrugged back. We ducked into the tent. Jursica looked up, honestly surprised. I checked her feet this time, curious. No WarBoots. None in sight, even. Stranger and stranger. No time for it just then, however.

"Jurs," I said, trying to sound coherent and calm, "you left before we could finish talking. Well, I say talking. I mean grabbing you and taking you back to the Queen."

"Well done, both of you," she said, acknowledging Anders for the first time as a person of interest. "But I don't think that you'll—"

"Anders," I said, cutting her off. "Remember what worked outside?"

He laughed. Jursica looked confused just long enough for me to punch her in the face. Her shock embedded itself in my mind for the rest of time. That image would keep me warm at night, I have to admit.

She stumbled, and before she could recover, Anders hit her. Oh how she hated that. A 'normal human' laying hands on one of the Neverchildren. Sheer scandal.

Whatever.

I kneed her in the face. She hit the ground hard and I rolled her onto her back, unconscious.

CHAPTER SEVENTEEN

WE HOISTED JURSICA between us, and listened for anything that sounded like someone intended to come running. "Anders, we'll have to FastWalk her back to the North Tower. There's no way to keep her tied up and harmless and get back through this mess."

"Can you take three people with you?" he asked.

Smart question. "Well," I started, "not easily," I finished, and looked around the room. "Look for her WarBoots. If she had them on, even unconscious, maybe I could link them and it would help."

We both looked, still awkwardly holding Jusrica's limp body, but didn't see anything. I didn't expect to. If she still had them, they would be on her damned feet. So I'd have to do this the hard way.

"We need to go," I told Anders. "Just hold tight to her and let's try to keep in sync."

He nodded, and took a deep breath.

We stepped forward, his leg matching the swing of my own.

The world shifted, violently. We just managed to bring our feet down at the same time, and started another step. FastWalking with another person could be tricky, but the WarBoots could compensate. Three people, more so if one was being carried, strained everything.

Added to that little problem — the energy not spreading evenly and forcing me to find ways to compensate, like a motocross rider going into a constant ninety-degree turn at three-hundred miles per hour — we needed to cross the battlefield.

Normally, no problem — FastWalking phases you out enough we wouldn't be in danger. Except a bunch of the front lines we'd passed had folded into their own side universes, on and off. Which meant we'd have to walk through them. Figuring out how big they were from feel couldn't be an option. Walking past them, without entering them, might be the default while normally walking around the forest, but FastWalking meant we weren't in phase with normal space *or* the folded spaces.

Wobbling, almost falling out and skidding to, if we were lucky, only decent injury, we tried to keep moving. I almost dropped Jurs, and then I felt Anders do the same a step later. I suppose our problems would be solved if we did drop her. But if I wanted Jursica dead I could've done that at any point along the way. No, the idea remained less violence, not more.

As I tried to judge how far we needed to go, we hit a snag. Literally, my foot snagged and we skidded to a halt, hard. Anders and I both dropped Jursica, which, sorry about that, and looked around.

All around us, the world erupted in color and light. Rocks with wings attacked clouds with teeth. Lightning and thunder went off in record amounts, bolts seeming to not only be choosing targets but also trying to strike each other out. The ground started to melt under my feet. "Get her!" I yelled to Anders as I struggled to get upright.

We gathered Jursica, quite awake now, and looked around for another second. "Jurs, we're FastWalkling out of here. We'll carry you. But if you struggle, *so help me*, I will leave you here. Bound. You'll die on your own battlefield, in a pocket reality that won't exist for much longer. So, going to cooperate?"

She nodded, glaring at me, and I considered adjusting her gag so she could speak but decided against it. She had nothing I wanted to hear anyway.

The ground started to suck us in, and Anders and I kept lifting out feet and shifting our stances, while lifting Jursica, so we wouldn't be stuck here. A rock got hit by lightning and the shards rained down, hot and sharp, on us.

We stepped forward. Hoping.

Another stumble as we crossed over into normal space again. Well, normal for the Ascension, but it'd do. It happened *as* we stepped, and I was expecting it, so we stayed upright enough to keep moving. A few more successful steps after that I *really* started to feel the burn. FastWalks under normal conditions could tire you out, but this low on sleep and food, and just the problems involved in this, and yet again I felt like I needed to push past my reserves to keep going. I didn't like the theme evolving. But we'd get there.

I stopped us and realized we'd overshot the North Tower by half a mile, but could at least see the thing, and were on the other side of the fighting. Getting back proved to be a relatively simple half step.

The guards that greeted us looked confused — by Jursica, I assumed.

"Could we get some help?" Anders asked them before I could say anything. I managed to stifle a laugh. The guards, still confused, called for assistance, and two more showed up to carry Jursica as we walked to the Chamber.

I appreciated that someone — well, obviously Mitlan — had prepared the guards for our return, even if no one knew when that might be. His faith wouldn't heal the wounds between us, but it went a ways toward opening the door to even start the process.

Mitlan himself met us outside the Chamber. He looked at Jursica. Then at Anders. Finally at me. "*This* was your solution?" he asked me.

"You wanted me to, what, kill her? I'm not your assassin, Mitlan, and I'm certainly not the Queen's."

"So you expect us to—"

"I expect you to get the Queen and let me hash this out with her," I said, turning away to look at the guards with us. "Follow Mitlan, he'll take you to somewhere she can hang out, safely."

"Paige—"

"No, Mitlan," I cut him off again, "nothing happens to her." I looked at Jursica, whose face betrayed nothing. She might've been accepting her fate as a prisoner, or assuming a double-cross and death, but wouldn't give anyone the satisfaction of showing either. "You lock her down — and nothing happens to her, no harm at all, or you'll have a much worse problem on your hands. I solved your war, I took one of the players off the board, when *no one here could*, it seems. So you'll play this my way or I'll keep bringing down people in charge. Get me?"

"I will alert the Queen, after I secure Jur—the prisoner," he said stiffly. Good, he needed to realize the actual threat in the room. Though no one but me did, yet. "You two stay here," he told me and Anders, and left. I knew other guards would be by in a second, and we had nowhere to go, anyway, so fine, we could hang out.

"Anders," I said softly, "I'm going to need your help."

"Of course," he said, matching my volume.

"You've gotten better at working with all of this madness, but all you've been doing, really, is playing with someone else's working. That only gets you so far. Real work — the stuff you want to learn, to help people — that requires your own personal touch."

"Is this the right time for school, Paige? We're waiting for—"

"This is the *only time we have*," I stressed. "The big thing I found when I was younger, to make this my own, to really find out what I felt most natural at—"

"Talking instead of actually doing big things?"

"Big things have big cost, Anders — you saw that in the forest. Work small and smart, and you can change the world without also killing it in the process. But that's only part of it. Make it *yours*. It's why I like to clap my hands before I start working on a big energy pull or shaping."

"And then you use part of it to make them glow because you like a nice show?" he asked, leaning against the wall. We tracked new guards heading toward us to watch the Chamber doors so we didn't slip inside.

"You're being snarky today," I laughed.

"Sorry, just worrying about time. We need to stop the Subtle Knives, and so far we've made no progress to help us there."

"We have, you just can't see it yet. But stay with me. Find your thing. And for the record, the hand glowing is just residual energy, and it's less work to let it happen then to dim it. But Anders, I think you might need to find that thing soon. No one here is expecting *you*, but they're all afraid of me. So if I throw the ball to you, you *need* to catch it, you got me?"

"I think so," he said. Unlike Jursica, Anders let his concern show, at least to me.

The new guards took up their position, staring at Anders until he moved away from the wall, and we passed the rest of the wait in silence, standing like good supplicants. A little while longer and the doors to the Chamber opened. Mitlan stood there, looking grim. Not a big change. He'd obviously briefed her already, as he nodded and led us toward the front of the room.

"So, Neverchild," the Queen began even as we stopped short of the throne, "you feel this ends the war and fulfills your promise?"

"Doesn't it?" I asked her. "Without Jursica leading them, her soldiers will lose all desire to keep fighting. Worse yet, they fear that I have entered the field on Kental's side."

She raised an eyebrow at that, literally. "Are you *not* on his side in this?"

"We both know better," I said simply.

"Fair enough, I suppose, as these things go. But why will they not hold her a martyr and push harder against Kental and his forces, or worse still, *my* people?"

"Aren't your people also Kental's?" I asked. "Isn't that the point of this? He wins and you step down?" I smiled at her. None of us truly believed, not an ounce, that she would ever keep her bargain. Kental certainly wouldn't. Which made me wonder why he even fought this stupid war. Unlike Jursica, he didn't seem to want to burn everything down. Maybe he just wanted to take her out of the picture so he could eventually take power, *someday*, but there would at least *be* an Ascension to take control of. I wanted to think that of him.

"Yes, yes of course," she lied smoothly. That's the thing about being in fairly secure power — people will let you lie to their face and sell you back your own bullshit just to keep things running. If I'd doubted why I left, this conversation reminded me, starkly.

"Well then, they won't treat her as a martyr simply because with Kental rising to the throne — or at least, until the transfer of power, which I understand might take a while—" I smirked as I said it, and was rewarded with the barest hint of a sneer from the Queen, "your power, his army, all combined — they'd have no chance. With Jursica there to whip them up, they might have continued to push, stupidly, but without her around to lend them her strength—"

"And how did you stop her, then?" she asked.

"We hit her until she fell down," I said, shrugging. "Turns out, Jursica is great at a lot of things, and powerful, but she always did underestimate the simple ways to get things done. Regardless, mighty Queen Leoras, our deal is complete and per its terms I ask for our reward. Assistance with the problem I face on Earth."

"Oh, no, Neverchild, I can't have you run free any more than I could release Jursica. You will stay here with us, until you learn to be a loyal, and true, subject." She smiled when she said it.

Then again, so did I. Bitch. As if I hadn't seen this coming. I bowed to her, slowly, and clapped my hands as I straightened, letting the glow shine brighter than normal. "If that's your call, oh high and mighty one," I said.

The guards started to move in. They'd prepared for me. Of course. Everyone in the Chamber knew how this would play out. Well, they were certain, given the shit information they possessed, how this would go.

"Anders," I said, "now."

He held both hands up, bent at the elbow to shoulder height, and snapped his fingers. Both hands, simultaneously.

His hands started to glow.

Everyone except me and him froze. Anders didn't look at me, good, he looked at the Queen. "Queen Leoras," he said, "we had a deal." He didn't sound angry, or tired. Just level.

No one took it well.

The guards, both behind the throne and near

the doors, started to move. Mitlan himself started to reach for Anders. The Queen simply glared, waiting to see who would bring her a fresh head. I just waited to see how Anders would handle it all. Sure, I stood ready to jump in, but he needed to try this out, first.

Anders moved his hands slowly, fingers twitching. A shield formed, not around us, but around the throne. Oh, smart.

"No one wants anyone to be hurt," he said. "But I'm pretty sure, Majesty, you need air."

I smiled and turned to watch Anders' back. "Hey, Queenie," I said over my shoulder, "we had a deal, like he said. So how about we hold to it and no one has to do anything you'd regret?"

I nudged Anders and whispered to him. "What else you got?"

"Just let me know when we're leaving," he whispered back.

Fine, let him keep his secrets — I would've done the same. No need to risk being overheard.

"Neverchild," the Queen said, "we both know this shield would never stop me, and my guards could—"

"Now," I said, before she could finish.

"Eyes," he said back. I shielded my face just as Anders exploded the shield into a blinding light show. I tapped his shoulder and started to run back toward the main doors. He followed, keeping a hand lightly on my shoulder.

We burst through the doors, and even as we did, I felt tendrils of energy snaking for us. "What now?" he asked as we hit the hallway.

"We get out of this place," I said, heading down

for an exit. We passed guards, and I stopped long enough to tell them someone was attacking the Queen and they needed to go help. Thankfully they'd seen us come in with Mitlan and hadn't yet heard anything else. That scam would hold maybe a few seconds.

CHAPTER EIGHTEEN

Pretty soon we'd be hunted down, total enemies of the Ascension. Familiar ground, for me, sure, but we still needed to get out. "So this whole thing was a waste of time?" Anders asked as we left, bursting out into open air but not stopping.

"How do you figure?" I asked him, pointing down a small road. We made off in that direction.

"We came here to get help. We got nothing, just wasted time."

"Oh Anders," I said, "we still have all the weapons in the bag at my back. And that's how we'll get out. Stop up here." I pointed to a small alcove set into the side of a building. "We can't use the same path back. That's just too hard a walk. But we can make them think we took it."

I gathered a bunch of energy. "Match me on this, feel what I'm doing." He nodded, and with his help I opened the tear to the walkway between Earth and the Ascension.

"They'll feel this breach open and assume we were exactly this dumb," I said, and threw my bag of weapons into the fold. It vanished and I closed the breach, smiling at Anders.

"Don't we need those weapons?" he asked.

"Yup," I agreed.

"And wasn't that our way home?"

"Nope," I said, and pointed, "we need to go that way. Look, they'll sense the breach and assume we used it again. They won't follow — they know how bad we had it getting here. They'll let us roast, probably check in a few hours, maybe a day at most. By then we'll be back on Earth and will be waiting."

"Waiting for what?"

"We get back, open the breach. They'll have to turn off the protection, for themselves. Then we can make the bag come to us. Simple." We made our way into a haberdashery. I nodded at the shopkeeper and tried on a few ugly hats.

"Won't they still come through for us?" he asked, shaking his head at me when I tried to stick a hat on his head.

"Probably not," I said.

"Probably?" he asked. The shopkeeper looked at us. We didn't want to make a scene, so I led us back out of the shop. Wrong place, anyway.

"They didn't last time," I told him, "and I assume it'll be the same this time, except they'll make it even harder to get back — not that I intend to."

"But, wait, Paige, how can you even time that, to get to the breach hall at the same time they do? This plan, it's—"

"Hey, relax, Anders. I got this. I really do. Now which store was it? They've half-changed, I swear." I looked up and down the block, knowing we didn't have that much time before someone recognized me, some guard off duty, or hunting around just in case, and so on. But I couldn't find the right store.

I knew the door couldn't have vanished, or been destroyed. Covered up, plastered over, bricked in, sure. I had to hope it hadn't been.

"What are you doing?" Anders asked as I

stood in the street and spun in a slow circle with my eyes closed.

"Trying to remember where I left a door."

"A door?"

I stopped and opened my eyes, then turned a bit more to face Anders. "Our escape route back to Earth. There's a door — not many people know about it, to the point the Queen wouldn't even begin to think I would know about it — that'll get us back to Earth."

"Wait, what?" he said, frustration in his voice. "Why didn't we come here that way then? Is it worse than walking through fire? Because, Paige, maybe we should take the hallway then, right?"

"It's painless, but Anders, seriously now, this is a secret big enough I *really* don't want anyone knowing I have it. Nester and I found it once when we were *much* younger. Never told the others. Never told anyone. Shit, we almost didn't make it back. The Walker didn't like that we had a door she'd never known about."

"Walker?"

I sighed. How to explain without taking up time? "Anders, there's a city on Earth, Mur. The first city humans ever started up. But it was cut free from time and space, back when you guys were all new. There are only seven ways into the city, and normally, on Earth, random chance more than anything determines if you open a door and end up there. But—"

"Paige," he said slowly, drawing my name out as his brain worked through what he was hearing, "what are you even on about?"

"Can we find the door, *please*?" I asked,

knowing he couldn't help. "We need to find it fast. It's used, very rarely, but it must still be used — the Queen wouldn't cut off a secret door, not to Mur. Still, yeah, Mur is protected — it's got a person, tied to it, known as the Walker, not a fan of there being a secret way in and out of the city. I think the Queen herself opened it, made it a stable point here. Which should be close to impossible, given Mur doesn't stop moving, even for a picosecond, in space and time. But then again, this whole place should be impossible to keep up. The power they use to ensure it, when things are stable, is immense. I guess one more stupid thing is fitting."

I walked us around, poking my head into various stores. Dumb move — by now anyone who did try and track us would hear about this, and tell the Queen, who would then know for total certainty that the door was a known object. She'd probably move it, which would suck — I couldn't guess how to find it a third time since I couldn't find it for a second time now without it theoretically having been moved.

I closed my eyes again, stopping near the side of a building. A shoe store, I think. And I tried to remember my steps, that night with Nester. We were running from Kental — and Mitlan, really, who thought we needed a firmer hand yet to learn to behave. We found the door in the back of a clothing shop — not guarded, but the person who owned the shop obviously worked for the Queen. He had that air about him, an asshole used to being in charge of more than a shop.

We snuck around the store, just enjoying the freedom, not planning anything, ended up in the back room of the shop, and found a door placed against a wall that we saw on our way into the back room couldn't have led anywhere.

That's the sort of door you open. At least if you were us. I'd like to think more people would have, but knowing the Ascension, they would claim to but never risk it. Not really. Of course the door stood locked, secured and all of that, but we were good at what we did and opened it, stepping through. We found ourselves in Mur. Imagine a city built from ideas and scraps of technology from every point in human history, and every culture and design sense. That was Mur. It was a wonderful, maddening place. We loved it. It was like what we'd been told about Earth, in terms of laws of physics and all.

We ran into the Walker, a nice enough old woman who, somehow, knew we weren't from anywhere she could pin down. We did *not* belong, as far as she was concerned, but she still wanted to help us. So long as that help ended with us leaving. We told her about the Ascension and the door but refused to show it to her.

In return she told us about herself, a little bit. Enough that we could call her the Walker and sort of understand what it meant. She helped protect the city, to keep it a stable and working impossible metropolis. She was impossibly old, even by Ascension standards, but didn't seem to do any energy workings, though she didn't seem surprised by the concept — only that two kids were doing it.

We held to our part of the bargain and left not long after that. She tried to convince us that the gates out of Mur, the seven she knew about, would dump us randomly somewhere and somewhen, but we told her we'd take the risk and snuck back to *our* door.

After that, I ran into a Knocker once on Earth. They were the people in Mur who could control where the gates dropped you, and get you back to the city as well. The Walker'd told us about them, in brief, so when I heard someone mention needing to get back the Knocker they'd hired, I followed and put on enough of an act to be allowed to pay to come along.

That time I stayed smart and didn't do any workings, just hid out in the city for a while. After a week of that, I realized it wasn't a place for me, long term — no tears ever happened there, so I found that same Knocker and paid to go back to where I'd left from. I never told Nester about that, just that I 'd needed a small week off. He shrugged, and I wondered for a while if he'd known. No way to find out now.

But that first night, when we found the door. The place had been…right! I smiled at Anders and started walking. I let memory guide my footsteps and we landed right in front of a run-down old curiosity shop. The kind of place that sold supposed antiques. Celebrating the past by selling you probable knock-offs of what you think it might have looked like.

We went in and I remembered what the place had used to look like. The shopkeeper wasn't the same guy, but the woman behind the counter certainly also worked as a guard: the squint, the line of her jaw, all of it echoed too strongly. That and the fact she'd left part of her guard outfit in view on the floor near her, badly stuffed into a duffel. It's the little things.

I nodded at her and picked up various things to show Anders. "See this?" I asked him, shoving an elephant statue toward him. "Never been elephants here, not sure why people think they're part of the history of this place. But what can you do?" He shook his head at me and started to say something, but I added, in a whisper, "this is the place. Just go with it and pretend to care about this stuff for a minute."

I kept picking up things and pushing them toward him, and he started to mmm and ahh in return. We worked toward the back of the store and lingered just enough that the shopkeeper started to ignore us. The door stood locked, of course, and I could feel the energy around it that would tie to the counter.

That could be forced, easily enough, even looped into a small feedback state so no alarm would go off for a few minutes. But once we hit the back room, a clock would start. The shopkeeper would notice we'd vanished and come looking. Then, entering the back room, would obviously notice the door to Mur unlocked as well — I assumed bigger and angrier locks on that.

But the idea still stood as sneaking out, making everyone think we'd left via breach. So how to get both done? I nudged Anders and we left the store, after I slipped something out of my bag and dropped it in a corner.

"I thought the door was back there," he said when we were outside.

I explained the problem and he sighed a bit, but nodded. Then I explained my solution. We went across the street and got a table at a small café, waiting. We tried to sit so we had a view of the target, but still weren't easily visible ourselves from the street. After about twenty minutes, a couple wandered into the store and I set down the coffee I'd been drinking. Working a tiny bit of energy, I made the small box I'd dropped in the corner of the store go off, making sure to entangle it with the energy of the couple who'd entered. That small an energy use no one would notice, not here.

They'd be too busy dealing with the fire. The smoke started billowing out of the store quickly and I started counting when the couple ran outside. The shopkeeper caught up with them, telling them to wait. Perfect, she'd thought they'd set off the mess.

People showed up to fight the fire, and that's when Anders and I got up and walked around the block. We stood behind the store, flames and smoke filling the air around it. "Why do you keep insisting I go into fire, Paige?" he asked.

"Twice, this is just twice, give me a break, Anders," I said. The box I'd left behind to start the fire would consume itself so it couldn't be easily detected, that would be the whole point of it. Sneaky, terrible device, really. But that would buy us time. They'd be untangling this little mystery for a few days longer than I felt sure we'd need. Now we just needed to get in and through the door to Mur.

"Anders, I need you to break down this wall.

Your signature won't be known, and I can layer mine over it to confuse people, and help you, but I need you to do the heavy lifting."

He looked at me, then at the wall. He snapped his fingers and let his hands glow. I didn't want to tell him how much I loved that, watching him find his own space with which to work. I didn't give him any advice or hints on how to get through the wall. He just tried a few things, most of them useless, and then he decided to attack the mortar between the bricks. I blinked. I would've set the brickwork to weaken, eaten at it, but he ignored the bricks themselves. His weakening started to work, and I joined in to help and speed the process up.

"Don't push it in," I told him, "we want this to look like the fire did it, the bricks need to fall out."

We moved some energy around and I egged the fire on a bit from outside, letting it lick along the wall we were working on until it actually did collapse part of the wall directly at us. We had to dodge a bit of a backdraft, which, my fault, oops. Still, the wall no longer presented a problem. And basic fire I could hold back with a well-constructed shield. I'd started to feel the lack of sleep and food again, but I could hold this long enough. We got inside and moved quickly — even a shield won't keep the heat off fully.

The door to Mur stood against a wall, the fire not touching it. The locks on the thing were *that* good. I was still better. The trick would be to open the door, get through, and collapse the door on our way. The Queen could fix it — the doorway would hold, just the wall it was attached to would fall down. That would be enough to make sense out of why the door'd been open when everything fell.

Sense enough, at least, for a little while.

I broke the locks, not having to worry about anyone finding out. Of course they would know the door fell open when the wall collapsed. We looked out into a dark space, and I waved for Anders to go through. "Just step through and hold on."

He did so, and I started to step through, but not before I egged the fire on a bit and tore at the wall around the door, making it fall even as I stepped fully through.

We stood in a small, dark, closet with a now-closed door behind us as well as in front of us. The door behind us opened to just wall, and would, I assumed, until someone fixed the Ascension end. I opened the door in front of us instead, and we stepped out into an alley. Exactly as I remembered it. A small closet off an alley, because it made as little sense as one might like in this situation.

Regardless, we were here: Mur.

CHAPTER NINETEEN

WE STEPPED OUT into the street and almost immediately bumped into a couple of people. His hair seemed to be on a mission to do its own thing, and she carried some kind of instrument in a case with her. They seemed too drunk to care about us. I was tired, and hungry, and stressed, honestly, about making this all work.

"Could you not?" I asked the guy, wishing they'd been a little less drunk and a bit more attentive, regardless of the time of night. Because it was night, here. Not that I understood how their access to a sun worked.

"Lady," he said, "you hit me." He shrugged as he said it and I knew the only answer would be to keep walking.

"Sorry," Anders told them both, "we're on business here." I managed to keep a straight face, for the moment.

"Oh, well, then in that case," the woman said and waved her arm to let us keep walking, "don't let us keep you from your important, ascot-related business."

I smoothed my suit and rolled my eyes, refusing to give in and start a useless fight with two drunks. I glanced at Anders and just started walking, quickly.

We crossed the street, and Anders got a good look at the town. "The streets seem…off."

"Yeah it's a strange maze-grid idea. I have no

clue why anyone thought *that* would be a good idea. Probably those two back there. They must love it."

"You're just mad they don't enjoy your fashion sense," he said.

"That's where you'd be wrong, Anders. Couldn't care less, just not a fan of drunk people in general. But then again, I didn't bust out a 'we're on business,' either. So what do I know?"

"I just wanted them to move," he said. We both laughed.

"All right, we need to find a Knocker — I'll explain, but we need to do it fast. Well. Fast enough. I'll get information and we can wait for them while we eat."

"Do we have time?" he asked as I led us into a random nearby diner.

I opened the door, and the smell of food hit me like an otter shot by a rail-gun. "Do we have time to *not* eat? Anders, all of this — energy work, just breathing — it takes fuel. We've been spending and not recovering. We need to stop for a few, eat, rest, and just breathe. We're going to need to wait for a Knocker either way, so might as well get something out of it."

I sat at a table and handed Anders a menu as he joined me. "You also like diners," he said, flipping through the menu.

"Doesn't everyone?" I asked. "Either way, eat."

"Is our money even going to be good here?" he asked, and I stopped, trying to remember how this worked. Fuck, right, I needed to find a way to exchange what I had for something worthwhile here in Mur. I flagged down a waitress and asked, showing her the bills Anders and I collectively could account for. She shrugged and said if we were willing to trust her she'd take the cash we had, substitute some of her own money, and take care of it for us.

An old scam, I felt positive, but one I didn't have enough time to bother circumventing. I agreed, even as Anders gave me a look. Yeah, her idea took the unwary, new, and hungry for a bit of profit — but right this second, could we be bothered to care? In the scheme of things, did losing a few extra dollars matter? It did not. Besides, as I pointed out to Anders in a hushed tone, a bit of grift makes any city work smoother.

We ordered and I followed the waitress toward the kitchen, handing her more money to let me use the phone. They kept a directory nearby, in the back, and I looked up Knockers. Given that Mur didn't have too high an atmosphere, as near as anyone could tell there were no planes, and certainly no wireless cell towers. So the city happily ran off landlines, which, when you consider how much of human history happened before them, meant that for many people living in town they were magical advanced technology.

That taken care of, I got back to the table and waited for some food. Just being able to sit, in peace, was a gift right then. We ate in silence, and I think both of us worked hard to be polite and not just shovel food in our faces like maniacs. Proving we were fit to be out in public, we finished our meal and paid the bill, moving to stand around outside and wait for the Knocker.

"So let me get this right," Anders said as we

leaned against a wall, waiting, "we can leave here to any place and time on Earth?"

"That's the way it works, yeah," I told him.

"So why not go back to before the Subtle Knives even attacked us, and—"

"Changing events is not a thing we should even consider," I said quickly. "Honestly I don't even want to go back to right after we left. We were in the Ascension for a few days, so we should go back a few days after we left."

"But we could show up and help Shealano," he insisted.

"We could, but we'd also be showing back up at a time we were technically around for, even if we were in a pocket dimension." I wanted to agree with him, but I couldn't. "Mur exists, sort of, outside of time for practical purposes. But the Ascension doesn't."

"So what?" he asked. "We weren't on Earth, technically, right? We were in a pocket dimension, so we should be fine. We can't run into ourselves — we know we weren't back on Earth then."

"Hey, buddy," a voice said, "I dunno about pocket dimensions or whatever, but I'm also not sure loops are smart." We both looked over to see a rail-thin guy, dressed in a perfectly nice suit jacket and slacks over a t-shirt. I liked him already. "I assume you guys are waiting for me?"

I held out a hand. "Lloyd?"

"Yeah, Paige, right?" We shook and he held his hand out to Anders.

"Right. This is Anders." They shook. "So you agree, then? Going back to a time we were in," I asked Lloyd, "even if we were provably not in the same location is not the best idea?"

"I gotta tell you, I'm not sure," Lloyd admitted. "And I'm sure that I've gone back to the same times, if not the same places, right? But only for a little bit. I don't know any time travel experts. You'd have to find one to ask."

"Paige," Anders said, "you loop causality whenever you feel the need, but this is a bridge too far? It could save Shealano."

"It's obvious you two need a bit of time. I'll wait over by the corner. Come get me." Lloyd walked away and I sighed at Anders.

"We're burning more time now, Anders. And yeah, sometimes I take risks other people would call dumb. Like a possum building a rocket, I admit. But this one, it's messing with time itself. I don't like it. We knew we'd be coming back a few days after we left, right up until—"

"Right up until you told me we might not have to," he said.

"Sure, and given that no one, not even the guy helping us, knows if it'll work — when I loop causality, I know what I'm doing. But I don't want to try this, not when we're not even sure what the Subtle Knives are up to."

Anders looked frustrated but nodded, managing to work in a petulant shrug to go with it. It'd have to do. We walked over to Lloyd, grabbed a cab, and made our winding way through the city to one of the gates. Lloyd paid for the cab, part of his fee, I assumed, and asked us exactly where and when we needed to go. I gave him Shealano's address — he could get us close, at least — and a date a few days after we'd left. He nodded and did

the thing he got paid to do, opening the gate for us.
We stepped through, back to Earth.

CHAPTER TWENTY

Back in Queens, we hurried the few blocks to Shea's place. I wasn't sure what to expect and didn't want to ask Anders, knowing how he currently felt about my choice regarding time. The building came into view, crisscrossed with yellow caution tape, burnt and half collapsed. Even if we wanted to sneak in, the place seemed ready to fall on the head of anyone willing to duck inside the mostly collapsed doorway. Not that you'd need to use the door — holes in the walls opened the place up to the street nicely.

Well shit. "Don't say it," I told Anders as we approached the wreckage.

"Can you find her?" he asked, skipping right over recriminations. Nice of him — I'd have them all by myself. What if Anders was right and we could've come back earlier? Would it have made a difference? Would it have been safe?

I pushed it all down and reached out to try and find Shealano. I got...nothing. I felt around for energy in general and got what felt like background radiation levels, not anything close to what New York felt like on a normal day.

"Anders, you try," I said, inching close to the debris. Maybe I'd simply gotten too used to the Ascension, and how easy working with energy was over there, that I'd forgotten the feel of Earth. I'd love for that to be the case, but in my gut I knew that was bullshit. Still, worth exploring. Much like the remains of Shea's place.

I eased my way under the warnings and into the space, where — yeah, this place seriously exploded from within. By now any bodies would've been moved out, so there was no point in looking for them. I checked for anything Shealano might've left behind that could be useful. Grim? Sure. But necessary. Nothing caught my eye — nothing intact, at least.

"I'm not sensing anything," Anders said, joining me. "So did she blow the place up, or did the Subtle Knives?" he asked, nudging some charred lump with his toe.

"Normally I could tell you," I said, "but right now I'm getting nothing, either. And that bothers me. Anders, even if there were low amounts of energy in use — almost no breaches, whatever — this place should still radiate. It's only been a few days. Think of it like a battery — the energy used in that fight would've charged the area up, like the excess bleed in that damn dead forest, though less destructive. That doesn't dissipate in hours, or days. We're talking weeks, minimum. And yet neither of us can...hold on." I carefully picked my way back out and stood on the street. "Do you hear that?"

Anders joined me after a few seconds and stood and listened. "Normal city noise," he said.

"Is it?" I asked. "Listen closer. I hear cars, I hear people moving, horns, busses, electrical hum, a plane or two overhead."

"Sure, normal city noise, like I said," he replied.

"But I don't hear any music," I said.

"I...hey," he said, "yeah, all right, that's odd —

but not unreasonable, is it?"

I started walking down the block, listening. "It really is — when was the last time you were in a city and heard no music, not from a passing car, or an open store, or anywhere? No one in the area happens to have an open window while they blast sad music over a break-up? No one?"

"So what are you saying, someone stole music? Is that possible?" Anders opened the door of a bodega for a second and listened. "All right, nothing from there, either, and that *is* odd."

"Exactly. We need to work out what's going on here. I'm not sure this is all linked—"

"You think the lack of music and the dulling of energy is linked?" he asked.

"I'm saying," I told him, "I'm not sure. Fuck, I'm not sure which would be better, even, not yet. But either way we need to work out what's going on." I headed toward an old motel I hoped was still open.

"Shouldn't we focus on finding Shealano, and the Subtle Knives, first?" Anders asked.

"If we did find them, Anders, what could we do this second? Until there's a way for us to sense energy, I don't know if we can find her, and if we ran into the Subtle Knives — sure, we can punch them a whole lot I suppose, if we're lucky, but punching isn't my thing, generally."

"So without your other skills, you're giving up?" he said as we reached the motel, to find it had closed and reopened as a supermarket. I shook my head at Anders and ducked inside to ask if anyone there knew of a place to get a room. Answer in hand, I rejoined Anders on the street and scowled.

"First of all, I'm not giving up, I'm attacking the problems in the only order that makes any damned sense. And secondly, if I don't get a good night's sleep sometime soon I will eat your leg in protest."

"My...leg...what?" he asked, shaking his head but following me down the block.

It took us another fifteen minutes of walking, and sniping at each other here and there, to find the motel suggested to me. We checked in, got to our room, and I fell down on the bed, only just remembering to remove my jacket and cravat first.

"There's a good chance this energy lack is just us both being too tired to do anything meaningful except by cranky," I said. "So get some sleep, and we'll see about all of this in the morning."

"Paige, it is morning," Anders said. I heard him settle into his bed.

"Then we'll see about this tonight, stupid Ascension time sync — no wait, worse, stupid Mur time sync. Both of them. Stupid," I said, and promptly let go of consciousness to try the other side of life for a change.

I woke up, having no idea of the time, and promptly, if sleepily, checked for any energy surrounding us — any breaches and so on. Nothing but the background radiation feeling from before.

Anders still slept, and I intended to let him, but I turned the clock radio on softly, scanning stations. News, sports, sports, talk radio, news, sports, news, news, weather, talk radio, and nothing else worth mentioning. No music, nowhere on the dial I could find, AM or FM. This was starting to feel creepy.

I decided to fill the void and hum a song, one I learned back in the Ascension as a child. I knew how it went like the back of my hand. The first note was...and my mind skipped over it and I couldn't think of it. All right, I was getting old. But that stupid ad jingle I'd heard far too many times in shitty hotel rooms across the country, that one for those ribs, that would be easy enough.

Nothing came to mind.

No music. No notes.

Nothing.

I woke Anders, quickly, by kicking his bed until he startled awake.

"Quick," I said, before he had time to fully regain consciousness, "hum me your favorite song."

"Wha—?"

"Just do it," I said, feeling that prickly feeling along my skin, the sort of thing you feel right before an animal closes its teeth around your throat.

He slumped back against a pillow and opened his mouth. The look of confusion on his face told me everything I needed to know. The music wasn't there for him. Just silence where the sound should've been.

"I can't...wait, no, all right, how about this one?" he muttered. No change. That made him sit up, all right. He looked alert, and confused. I matched the alertness, but my confusion had turned to full-on worry.

"How do you steal music?" I asked, and started to pace around the room. "We need to go work on this," I told Anders. "I'll grab the first shower."

We hurried our way out, dressed and refreshed. Walking the streets did no good. I couldn't sense anything, on any level. I knew my WarBoots still had a store of energy but didn't want to use it, for fear of it being the last I could work. But without using it...

"Set the bag down," I told Anders. We'd collapsed both bags down to one, and were taking turns lugging it around. I rummaged and took out a few odds and ends, all of them devices that used their own stored energy in stasis to produce wildly different weaponized effects.

"If we can get the stored energy out of these, safely, we can use it to search for a cause." Anders knelt down on the street to help. Luckily we were in Queens, and no one is going to really stop you when you sit on the sidewalk and fuss about with electronic-looking devices. So long as you don't seem to be building a bomb. In general.

All right, we got a few stares, and forty-three cents tossed at us, but otherwise the work went quickly enough. I unspooled the energy and Anders caught it, keeping it moving around his hands. As soon as we had it, the stuff started to dissipate, which, I admit, freaked me out some.

That's just not how the energy works. But that was, in effect, the problem. "The music and the energy problem are tied," I said, "they simply have to be. I'm just not sure how yet. But at least I can use this little bit we have to try and find out, and enough left to maybe hunt down the Subtle Knives."

Anders spun me the energy, though the stuff was still losing coherency, and I wove it as quickly as I could, tapping into it to try and sense where it was bleeding to while it seeped away. I got an answer that unsettled me to my core.

The rules of the world were different. The very nature of energy and how the world worked were changed. We were on Earth, not another pocket dimension, not some other place entirely, but the universe no long functioned the way it had when we'd left.

I had utterly no idea of how anyone could pull that trick off. Small problem, there — if I couldn't figure out how, then I couldn't work out what I needed to do to put it back. I shook it off and used the last of the energy to try and trace the Subtle Knives. They wouldn't give off energy, not now, but working in what felt like close to a vacuum actually made hunting someone easier.

A decent enough location sprang back to me: Boston. Good enough. I felt sure we could get a closer read when we absolutely needed to. But for now, it would more than do. I told Anders only about the Subtle Knives, at first, and he assumed we were going to FastWalk there. That brought up the other problem.

Calling it a problem feels like the undersell of the century, but whatever. The point remained we needed to get to Boston and work out what had happened. Though, seeing a cop, I already knew.

"They won," I said, as we started to walk to a train station.

"What makes you so sure?" Anders asked me.

I shifted my glance back to the cop and raised an eyebrow at Anders, daring him to look, too. He did. Then he cursed a lot, very softly.

"Pretty much," I agreed. The cop's uniform said, fairly small, 'Subtle Knives of the Eternal Blossom' around the normal NYPD logo on the shoulder. "Though it confirms my other thoughts. All of this is their work."

"So that time we spent—"

"Anders, please, right now don't go into telling me why we should've done things different. I stand by my choices — they were made with all the information I had, and really, even knowing this now, I think avoiding the risk of messing up time still made for the right call."

"I wasn't going to," he insisted. "I just meant, they did that in that small a time? How?"

"I wish I knew. But we should avoid officials for now. For all we know, they're looking for us. I'd kind of bet on it." We waited for a train on a platform in much better repair than many I was used to. We switched trains a few times along our route, and all of them, every single car and station we saw, were all deathly well-kept. It started to make me think.

The world seemed so much more peaceful. I watched normal folks on the train, and they all just rode in silence, calmly. Though I did notice that no one read a book. Of course no one listened to music, but books, too?

"They're not zombies," Anders said softly to me, "but they don't seem to be doing anything, either."

"No, they are doing things," I corrected him, "they're just not doing anything fun. I mean, at all. But on the other hand, look how calm and relaxed everything is. Could you imagine the subway like this? Ever?"

"No," he said, "and look at the newsstands."

I've always been convinced that newsstands in the depths of the New York subway system were their own special species. Crammed tight with the requisite newspapers, but also magazines, some novels, candy, phone cards, small toys, a few cold drinks, all existing in a tiny space — they could've been pocket dimensions themselves. Impressive really.

Except the ones we passed now were streamlined. No magazines, sure. A few papers, but none of them printing color pictures, much less pictures of any kind on the front. They still had snacks, of a sort, but each was simply labeled something like 'Sweet Snack' or 'Salty Snack', with basic gray packaging. Drinks were much the same.

I grabbed a paper, flipping through it while we took our last train. News and nothing else. No opinion columns, or reviews, no movie listings or comics, just the facts. Or at least, what the paper had determined to be facts. A lot of weather stuff and some sports, though none of it sensationalist in the least. My sense of what was going on grew but I kept it to myself until I had more data.

I didn't say anything until we stood in Port Authority, buying bus tickets to Boston. There had always been a familiar grime to the Port Authority bus terminal. A grounding in humanity, it was weathered and soiled in ways that could be fairly disgusting to some, but always made me feel like humanity was going to be all right, so long as we still had places along those lines.

The place almost gleamed. The floors shone,

the walls were spotless, and everyone walking through the station seemed calm and relaxed. No one rushed, no one yelled or stood slapping themselves.

"I don't know how they did it, but I know what they did," I told Anders as we found our bus. Only six other passengers occupied the bus, we'd gotten there just before the driver closed the door to pull away. We sat in the back, away from anyone, and I felt the familiar lurching as the bus started. I did notice it was an electric engine, fully, which felt new as well.

"They took over," Anders said.

"Yeah, they took over — at some point in the past, it seems. However they did it, they made themselves win, possibly since forever ago, but they did it by removing all creativity. No music — no books, either. No movie listings in the paper. They wiped it out."

"All right," he asked, "but why? Would doing that *really* let you control people? I'm assuming they did it as a way to keep control — otherwise, why?"

"If people have no reference point to rebel, no way to create art, even — come on, when we tried to hum songs we still *know*, we couldn't, right? They didn't just remove creative things, they made it so that they couldn't exist. And that would explain the energy problem as well."

"Energy is energy, even if you're not being creative with it," he insisted.

"Shows what you know," I said, smiling. "No, fine, yes, most energy works like that — light, sound, all of that good stuff. But the energy we use, that we work with and shape? That's all creativity bottled by the universe. Remove creativity, however you could do it, and you would probably, and look around, remove that energy access as well."

"Well, we'll undo it," Anders said, and looked out the window.

Lacking a window seat myself, I took to looking around the bus. The other passengers each sat, silent and looking conformable and relaxed. I shifted in my seat and turned to look out a window across the aisle. Everything seemed so normal outside. But of course it would. The trees don't care. Not really. At least, the few that might give a shit wouldn't notice.

"Should we, though?" I leaned back as deeply as I could in my seat. I didn't want to look at Anders because I knew he'd react from his gut, and seeing it would spiral both of us into this discussion going somewhere wrong.

"Of course we should, we have to reset the world," he said, and I could hear the surprise in how he said it.

"Why?" I asked, making my voice as calm as humanly possibly.

"Because it's how the world was," he said.

"But," I offered, "just because that's the way something was doesn't mean, by default, that's the way it should always be, right? For thousands upon thousands of years, people moved at the top speed of their legs. Then came taming and riding animals, and the wheel and engines, and now we're on a bus going at least," I looked out his window, "forty — is there traffic I don't see?

Shouldn't we be going faster? But my point, right, sorry, my point is just because a thing *has been* done a specific way doesn't mean it has to *be done* that way for eternity. And maybe some betterment can come of that change. Isn't that just what human history is?"

"You're arguing for letting the Subtle Knives win," he said.

"I'm not," I said, "I'm just asking the question." I shook my head, rubbing the base of my skull against the back of the seat. Even though the bus remained the cleanest bus I'd ever been on, I still regretted the movement. Habit, if nothing else. I opened my eyes and studied Anders's face as I spoke. "Shouldn't we, as the people who are going off to, at least this second, revert the world to a different state, ask if it's the right move? Think of it this way...we're acting as doctors, we want to fix the world. Shouldn't we be conscious of the effect, and the cost, *and* the dangers, *and* the—"

"If the patient has a tumor, you remove the tumor," he said. "That's the danger in front of us, and we fix it."

"But if the tumor is large enough you can't remove it, not always. Maybe there's a better treatment. Maybe the tumor is benign. You have to know first. Otherwise you're just going slaphappy, right? And you can end up causing more problems than solutions, just by meaning well."

"Are you *seriously* suggesting we just leave the world the way it is now?" he took a deep breath and exhaled slowly. I liked that he seemed willing to have the discussion, even as it baffled him, instead of just planting his feet in surety.

"I'm suggesting we consider it, at least, before defaulting to a choice," I said. "Look around, think on what we've seen so far. The news, did you read any of it? Peaceful. Science is advancing, people aren't at war. Incredibly low crime. These busses, the trains, all so clean and nice. Isn't that how cities wanted to be? I have to assume the rest of the world — if everywhere has been affected in the same way, and there's exactly zero reason to think that *isn't* the case — is in the same boat. A good boat. A nice, clean, quiet boat. Would people be thankful for us tipping it over and returning them to the mess, the utter crapshow that we left?"

"But we can't even make our case," he said. "They wouldn't remember the way things were, so we can't ask people. If music, if creativity is bouncing off of people's consciousness, how could we explain? So all we could ever do is ask if someone wanted a worse-feeling world in return for the promise of a thing they can't imagine right now. Of course no one would say yes to that. And on the flip side, if you offered people an easy solution to the grime, the wars — all of it — in return for the loss of something they take for granted, that they...I don't think people could imagine this world if they tried, not really. So how could we ever know, really?"

He looked at me, honestly, searching for an answer that would make this simple. I felt bad for him. Simple answers weren't the sort of thing that I encountered that often. "That's why *we* have to decide for them. Consider, creativity is gone and it's refusing to come back. But here we are having a creative discussion. There's science in this world. So there must be creativity. Just highly specialized? I'm not sure. It doesn't actively track, not in a way that fully makes sense. Which means the answer is stranger than we think," I laughed lightly. "Which is normal for my life, and, if you're going to keep up, it'll be the normal for you as well. But that just makes it more important, to me, that we mean to do the damage we do as much as the damage we *undo* — if not even more. We can't consult with the patient. We can't...shit, Anders, there's not much we can do except try to see the problem as best we can, make a choice, and be ready to accept the consequences of our actions."

He let out the softest chuckle ever created by a human. "Accept the consequences of your actions? Paige," he paused, and I saw him consider stopping there, but he pressed forward, "didn't you leave the Ascension to not deal with consequences?"

"I wish — no, I left because it seemed the only way to not play the game. Which, given what we just dealt with, seems to have not worked at all, only delay my next move — but the impetus wasn't to bail on the consequences."

"Splitting hairs," he said, "and then, after Nester—"

"Yeah, all right," I had to laugh, myself, "shit, Anders, *you* sought *me* out, remember? I never claimed to be good at this."

"You claim that all the time," he said.

I waved a hand dismissively. "At the jerks we're trying to stop, sure. But I know I'm as good as I am today, and that's not going to be as good as I am if I live to try again tomorrow. Or, at least," I amended, "I know that in my better moments. But

I'm just a person. That's it. So, yeah, of course, *of course*, I fuck this all up sometimes."

"But you want to make this choice, for everyone on Earth."

"Nope," I told him, "I don't. I do not, let me be clear, want us to make this choice. But, Anders," I asked him, "if not us, then who? The Subtle Knives made a choice, and this is the result. Now we have to decide if we're going to undo it or not, because we're the ones standing here. We're it, as near as I can tell, and I don't think you know someone else who can make it, or you would've — I mean I hope by now you would've suggested them. Give me an address, a name, a phone number, something, and I'll rope them in and ask. But unless you have that, I'm not sure who else there is. So we have to do it. And opting out is a choice as much as opting in. So what's left?"

"I'm just not sure I see how leaving things the way they are could be the right choice," he said. "And I'll give you this, you're right that we need to choose, I'm just not sure I'm seeing the other side, right — so how can we choose if we only see one side?"

"Different can of worms," I told him. "Understanding the option, that's a trick, too. Think of it, though — a quiet, good life. Isn't that what you want, really? Isn't that why you want to help people, so they can life a life like this?"

"Not devoid of art," he said. He looked out the window while he spoke. "The cost is too high, I think. Not for me, though yes also for me, but in general. For the world. The Subtle Knives might control everything and keep the peace, but the cost of it all is horrible. I can't think of it as peaceful so much as stunted."

"Then you do see both sides," I told him.

"No, I only see one as correct," he said, turning back to me.

"I said you needed to understand both, not convince yourself both are right. But know that the choice you make here is for everyone. Regardless of whether we pull this off, you have to live with that."

"I can live with music being back in the world, with art, with—"

"War, and crime, and that constant weight over the heads of everyone that the world might be ended by someone they can name, that death and despair lurk around any corner?" I asked.

He sighed, shaking his head and looking down at his lap. We rode in silence for a while, then. Eventually he rubbed neck slowly, turning back to me. "I thought this was *our* choice, not mine."

"Anders, I'm not from here," I reminded him.

"But you've made this sort of choice before," he said.

"Oh, I totally have. One hundred and thirteen percent I've made that choice for people here before. But what choice did I have when standing back was also a choice, right? Thing is," I shrugged, "this time you're here, too. And this scale…it's *big*, big enough that I think someone involved in a way I just can't be needs to make it. Obviously, if you weren't here, I'd make a choice, yes. But you *are* here. So I think it needs to be you."

"That's—"

"Not at all fair," I finished for him. "Not in the

least, nope. But it is what it is."

He fell silent again and I started to go back to people watching. Boring, boring people watching. Used to be one of my favorite things, but now? Boring people, leading safer, dull lives. I knew which way I'd choose, and selfishly, at least part of that choice...no, to be honest, a lot of my choice hinged on my own enjoyment of the world. Totally unfair, but honest, at least.

Either way, though, I'd go along with him. Couldn't very well let him make the choice then override it for being wrong. I didn't even want to debate the options anymore, and risk swaying him to one side. I felt, in my gut, what choice he'd *been* sure about, but the longer we talked, the more the doubt crept into his voice and body language.

The bus slowed down as we entered the Boston area, and the city moved past the windows, looking, from the outside, much like it always had. The Subtle Knives may have found a way to rewrite — fuck, I don't know, most of human history somehow, but they'd managed to keep far too much intact.

I just felt more should be different. The way things stood, I felt like they hadn't put their heart into things. Not enough thought given to how the world would change, based on whatever rules they'd cooked up.

Everything I saw made me more and more curious about how'd they achieved the changes. I also started to wonder why they hadn't affected Mur. Then I got that piece, at least: If they'd changed how humanity worked but in a sliding scale — instead of removing all creativity of most types, or suppressing it at least, they'd just eased back — they would've missed the founding of Mur, at a guess. Once the city sat outside of time it'd be immune, the way Anders and I had been while we were there. In fact, depending on when they'd made the actual change with respect to our personal local timeframes, being in Mur might've been what held us this way.

But that would mean anyone leaving Mur, or entering it now, would see the affected world, or have been affected by it. And that would've been noticeable. Maybe not to us instantly, but still. No, Mur had been left alone because they didn't know about it, so they hadn't reached out to it.

Which still left the problem of anyone entering or leaving the city now. My head started to hurt attempting to run those numbers. I knew just enough to run myself in very certain circles that would each blow apart after a while. No way to solve the problem until we knew the problem. Assuming we were going to solve it.

We got off the bus and wandered out among the Boston crowd, small as it happened to be in the bus station. Anders still hadn't spoken since he'd started to really ponder his options. I walked, knowing he'd follow, right to one of the eating areas in South Station.

"What if," Anders said as I handed him a hotdog, "I chose you to choose?"

I laughed at that, spraying some hotdog onto the table in my sudden surprise. "Really, Anders? You're better than that, come on. All right, then I choose to only do what you choose. So we deadlock. Or I tell you if you try to abdicate, I'll just do the same. Which is the same as you choosing to not do anything. You won't weasel out of this. And I'm sorry, I really am. I'm laughing, I know, and it's hard to look sorry while you do that, but trust me here. I am not pleased with myself for putting you in this spot. I just don't see a choice that's at all fair to the *rest* of humanity."

"If I do this, I'm responsible for everything that happens after," he said.

"This is what you wanted — this, right here, is what you spent your life chasing, Anders," I said. "Every choice, big or small, every time you save a life, you find yourself here. You know that. Isn't that why you hunted me down? Because in some sense I'm responsible for making you want to help people? You put it on me, and this is how the wheel turns. No, it isn't fair — no, it isn't fun. But it is what we do. So do we get used to the world, or do we push back?"

He wadded up his napkin and threw it at a garbage can. The paper went in, but the points from the shot wouldn't matter, not to either of us. Only one thing mattered. I watched his face, trying to do it without looking like I was studying him for clues. No, that's silly. This was Anders. Only one thing he could do.

"We push back," he said. About time.

CHAPTER TWENTY-ONE

Wandering the streets of Boston, I thought about what to do after we found the Subtle Knives. I could use a bit more stored energy to find them, no problem. The closer we were to them, though, to one of their bases, the more they'd be looking for us and for energy use — even that would be noticed, I had to assume.

Then they would, what, swarm us? And what could we hope to do then? No, we needed to be either much smarter or much stupider than that.

"Anders, do you trust me?" I asked.

"Of course, but I also feel that's a hell of a set up, Paige. What are you about to do?"

I smiled at him. "Get us noticed in a way they won't see coming. Hopefully that'll confuse them enough to make a few assumptions in our favor."

"And if it doesn't?" he wanted to know.

"Then we're no better off than if they came after us guns blazing," I said. He nodded consent, and I took a deep breath and set us off down the street. Two cops stood by their cruiser, having coffee, listening to the radio to give them a purpose in their day. They'd do fantastically.

"Excuse me, officers," I said, cheerily.

"Really?" I heard Anders mutter behind me.

"Can we help you?" one of the officers asked. She was the taller of the two, and her partner took her coffee and set it inside the cruiser for her, along with his own.

"I sure hope so. I'm Paige Never, and I'm pretty sure the Subtle Knives want to talk to me."

"Excuse me?" the shorter cop asked. His hand reached back around for, I assumed, handcuffs. "And who's he?" he asked, lifting his chin in Anders's direction.

"Oh, that's Anders. He's with me and just as interesting to your bosses," I said.

"Don't move," the taller cop told us, and she grabbed her radio, walking a short distance away to have a conversation with someone that she didn't want us to hear. Dispatch would check the names, be truly well and confused, and we'd see what happened next.

What happened next was a lot of shouting and orders to get on the ground, arms behind our backs, to not move, to not *breathe*. Well, at least we were being treated like the threat the Subtle Knives knew we could be. I took some comfort in that — no, not comfort. Pride.

They shoved us in the back of their car and slammed the door, and the entire time I could see the shorter cop's hands shake a bit. They were nervous. Good. The Subtle Knives thought I'd make it clear of their machinations, and that I'd do so with all my abilities in check. Which meant they'd assumed I'd have a way to still work energy even though it'd been dampened down to nothing. Which told me they weren't *sure* their plan had really worked as well as it had.

However they'd remade the world, they were wary of it. Could mean they'd had help, which would make a lot of sense. The Subtle Knives of the Endless Blossom were never known to be this dangerous or competent. So if I assumed someone else had arranged this for them, then it left me with the questions of who and why. What did their new benefactor get out of it?

On the other hand, the help could have been inanimate. An object of stored power and a helpful handbook. Throughout history, well-meaning smart people have stumbled on ideas they knew were simply terrible. Some of them went the extra distance of being incredibly shortsighted and wrote them down for future generations to misuse.

I'm not saying you shouldn't leave knowledge for future generations, even if it's dangerous. Don't get me wrong. I just wish people who did would include the warnings up front, in the middle, and at the end. Really drive it home. Most people, though, they would write an entire treatise on this *really cool and dangerous idea* and then, in the small print at the end, leave a 'but seriously ha ha don't *do* the thing, that would be foolish' and hope for the best.

The police station was as clean and calm as everywhere else around, and just as creepy for it. Perched above the standard Boston PD sign out front, a Subtle Knives logo and text stood out. They really weren't hiding it. And yet in the papers and all they got no mention that I'd seen. I suppose that made a sort of sense. The world knew who ran it, so why mention it every other minute? Their complete control simply stood as normal, now.

We were fingerprinted, read some more rights, processed in all the ways police departments learned to move people through a system grown expert at dehumanizing people down to the core so they would sit and think about what they'd done. Or at least sit and stew, and gain nothing from it.

The holding cell was brightly lit and sparsely decorated, as such things often are. Anders and I were left together, but otherwise alone. Lucky us, they seemed to not care about normal gender separation procedures or, really, much of anything outside of locking us away. Two cops stood nearby, I'm not sure what they thought they could do if their fears proved right, that we could still pull all our old tricks — but then, what other choice did they have?

Obviously they weren't supposed to kill us, or they would've tried by now. But I felt sure that if we did try anything they'd shoot us — a leg, maybe. Then again, most people, even good marksmen, couldn't be sure a shot to wound would kill or only wound, so they might be afraid to try it, depending on their orders. Didn't matter, since none of them intended to try anything, and neither of us really could if we wanted to.

That was a lie.

We could do a few things. They may have confiscated the bag of supplies, but the WarBoots still held a charge, and that might've been used, but I'd gotten us in here on purpose. Instead, we sat and waited.

And waited.

And waited some more.

We waited long enough they had to bring us food.

I considered taking a nap and almost told Anders to do the same when three Subtle Knives came down the way to see us. They'd upgraded their outfits, now that they ran the world. They sported pristine, almost shiny, suits of a grey material, with a cherry blossom on the lapel. They each also wore a black bracelet, about an inch wide, with a red centerpiece. Not a stone, and it didn't blink, but the whole affair screamed 'I should be blinking' in the way that bracelets shouldn't.

I noticed it if only because it looked strangely out of place, and then to see it on all of them... As I watched, the center red bit of the bracelet shrank but a tiny amount. I mean tiny, but you could catch if it you happened to be staring at them, wondering what the hell was up with the strange jewelry.

"You need to come with us. For processing," one of the three said. They all sported similar haircuts, were close to the same build and height — might be from the same vat and batch number, I guessed.

"We were processed," I told them helpfully.

"Not here. You'll come with us," the lead Knife said.

"Do not try anything, Paige Never," the one to his left said, "you or your friend. Or we will be forced to damage you."

"And let me guess, you're not supposed to damage me?" I asked.

"It would be unfortunate," he answered, "but acceptable, if you give us a reason."

"Why won't you," Anders asked, as a cop unlocked the cell door, "just beat us up a bit on the way and *claim* we gave you a reason?"

The Subtle Knife shrugged and waved for

us to start walking out of the cell. One of them, their leader again, walked ahead, the other two behind. They loaded us into the back of a sedan. One of the Subtle Knives sat next to me, the other riding shotgun, and their leader drove. Anders tried the door in a very subtle way, I noticed, but the parental locks were engaged, and the door wouldn't open. Which was fine — we didn't *want* to escape. I nudged his ribs and shot him a look when he tried, and got a semi-sheepish look in reply.

We drove, and drove, and I kept watching the signs as we got on the highway and left Boston. Then we left Massachusetts and headed right toward points south. If we ended up driving all the way back to New York, I might've had cause to scream.

They did not give me cause. After about an hour, we slowed down as we approached East Greenwich, Rhode Island. Not something I saw coming. Not at all. I whispered and asked Anders if the place meant anything to him, and he shook his head. The whispering caught us a reprimand, but who really cared what those goons thought?

The whole ride, I tried to sense any energy, off and on, and got a few blips from the Subtle Knives in the car with us, centered on those bracelets, but nothing really strong or what I could call normal.

I tried again as we entered East Greenwich, and no joy from the universe. On a whim, as the car turned off a main road and approached a large estate, I tried again.

Holy fuck.

The place was practically radioactive. Not

really, but it bled energy like a giant, leaky battery. The energy dissipated quickly, unnaturally, the way it had in New York, but the grounds kept putting it out. Switching my vision down so I could really see, I caught sight of a large dome made of energy, passive and huge, covering the entire six- or seven-building grounds worth of land.

I nudged Anders and wiggled my fingers. He caught the idea, I'm pretty sure, given the way his face changed, and then changed again as he caught sight of it. We drove right for the dome and I braced myself for hitting that wall, but we passed through it without incident.

Except, that is, for two things.

The first thing simply being the red centers of those bracelets, or at least the one I saw, grew and brightened. Fine. So they stored energy taken from this place. For what, I didn't know just yet.

The second thing, though — I could feel and work with the energy. These idiots just took me right to where I could be dangerous. I supposed they didn't care — they believed I'd always been able to draw energy, even outside, given how they'd treated us. But they'd just accidently made it true. Fine by me.

The car stopped by a long and winding driveway, and we were ushered out without ceremony. Guards, obviously Subtle Knives, dotted the landscape like crap topiary. They led us inside one of the houses and sat us down in a waiting room. I'm sure the room had a better name that that, but I'll be damned if I cared. Shit, let's call it the sitting room. We sat. It was a room.

I figured the next person to enter the room

would be the ringleader — the shadow behind the throne, as it were. The person who'd managed to actually pull this off. They'd taken the Subtle Knives from an annoying cult right to the top of the food chain. They'd actually won, so far. I expected them to strut into the room and tell me how they were going to kill me.

And then Quince walked in.

CHAPTER TWENTY-TWO

QUINCE, I REMEMBERED, was dead. Back in the Ascension. So he couldn't be here. Someone must be messing with me. But there he stood, in a crisp, mint-green suit. With his WarBoots on, I noticed. He was tall — the tallest of us, a few inches over six feet — and bald. His skin remained so pale it could impress goth kids.

"Hey Paige," he said, warmly.

"You're dead," I said, by way of greeting.

"What is it with you and people you think were dead?" Anders asked.

"Hey, you *were* dead, and Quince here is supposed to be. Don't blame me for the universe being strange. I found it like this," I told Anders.

"Oh, so you've been back home, I guess," Quince said, sitting down across from us. One of the guards brought coffee and poured for all three of us. "You understand why I needed to appear dead, Paige. You, of all people, must understand."

"I get the why," I admitted. "If you can get out of that crapshow, you get out. But how?"

"Simple," he said, "they wouldn't listen. I just wanted peace. We tried for it, after you and Nester left. I was sorry to find out he died, by the way. I hope it was a good—"

"Shut up, Quince — you wanted peace, my ass. You wanted peace so you could take over. Don't drag Nester into this. Shit, how'd you even—"

"It's not hard to keep tabs on people here —

doubly so when they don't even suspect to look for you. But I did want peace, Paige. So I left, and faked my death, and found some allies I could work with to get my goals met."

"The Subtle Fucking Knives of the Endless Blossom, Quince? These dopes couldn't hold a meeting without messing it up."

"Which is why they needed my help," he said, "and were grateful for it. They couldn't dream of the things I could help them achieve."

I sipped my coffee, noticing Anders didn't touch his cup. Quince was *not* about to poison us — not just then, at least. I gave Anders a look and he grabbed his cup, sipping briefly, but only after I did.

"And you also made sure to have them try and kill me, and all my friends, from the jump," I said lightly. "Hell of a way to get peace."

"I didn't *want* to, you understand—"

"As if I give a fuck about how heavy the choice to kill me weighed on you," I said, chuckling. "Get over yourself."

"Fine," he said, "but I didn't want to. You — even supposedly gone missing for as long as you were — and your friends, all of you, were trouble waiting to happen. Each of you felt so dedicated to doing what you considered right, none of you would listen, not even give my idea a chance."

"Your idea — the one we're in right now, where you take over the world and reduce humanity to sleepy drones? Yeah, can't imagine why we might not have gone along."

"Where's Shealano?" Anders asked, before I could get there.

"I wish I knew," Quince admitted. Good. Anders and I relaxed a bit at that. "But you see what I mean? You all claim to want to keep things safe for humanity, in your various ways, but none of you would have let me work this to bring peace. The world was a nightmare. I merely woke it up, so that we can all live the dream."

"A dream of peace with you and these mooks at the top," I said. "Sounds great. Oh, wait, no, it sounds like *utter bullshit*, Quince. What are your plans for the Ascension?"

"Oh, them?" Quince said, trying to act nonchalant about the whole affair. "We will visit them soon enough and bring them to peace as well. These things are trickier than you might imagine."

"Doubtful. I can imagine a lot. Want to know what I'm imagining right now?"

"No, Paige, and no one else wants to hear your empty threats. I can see you have your abilities here, of course. But you haven't tried to draw any energy toward you at all, yet. Why is that?"

"Wouldn't you like to know?" I asked, smiling. I set my empty cup down on the table between us.

"There's the Paige I knew," he said. "Always a step behind, and playing a card she hasn't been dealt yet."

I smiled and shrugged, leaning back. "So now what?" I asked, fairly certain of the answer.

"Well, even if you said you wanted to join me, I couldn't believe you," he said.

"Of course not," I agreed.

"And keeping you locked up would be delaying the moment you decided to try something stupid," he continued. "Brilliant, if I know you, but stupid, and useless."

"Sure, sure," I said.

"So I suppose I must kill you. Both of you," he said, nodding at Anders. "Sorry about that," he told Anders, "standing in the wrong place at the wrong time and all."

"I'm standing in exactly the right place," Anders said. "So no worries."

"You are both being extremely polite about this," he told us, "which means you already have a plan. Too bad for you," he went on, "I'm far more powerful than you are, Paige. So please, don't make a scene. This is nice, sitting here."

"But it ends in our deaths, Quince. You see," I said, "how that might leave both of us disinclined to go along with it?"

"But I also know you have no choice. You can't even start to weave energy without my noticing. And the second I do..." he left the threat there, hanging. Fine by me. Our bag of extra goods was, at best, in the trunk of the car that brought us here, assuming they'd gotten it back from the cops in Boston. He was right about my ability to sneak attack him here. And, unlike the Ascension, he wouldn't assume Anders knew nothing. So he'd look out for that, as well.

"Can I, at least, ask how you did it, before we die?"

He laughed at that. "No, of course not. I'm not a movie villain."

"All right, how about this. Why Rhode Island, of all places, to put your seat of power?"

"Oh, that, sure," he said. He looked around

the room. It was a nice house, I'll give him that. "I've lived here for years. Why should I move just because I run the world? That seems silly."

"That's it. You just happened to live here?"

"That's it," he agreed.

"In Rhode Island."

"It's a nice place," he insisted. "Even before. It's...peaceful." Christ he annoyed me. "But now, as we agreed, I suppose this is the end."

I smiled and shrugged at him. I'll admit, the plan I'd come up with sucked. No time, no good avenues out. Except one. I tapped down on the heels of my WarBoots as slowly as I could while he talked.

Quince stood, and I stood to match him. Anders joined us, and there we all were. I didn't know how he intended to kill us, but I had to assume it'd be simple and direct. No room for mistakes, nothing fancy. Fine by me, since I didn't intend to be there to be killed.

I grabbed Anders arm. I glanced at him and mouthed "Step," and started to take a step forward. He joined me and we shifted.

As soon as my foot raised up, I brought it back down.

This is what is known as a terrible idea.

We appeared, mostly, in another room in the house. Mostly, because a small chunk of my right hip was now merged with the wall.

FastWalking will let you generally go through things, but something as harsh and aborted as I pulled off...mistakes happen. I swallowed the scream and told Anders to run, any direction, so long as it took us out.

I limped behind him, knitting energy to cauterize my wound. At least the new hole in the side of my pants was covered by my jacket, when buttoned. Otherwise everywhere we went, people would know something was wrong with the woman with the gaping, freshly closed wound. Mind you, it still hurt. But death hurt more, and that gave me the energy to move my ass and catch up with Anders. We wound our way through a hall, shouts gaining on us and Subtle Knives in front of us.

"Another FastWalk?"

"We can't go through that shell that way. The sudden energy loss, we'd go down in flames. Literal flames," I said quickly. "No, just shove them clear," I said, and twitched my fingers as Anders snapped his, and we wove a shield, one big one shaped to a point in front of us, battering our way through.

We only had a minute, maybe less, to get clear before Quince would be on top of us. The grounds opened up in front of us as we made it outside. Still not clear, though — we had to get outside that field. Quince would be right behind us, and the Subtle Knives closing in from all sides. The sedan — black, standard detective-issue car that drove us here — sat in along the path, in our way. Perfect.

Anders dove in behind the wheel and I rode shotgun, and we drove out of there as fast as possible. I put the WarBoots on heavy draw before we passed through the field, just to fill their tanks, and like that we were back in a boring, safe world of nothing.

Of course they'd follow, but we could ditch the

car and steal another. It'd be easier to lose them, actually, with the world in the state it was. Except, of course, Quince and his blockhead army could still use energy. To an extent. I thought.

"All right," I said as we sped down the road, Anders taking random-seeming turns, "work through it with me."

"Work through what?" he asked.

"Quince's plan, how they did it, how we're gonna stop it. The whole party. We saw enough in there, we should be able to get there off of it."

"Seriously?"

"Dead serious," I said. "Why would they need a shell to protect them and enable energy work?"

"Because Quince doesn't want to give up any power, and because he expected you," Anders said.

"All right, let's run with that. An entire area unaffected. Which means something did affect the world, and still is. But they planned for it. Why not just have whatever did this leave a spot — why set it up, that barrier is being held in place by something."

"Maybe whatever they used isn't precise?" he ventured.

"Seems like a good guess," I agreed. "Pull over here, let's get another car."

He did. We checked the trunk before we left the sedan, and they'd managed to shove our bag of supplies in it. We broke into a small two-seater, trying to shatter the driver-side window as softly as possible. Meanwhile, I kept up our actual work.

"The bracelets the Subtle Knives all wore. Quince didn't have one. You noticed the red bits on them?"

"They shrank and grew, depending on if they were in the shielded area or not? Yeah," he said, as I reached over to the starter button and pressed my hand over it. I used the tiniest sliver of energy, drawn from the WarBoots, and jumpstarted the car.

"Except the Subtle Knives aren't generally energy workers. There's no way they'd need that sort of thing. I'm assuming they stored some energy for use, but the way it drained...about as fast as the energy we released when we were testing what had happened, would you say?"

"I didn't time it," he said, "but probably, yeah, about that." We drove off again, Anders rolling down what was left of the window, hoping no one would notice.

"A drip that slow, given how little energy they must be able to store and how slowly they were draining, that wouldn't be useful for anything. *Unless*," I added, "you needed it for stabilization."

"You mean the effect is ongoing, and without constant energy to keep them tethered, the Subtle Knives would be swept into it?" he asked.

"Exactly, so why aren't we? And why wouldn't Quince need one?"

"Because we weren't here to *be* affected." Anders said. "So it can't retroactively grab us. But the Subtle Knives were."

"All right," I said, "And Quince?"

"Who says he was here when it happened, either? Maybe he made a pocket dimension because he knew. But he wasn't powerful enough to grab all of his soldiers with him, or needed some to remain behind. Either way, that'd do it, right?"

"It would. Good. So let's think of why. Why would Quince do this at all? He left the Ascension, wanted to opt out of the whole thing. But not really, right? So what better way than to come here and infiltrate a small, worthless cult and take them over, then use them. Use them to take over the world and make it cold, dull, and sterile."

"Best way to turn them into an army," Anders said. "They won't question it, will they?"

"No, they won't," I agreed, "but it takes time to make sure they're all used to things and the plan is stable. Then he can move on the Ascension and control both places. Hell, fuck, he could use whatever he used to rewrite Earth *on* the Ascension. So that's the why."

"But how. Paige, how can anyone do what he did? That kind of power..."

"I know, we'd have no chance which — Anders, watch the road — Anders, that's where I stand more often than not. That's what you wanted in on and where you are right now. So, don't worry about it. Just accept that. And then make it work."

"There has to be more to it than that," he insisted, taking a road and heading back toward Boston.

"Getting creative is a lot of it," I admitted, "and willing to look stupid. But why are we going back to Boston?"

"Why did they have a giant base there you could detect if it wasn't their actual base?"

"To lure me in. No, Boston is a wash. Whatever Quince did, he'd keep it closer. Also, I bet he'd think of that, too, and be on the roads looking for us. No, get off here, there's a diner."

"Are you kidding me?" he asked, but signaled and got off, heading for the diner's lot.

"Why would I joke about food?" I asked. "And don't worry, I can spark up the car again when we need to."

"What about the window?" he asked.

"Crap, right, park in the back where the car isn't easy to see. Then we'll steal something else, or grab a ride."

He nodded, and soon enough we sat ordering large amounts of food and sipping coffee. "So, really, how could Quince pull this off?" Anders asked.

"He couldn't," I said. Simple but true. "The question is then who, or what, could. We're looking for something...someone...that could overwrite the world, to spec, and maintain it. But that would also manage to not do *too* good a job, which gets us Mur and the Ascension being excluded. Plus that dome of Quince's."

"Don't ask me," Anders said, nudging some food with a fork, "I wouldn't have the first clue about what's out there."

"Oh come on," I said, "you have the first clue. It's the *second* you're missing. But you're right. So let's see, then." I pushed my plate away and drummed my fingers on the table. "Let's toss out any org that could even approach this, simply because they wouldn't partner with the Subtle Knives, or Quince. If they would've been open to it, he would've used them. Artifact-wise, there's nothing strong enough. Maybe if he gathered a bunch together and then linked them all up somehow, though." I waved the waiter over for a coffee refill. While he poured, I kept my brain running.

"How would you do it," Anders asked.

"Ha! Sure," I sipped my fresh coffee greedily, "I wouldn't, like the idea wouldn't occur to me — unless I stumbled on something that screamed 'This is what I'm here for' at me. So Quince flees to Earth, hangs about, hides a lot, dreams of revenge. He studies up, researches things, that'd be a very Quince thing to do. And he finds something."

"Or someone."

"Right. A whisper, maybe, a hint of a hint. And he tracks it down and here we are, basically. So what did he find?"

"Could we retrace his steps? Do the work he did?" Anders asked.

"I don't even know when he got here, much less where he landed, so no. We'd need a lot more information for that. But I do know I've been here longer, and done more digging for strangeness than he could have, really, right? I spent time plugged into a community, instead of lurking. So what have I ever heard of, something that...oh." I stopped and shook my head.

"What've you got?"

"I just remembered a legend I heard about, but that was it, a legend. It isn't real."

"Paige," Anders said, staring at me, "isn't that *exactly* what we want? Something anyone else would've tossed out?"

"If that's the case, then we're looking for The Boy Who Dreams," I told Anders. "Thing is, the whole idea never quite made sense. The idea was there was a kid born in the last few decades who had the ability to dream reality. What he saw in his dreams could become our reality. That'd do it, right?"

"So that's what we're looking for," he said confidently.

"If, and I stress *if*, such a person ever existed, why hasn't anyone—"

"Because everyone else dismissed it," he said.

"Even then, Anders. A person with that kind of raw power would've been noticed by the Tide."

"The what now?"

"The Rising Tide. A bunch of...they're really... oh, how to explain the Tide. They're sort of possibly universal forces given human form? That's close, at least. Just go with that. And if something like the Dreamer existed, they would have intervened by now and taken the kid somewhere else, or whatever it is they do. I don't know. I only ever met one of them once. Too long a story for now, but trust me on this, they wouldn't want that sort of power around."

"Even if everyone thought they were a myth?" he asked.

"If the power was used, even once, it should've been a huge signal in the sky, so to speak." I thought about it for a few minutes, in silence.

We finished eating, in that same silence, and I paid, after draining my cup dry. We wandered out to the parking lot, looking for something easy to steal. The back lot, where we'd parked ourselves, sat fairly empty, but the front lot could be seen from the diner so we had no other good choice.

I tried to hide my limp from Anders — getting a chunk taken out of your hip is never fun. It mostly worked. He asked if I was all right and to distract him I put us back on track. "What if," I asked quickly, "the power was used briefly, once or twice, when new enough that it hadn't fully developed? It might escape too much notice then, but enough that someone would've locked it down and, for the sake of argument, hidden the entire thing."

"Why would they hide it?" he asked. I used some draw from my WarBoots, as little as possible, to force the car lock to disengage and then start the car.

"If they saw that the power seemed to grow, wouldn't you want to keep it safe — for yourself, possibly, but at the very least safe — until something could be worked out?"

"What would be worked out, outside of how to use it for yourself?" he asked as he started toward the highway.

"A way to harness it, sure, possibly," I said, "but it would also take time to work out how to control it, not for yourself but for the originator of the force. So they could not destroy worlds every time they slept. A chemically induced coma, maybe? No, wait, some people still dream during them, you'd have to suppress the dream state. I don't know, I would need time to think of a few ideas for *how* you could pull that sort of trick off, but if we assume that's the trick, everything lines up, more or less."

"So whatever is causing this is inside Quince's—"

"Outside the dome, so they didn't affect people inside it, but close by. And this effect doesn't use energy. If it did, we would sense it all going there, but instead we have no energy to speak of. So it uses another force."

"There are other forces?"

"Sure, lots of them. Some more closely tied to the universe, some not, but in general — not exclusively, but generally — humans are only really good at working with the sort that I've shown you. There are colors you can't see, either, but they exist," I said.

"Thanks, Paige, I know. And some people can't see the ones I can," he said.

"Right. So now we just have to find where Quince is keeping the Dreamer."

We entered Rhode Island and kept driving just at the speed limit so cops wouldn't be hungry to pull us over for anything. "So we're going with this?"

"It fits, it's the *only* thing I can think of that does. If I'm wrong, I should still be right *enough* we'll just have to do the rest on the spot."

"Oh good."

I smiled at him. "Anders, which bothers you more? That we'll have to possibly fly by wires again or that you realize you enjoy it?"

"About equal, if I'm honest," he said.

"See, it's good you can admit that to yourself already," I told him. "Now, let's go...do...something."

"Inspiring."

CHAPTER TWENTY-THREE

WE DROVE AROUND East Greenwich slowly, looking for all the world like totally lost tourists. The clock in my head ticked loudly. I knew Quince would find us. I didn't know how, but just as I knew if I looked for him I could find him, he would find us.

Before that came to pass we needed to find the Boy Who Dreamed, if he existed. And then it clicked. "Anders, pull over a second, I have an idea," I said quickly. Tires crunched along gravel and I leapt out of the car, grabbing the bag from the backseat. The trick wouldn't be to find the Dreamer.

"Quince," I said to Anders. "We need to find Quince."

"So back to his big compound? But with the dome and all—"

"No, that's just it. He'd know that I would search, and that I would be able to work this out."

"Are you sure?" he asked.

I looked at him the way cats look at humans who don't pet them right. "He'd count on me working it out, and he would have run right to the Dreamer to protect them in response."

"But wouldn't he know that you'd work that out and then he would…" Anders trailed off, waving one hand in that 'and so on' motion.

"No, he also has the ego to assume he can stop us," I said.

"The same ego you have to assume we can stop *him*?"

"The *exact* same," I said. "Difference is, I'm right and he's wrong." I dug around in the bag a while and took out a small, flat, black disc. I also took the second to fill my pockets a bit and had Anders shove something in his, as well.

"Paige, you know that's exactly what he would say in this situation, right? You're pulling logic in circles here."

I shrugged at him and cracked the disc open, handing parts of the shell to Anders to hold a moment. "You have to decide if you believe in us or in him, I guess. I back our team."

"I didn't mean it like that, Paige, come on. I just wish there was some more concrete answer than 'because,' you know what I mean? Also, what are you doing?"

"I do know, but that's all we got. Well, that," I said, "and this." I held up the core of the disc, a small green-and-blue blob that pulsed slowly. "Disgusting, isn't it?"

"...Yup."

"I could not even begin to tell you why anyone would design something to look like this. But, here's the fun part, it disrupts energy."

"What kind? Like an EMP device?" he asked.

"Sort of. But for the energy we work with. Which, I realize, right now is theoretically useless. That energy is basically gone, so why short it out? Well, much like the noble badger who loves to hunt pugs—"

"That is not even close to true," Anders told me.

"Whatever," I said, "I know badgers. And they'd *love* this idea. I can use the disruption energy, which is totally different from the energy we normally work with."

"You can use that kind of energy to find Quince?"

"Should be able to," I said. "Kind of. Mostly. If this works."

"And, Paige, if it doesn't work?" he asked.

"Then the WarBoots drain *and* we have no good way to find Quince other than checking every building in the area," I told him.

"If we think about it, for just a second," he said, "he'd need a place with a lot of electrical draw, medical equipment, and probably large enough to house a staff, right?"

"Sure," I agreed, "and this will point he way. Because otherwise we have to canvass any property that, even just from the outside, might be the right size. We have no way to gauge electrical draw, and he could own any building and have gutted it. No, there are a few great ideas there, Anders, really, but none of them happen to work *for this, right now*."

He nodded and looked at the little blob in my hand. "So how to get the stuff out, in the way you need?"

"Without the right tools, because of course we don't have *those*...anyway, yeah, grab the jumper cables from the trunk."

"Does this car even have jumpers?" he asked, rummaging around a strangers' trunk. I didn't want to tell him that I'd forgotten that part. Luckily they had some old, tarnished jumper cables.

I took them from him and carefully clipped one hot lead around the blob, clipping the ground to the metal car frame. Then I handed the other two leads to Anders and held out my hands.

"Clip them on, one to each," I said.

"Really?" he asked, but I shook my head to shush him and wiggled my fingers. He clipped the alligator clamps onto my fingertips and I got a hard jolt as the energy in the blob ran down the completed circuit into my right hand.

Fuck that hurt. The energy wasn't the sort I would ever choose to touch. It *burned* me, from the inside out. I felt like a fire raged along my tendons, my nerves, my skin. I shook my hands hard to dislodge the clamps and used the budding scream to focus my mind on feeling for Quince.

I couldn't feel a thing that resembled him, but I did sense a large, black hold of power. Large, and dark — powerful enough to reshape the world, possibly. That would more than do, and would have to, regardless.

Leaning over, hands on knees, trying to catch my breath, I tried to explain what I'd learned to Anders but it took a few tries until I could speak coherent English again. Eventually I got there, and we set off in the direction that I sensed the hole in the world. This had to be what we were looking for, *had to.*

A little over twenty minutes later, we circled around an apartment building — this being East Greenwich, the building stood only three stories, and stuck out with terraces and other quaint touches.

We parked a few blocks away and snuck up on

the place. Not that you can sneak up on a building, but still. I'd insisted we both stuff our pockets with a few things from the bag, just in case — not that they'd really help. The effects would be muted now, and last for only seconds. If Quince really could work energy outside of his dome, we'd be outclassed.

A few bored guards, Subtle Knives in their new uniforms, hung around the building — and *only* that building. So we were right on. I debated how we could go in. Knocking them out, physically or any other way, would just call attention to us. With no real way to get disguises and so on, though, it stood our only chance. We circled around and poked our heads out from around the corner of the building.

I whistled.

They came over to investigate. They really weren't the brightest, these folks. We hit them, a lot, in various places, when they turned the corner. It wasn't particularly quiet, and there remained no grace in it, no art or style.

We just hit them a lot.

Sometimes that's what a fight is.

At least, it can be when I'm involved. I never really got the hang of the whole deliberate, precise attacks that culminated in some spectacular landing of blows. I can make a fist, I can throw a punch, and can kick the crap out of people when I utterly need to. Most times. All right, a lot of the time it goes the other way. Anders, luckily, knew how to hold his own in a fistfight, and that got us through. Not that I didn't land a few blows. Of course I did. But.

Which doesn't matter, because we had a clear shot at the door and at least two whole minutes to end this. Plenty of time. The inside of the building... wasn't. The façade we'd seen, the apartment building, seemed to be a hollow shell. Inside the door there was a bunch of empty space and then at the center of the building a windowless cube, about the size of a truck trailer at most. Support struts ran from the top edges of it to the outer shell walls of the building we'd thought we were entering.

A single door in the box sat closed. No guards in here, nothing. So I opened the door. Inside was a mess of medical equipment, most of it looking very impressive if you didn't know what any of it did. If you happened to, and I knew most of it, you could see the stuff was set to a floor display pattern. All the readouts looked fancy, medical-like, important, but the machines weren't hooked up to anything.

That wasn't a *great* sign, no.

We wove through the equipment toward the bed in the back of the space. A chair sat near it, nothing too fancy, but far nicer than your normal hospital room chair. As we got closer I could see the old man in the bed. Late sixties, possibly seventy-something, he lay in the hospital-like bed, tubes hooked up to his nose and mouth, needles and wires going to his chest and arms.

And in the chair, Quince. Who stood as we approached, turning to us, with the smile of a door-to-door salesman who just landed a whale of a client. "Well that took entirely too long," he said. "I forgot that deprived of your normal tools you're not really good at this, are you, Paige?"

I shook my head at him. "Sorry, got distracted, Quince. You aren't worth that much to me, frankly, and I was hungry. So we went and grabbed some lunch. Honestly, would've stayed to be killed if not for the tummy rumblies," I said, letting a pause creep in, "you miserable fucker."

"Uhm, Paige—"

"I know, Anders," I said, "and yeah, that old guy is The Boy Who Dreams." I shrugged. "People age. But also, we should call him The Boy Who *Dreamed*, right, Quince?"

"I did not kill him," Quince said. "Well," he shrugged with his whole arms, not just his shoulders. A cartoon of a shrug, arms bending at the elbow and hands up. Playing cute.

"Without him, everything goes back to normal, though," Anders said.

"It's true," Quince admitted, "if you want to wait that long. Tell him, Paige."

"Anders, that energy we tracked here, that's going to linger something fierce," I said. "Long enough for Quince to raise an army here, take over the Ascension and put in real control. Though," I looked back to Quince, "when things revert, wouldn't that be a whole new problem you don't want interfering with your reign?"

"Always steps behind, and doubly so when you're so sure you're right, Paige," he said. "But I'm *still* not going to just hand you answers. Why would I ever *do* that? No, but you'll come with me, and I'll kill you, and you won't care anymore."

"Why should we leave here with you?" I asked him.

Instead of answering, he touched his thumbs to the third finger on each hand and Anders and I found ourselves unable to move, or speak.

Fuck.

Right.

Quince crossed the few feet between us and patted my shoulder with mock-sadness. "Because I can still work energy out here, obviously," he said.

Manipulating the binding he'd placed on us, Quince walked us out of the room, locking the door behind him. "The Subtle Knives don't know, of course," he said before catching himself and shutting up.

We all walked outside and, awkwardly, loaded into a car. Aiming right back to Quince's headquarters, I wondered why he was dragging us there to kill us. He wanted something else, something that he couldn't get in a largely empty building. Assuming we gave him the chance. We passed the dome marker — I could feel it, energy all around me again, and I decided to take advantage of it. Move now, figure out why Quince did the dumb things later.

I kicked at the door of the car suddenly, with the WarBoot. The door went flying. I dove out of the car, grabbing at Anders' arm as I did. He leapt after me, and as we rolled, painfully, to a stop, we could hear the car's tires screech as it too stopped.

I tried to spring up, heroically and shit, but diving out of the car I'd hit the wound on my hip so I managed to stumble upwards at excited sloth speeds instead. I got there, is the point. Something caught my eye as I stood, though. I glanced over and saw a boot, just laying there, knocked over onto its side, back a bit on the grass near the road.

A WarBoot.

And suddenly the dome made sense.

"Anders, I've got it — well, part of it," I said, throwing up a shield to deflect Quince's first attack.

"Can you tell me later, maybe?" he asked, pulling energy and feeding it into my shield, while changing the shape. He curved it convex, so it curved in toward us a bit. Then he pushed more energy around, while I did the same, and the next tendrils of energy Quince sent reflected back toward him some, tangling into the rest of his attack.

"Nice one," I told him, "but that boot, it's a WarBoot. I noticed Jursica and Kental weren't wearing theirs. Quince must have taken them. He's using them to form the dome. One at each cardinal..." I stomped my WarBoot and shook the Earth enough to stumble Quince. "Will you *stop*?" I said in his general direction. "...each cardinal point," I continued to Anders, "if we shut even one off, the dome goes bye-bye, I'd bet."

"And then we'd be powerless, but Quince can still work outside of it — how is that good for us, Paige?"

"It'd also mean the Subtle Knives would fall under the influence of the Dreamer's reality," I said.

"Really slowly," he pointed out. Damn it, he was not wrong. I nodded at him and thought about it. Taking down the dome still felt like the right move, but Anders was right, it would only serve to hurt us right then.

I needed a plan, which would require, realistically, a few seconds not under attack from Quince. We turned his attacks back easily enough, though, and the Subtle Knives hadn't joined in to help him.

"Quince," I said, loudly, "let's talk for a minute instead of trying to kill each other."

"So I can explain my plan?" he asked, laughing. "Paige, stop trying for that!"

"No, you giant stain, so I can explain your problem to you." That got his attention, and he dropped his arms to his side.

"Can we trust him?" Anders asked quietly as we walked over to where Quince stood, waiting.

"Of course not," I said, "but you should trust *me*." I nodded at Quince. "You're really this worried that if we tell your happy subjects here the truth about the Dreamer, they'll go sideways on you, aren't you?"

He laughed. A fake laugh, the kind you do when your crush tells the absolute worst joke ever but you know if you actually vomited it would end badly for you. "Don't be silly, Paige," he said, "you obviously don't understand—"

"Oh I do," I told him, "you're going easy at us, holding them back — you just don't want either of us to shout the truth, because they might just go look. You *didn't* kill the Dreamer after all, did you?"

"People get old and die, Paige — humans, at least."

"We do too," I said, "but you won't, if they find out. This is all spiraling out of control for you. Let me help you, Quince."

"What?!" Anders said, "Help him? *Him*? We need to stop him, not give him a hand."

"Besides, you've already helped me," Quince said.

"We have?" Anders asked.

Which is when Quince blinded us with a flash of light. Damn it! I got suckered, hard. I tried to throw up a shield, but not before I felt the heat of what Quince had built. He tried to throw everything at us. This would be it, no more holding back. Damn, of course — he could now happily blame us for the Dreamer's death and he'd just realized it.

The energy wave built, but I threw up my hands and smiled into it, still seeing only blackness. The energy burst felt familiar and I'd twigged to why. I folded causality and sent it back to myself, so I could use it to get back into the Ascension. Quince growled — he actually growled — at that one, and instead of trying again, leapt onto me and beat my head against the ground until I lost consciousness.

CHAPTER TWENTY-FOUR

I WOKE UP tied to a chair, with Anders staring at me. He, too, sat tied to a chair, and I could assume my bonds were as well-crafted as his. I could sense the energy in them, too. My head hurt. Being knocked out will do that.

We were in Quince's main house, I could tell by the décor. I tried to pull energy but the bonds stopped me.

"Anders, you all right?"

"What the hell, Paige?" he asked in reply.

"What?"

"You want to help him?" I've seen kids find out that Santa wasn't real. The look Anders gave me felt the same.

"And he wants to keep me alive, Anders, don't you get it?"

"Obviously no. Obviously. No."

"We're it, really. I mean Jursica will be dropped down a hole so deep she won't see the end of it. Kental will supposedly be groomed to take over, but I wouldn't sell him life insurance right now given he'll be in constant, and close, contact with the Queen, all right? Do you see now? There were ten of us, Anders. We grew up together. The only two to make it out, to make it to freedom of a kind, who are still alive are me and Quince. Could you kill your brother?"

"He's your brother now?" Anders scoffed.

"He always was," I said.

"And who says we have to kill him?"

I sighed. "What options are there? I can't lock him anywhere. Even if I could get him back to the Ascension, what do you think *they* would do to him? And if we stop his plot, right now, before we work out a way for him to survive and pose no threat to us, the Subtle Knives will realize they've been used and kill him."

"Can they? They couldn't kill us, Paige — why is he so much more venerable?"

"They tried to kill us because they were told to, and they came close at least once. But this — they'd make it their new eternal mission to see him pay for using them, for using their own goals against them. Giving them what they wanted and then for them to find out it was a scam? No way to do they forgive that." I struggled a bit against the ropes and energy that bound me, but just got a constant mild shock for my efforts.

"So you want to..." he asked, trailing off, trying to lead me to an answer.

"I have no idea, Anders, but I'm sick of losing every inch of my past," I said, admitting it fully to myself as I told him. "If we left things here, just for a bit, and worked with him to find a solution, then maybe..."

"...You don't get it," Quince said from the darkness of the room. "I don't want or need your help, Paige." He stepped into view. He looked sad — about how I felt, really. "When I did need your help, if you'll remember, you said no."

"You wanted to rise up and take on the whole—"

"If you, me, Jurs, Kental, Nester...if we'd all

worked together, maybe we could have done it. But you said no. And then Nester ran away and you followed. You left us all, so don't give me your fake concern now. I have this all under control. My control."

"So why haven't you killed us?" I asked. "You keep telling us you're about to, but you haven't really tried, not really." I thought about it. "All right, maybe twice — the first time and before, outside the car before we—"

"*I was there*," he said, snarling. "And maybe you're right, partly, about not wanting to kill each other. There is a sense of home to you, Paige. I just need to remember *I hated home*. So please, believe me when I say this time I really do intend to kill you."

"I believe you," I told him. "But I still don't intend to *let* you."

"And how are you going to escape this time? The bonds around your ankles should even cut off the WarBoots, for a while. And I only need a while," he said. "Besides, Paige — you escape, and do it badly, and then I catch you again, and how many more times will you make us go around this circle? Just stop. Stop fighting. Give in. I hear tell that was your plan, anyway, at the start of this."

That stung. "You're not wrong," I said. "I wish you were, but you're not. In the least. But Anders here pointed something out to me, a while back. I mean, he didn't..." I smiled at Anders, "you didn't *say* it, really, but you know, I picked up on it." Looking back at Quince, I clicked my tongue. "Anders showed me that I was incredibly dumb. Like you, he wasn't wrong. So I stopped being dumb, Quince — that was all it took."

"Fascinating. No, really," he said, "and I would love to hear more about how life-affirming this has all been for you, but..." he shrugged, "I don't give a shit."

"It's all good," I told him, then turned to face Anders. "Hey Anders," I said lightly, "I can't reach, but it looks from here like *maybe* you can. Still got it?"

Quince and Anders both looked at me, utterly confused, but Anders got to a realization and managed to fumble his hand just inside one of his pants' side pockets, just to the very opening, but the device inside sat close enough I could see it so I knew his fingers could get there.

The slim box in Anders' pocket was just a battery, essentially. Like the WarBoots, but smaller and less fun. It still held enough energy to allow Anders to overload his bonds' energy component and burn away the ropes at the same time.

My own bonds fell the same a few seconds later, as Anders shot a bunch of energy my way. This all unfolded in the time it took Quince to catch up. He started to react, to pull energy, but Anders hit him, full-body slamming him into the ground before he could.

"I have to say, I never really thought about just punching them before. We always tried to out-trick each other."

"Paige, you're ridiculous. Sometimes all you need to do is introduce someone to the floor as hard as possible. It's not elegant, but it's effective."

"I'm seeing that," I told him, offering him a hand up. "So, now we just have to work out how to undo all of this."

"I know how," Anders said. "Or at least, I think I do."

"Really?" I asked, then smiled. "Go for it. Tell me the plan."

"This Dreamer," he said, then stopped to look around. "We should secure Quince first."

"I'll get that," I said and walked over to him, weaving a nasty set of vipers around him. Not literal ones, but just as effective. "Go on."

"He had to keep dreaming to keep the world going his way. So I would think they hypnotized him, or something."

"Maybe? My guess would be an energy bleed to keep his subconscious on script. So what?" I asked, sitting back down in the chair. My hip hurt.

"Oh, no, that wasn't part of the plan. I was just trying to figure that out, too," he said, still standing. "Oh shit," he said, reaching for his side. "The cops, they never gave me back my bag. My journal is in it, and—"

"Anders, focus," I said, "we can go get it later. You had a plan?"

"Sorry, just not sure about it and stalling and... all right, so that strange energy the Dreamer put out, we could still feel it, even though he'd been dead a while. That energy must be what's keeping this world the way Quince wanted it."

"Full marks so far."

"What if we took the energy in those other WarBoots, he *has* to be using more than the one we saw, spaced out regularly, and used it as a bridge?"

"How so?" I asked, starting to grin.

"We could connect me to it, to the Dreamer's energy," he said, "with that bridge, and then I could reverse the effect."

"I don't think you can channel his ability, Anders — I'm honestly not even sure how he could manage what he did."

"I don't have to do what he did, I just have to disrupt it in the right way," he told me.

"And how do we know the right way? Anders, if you just disrupt it, you might bring back what humanity needs, but the past will still have happened his way — for centuries, possibly. We need to work out a way to undo everything retroactively."

"No, I know that, Paige, and I know how. Influences don't care about time," he said, as if that explained it.

"All right..."

"Just trust me? I don't want to keep talking when the Subtle Knives could come in here at any second, or Quince breaks free, or a hundred other things. Just trust me — I know this, I have this down. I can *do this*, Paige."

I took a deep breath and ran the numbers in my head as fast as I could. If he was right, we would be great. If he was wrong, we would have blown our best, and possibly only, shot at fixing this. Worse yet taking down the dome, using that energy, would leave us trapped in this world without another way to gather energy for a second shot.

I looked at Anders and thought. I considered everything we'd been through, right from him falling off a roof when he was a kid. Where he'd guided his own life. How he'd helped, and frustrated, me all this time since.

I nodded and stood, heading for the door. "Let's go then — I'll need one of the WarBoots to channel the dome energy to you."

CHAPTER TWENTY-FIVE

WE SNUCK OUR way, quickly as possible, to the edge of the dome. Subtle Knives were patrolling, but they didn't seem to be actively looking for us. I hoped we'd have enough time before Quince could raise an alarm to do this.

I grabbed the WarBoot and siphoned just enough energy to reach out to that blank spot the Dreamer had created and make sure I could actually bridge the two the way Anders would need. It hurt, but felt doable.

"We get one shot," I told Anders. "And I can't give you all the energy — I need to save some to hold off the Subtle Knives. Once the dome goes down, they'll notice, and they'll find us. Also," I warned him, "this is going to hurt. I mean really hurt, from the inside out."

He nodded and sat down on the grass. "Then I should get comfortable," he told me, and closed his eyes. "Do it."

I shrank down the dome, channeling almost all the energy from all four WarBoots into myself, and reached out to the blank space's energy. I interfaced them and then linked *that* to Anders. The rest of the energy I used to keep what was left of the dome, with its properties, around just us. Then I reinforced that with my own shielding and waited.

Anders started to scream, but bit off the last of it. I dipped a metaphorical toe into his energy stream to keep an eye on him and see what he planned on doing. It made sense, then. He'd used some of the dome properties to remember a bit of music. Just snatches of a song he'd loved dearly.

Then he'd pumped that song into the blank energy space, pushing it out to people — the world, really. And following that, they would be influenced by it and wake up, for lack of a better term. But it didn't stop here. Because as they remembered, they'd also remember the first time they'd heard the song, and who sang or gave it to them, and the chain of influence ran back in time. It'd spark off other memories in people, even people who'd never heard the song.

The spark flew like a lit fuse. People who never could have heard the original song or heard of the singer were caught by a related memory, even a few generations back, of someone who knew someone who had influenced an ancestor. That influence would reestablish a connection that would then go forward in time to today.

Influences don't care about time, Anders'd told me. He was not wrong. The more people who'd broken free, the more they freed. The more their own memories, and feelings, and influences along their own line spread, the stronger the spark got. Nothing to do with the original seed from Anders, anymore, the effect took root and undid the Dreamer's dream.

Subtle Knives started to come for us, somewhere in the middle, but my shielding stayed strong, and I held the line. I even punched a few of them when they got too close. My own WarBoots kept the ground shaking, as well, to add to their misery. Their great plan was tumbling down around them and they knew it.

Anders had gone too deep, though, and was drowning in the energy swirling around him. Too new to know how to really swim in waters churning this hard, his mind threatened to drift away. I took a screamer out of my pocket, my last, and, after making sure Anders and I wouldn't be hit, threw it to buy myself some time.

I linked myself to his energy stream and helped shore him up. His work was done — the spark couldn't be stopped now. Now I just needed to make sure he didn't die, physically or mentally, and we could be done with this.

I emptied the rest of the dome into pulling Anders free, unhooking his mind from the streams he'd created. It left us vulnerable — if the world didn't snap back into its rightful...being...fast enough, we'd be caught out. No time to worry, though, only time to do. So I did. Along the way, the rest of the pain from the raw energy smacked us both around.

Anders lay on the ground, panting in pain. I stood above him, feeling every day of my long life all at once. The Subtle Knives mostly lay on the ground or staggered along for now. A few of them had already recovered, but they headed away from us.

Shit.

"Anders, stay here. Don't get dead. They've realized what happened and are after Quince. I need to—"

"Go," he said. And I did.

Quince lay where we'd left him, though

conscious now. He was struggling to get free but hadn't worked out quite how yet. Subtle Knives closed in, surrounding him. "Paige," he said, spotting me, "do me a favor?"

"Yup," I said, starting to move toward him. I could feel energy start to seep back into the world.

"Not *that*," he said, smiling. "I want you to go away. I've got this. I still don't want your damned help. Not ever," he said.

I wanted to ignore him. Everything in me wanted to just barge in and solve this and then find a way to deal with him. But after a while, it has to be said, you need to let people determine their own fate.

Sure, I'd always be grateful Anders had ignored me when I said the same thing Quince did now. But that was me, and I was not Quince. I couldn't force him into the same box I lived in. I needed to trust him to know what he wanted.

So I turned.

And I left.

CHAPTER TWENTY-SIX

AS I REACHED Anders, still laying on the ground looking grim, the house behind me exploded. I gave it a fifty-fifty chance that Quince had managed to get out or survive, but that was being generous and hopeful. I'd missed being both those things, I gotta say.

Helping Anders up, I asked, "Feeling good about yourself, now that you saved the world? Was it everything you always wanted?"

"And more," he said, voice strained. "Did it work? I mean *really* work?"

"It really did," I assured him. "But we're not done."

"We're not?" he asked.

"We'll need a car — I don't want to try a FastWalk with you right now, but yeah. We have to find Shealano, for a start. And check in on Smythe. And maybe," I shrugged a bit, "find a way to deal with the Ascension...one day. But first Shealano. I want to make sure she's all right."

"Yeah. But maybe we can hit a diner first? I'm hungry."

I laughed harder than I should've. "Oh *now* you're ok with side-tracking to a diner."

"I guess I am," he said.

"We won't always work together, you know," I told him as we climbed, painfully, into a car along the driveway. "I mean maybe you want to hang out with Shae."

"*You* want to," he said.

I started the car with a spark of energy from my hand. "Maybe. But seriously, if you intend to keep doing this shit, Anders—"

"I do."

"Never be afraid to go off on your own, or with someone else, or—"

"I get it, Paige," he said, shaking his head at me, smiling. "You're sad you might have to let me go do my own thing, so you want to make it sound like your idea."

"Stupid. Dead. Anders," I said. "You shut up." I smiled, "And keep an eye out. There's gotta be a place with good coffee in this town. Somewhere."

"Somewhere," he agreed.

ALSO BY ADAM P. KNAVE

PROSE

Crazy Little Things

Stays Crunchy In Milk

Strange Angel

NYCWTF

I Slept With Your Imaginary Friend

This Starry Deep

The Endless Sky

COMICS

Amelia Cole

Never Ending

Artful Daggers

Laser Joan and The Rayguns

Sensation Comics Featuring Wonder Woman

The Once and Future Queen

ABOUT THE AUTHOR

Adam P. Knave has been telling stories since he was a small child. He never stopped, and hopes he never will. A New York native, he self-exiled to Portland, Oregon, not long before his fortieth birthday and now spends many evenings on his patio, whiskey in hand.

www.adampknave.com